Solar Labyrinth

Solar Labyrinth

❖

Exploring Gene Wolfe's
BOOK OF THE NEW SUN

Robert Borski

iUniverse, Inc.

New York Lincoln Shanghai

Solar Labyrinth
Exploring Gene Wolfe's *BOOK OF THE NEW SUN*

iUniverse, Inc.

For information address:
iUniverse, Inc.
2021 Pine Lake Road, Suite 100
Lincoln, NE 68512
www.iuniverse.com

ISBN: 0-595-31729-4 (pbk)
ISBN: 0-595-66399-0 (cloth)

Printed in the United States of America

"The unraveling of a riddle is the purest and most basic act of the human mind."

Vladimir Nabokov, *Conclusive Evidence*

"There's nothing worse than a labyrinth that has no center."

Jorge Luis Borges quoting G. K. Chesterton.

Contents

FOREWORD

This book is not meant for the casual reader of Gene Wolfe. But if like me and other longtime fans of the writer, you've learned that Gene Wolfe can best be appreciated and understood with multiple re-readings, perhaps you've come to the right place. Because over the years, and starting with the original publication, I've had the opportunity to read the five books of the Urth Cycle a dozen times or so, and as I have, I've proceeded from being near totally lost and confused about many of *New Sun*'s twists and turns to a comfort level where I can begin to talk about some of the pathways I've discovered into Wolfe's solar labyrinth. I'm therefore proposing you now allow me to be your tour guide for a while and can almost guarantee you I will reveal things about the book that you will not have realized before. And while you may not always agree with me, I do believe that the one thing you will want to do after you have finished this guide is go back and read Gene Wolfe's epic masterpiece yet again.

On the other hand, if you prefer ambiguity, like your mysteries unresolved, or desire to find your own way unassisted…Well, it is no easy path I seek to illuminate, reader. And all labyrinths—even well-lit ones—should be entered guardedly. So if you wish to walk no further with me…

ACKNOWLEDGEMENTS

Portions of this book have previously appeared in *The New York Review of Science Fiction*, edited by David Hartwell and Kevin Maroney; *The Internet Review of Science Fiction*, edited by John Frost; and the on-line Urth list, hosted by Ranjit Bhatnagar. If I have not expressed my gratitude before, gentlemen, let me do so now.

Special thanks also to Roy Lackey, whose sharp eye and unflinching dedication caught many of the early mistakes in the manuscript. Any untidy grammar, solecisms, or ill turns of phrase that remain are strictly the responsibility of the author.

A NOTE ABOUT CITATIONS

Shadow = *Shadow of the Torturer* (Simon & Schuster, 1980)

Claw = *Claw of the Conciliator* (Timescape, 1981)

Sword = *Sword of the Lictor* (Timescape, 1981)

Citadel = *Citadel of the Autarch* (Timescape, 1983)

(All four volumes comprising *The Book of the New Sun*, a.k.a. *New Sun* or *The Book*.)

Urth = *Urth of the New Sun* (TOR, 1987)

1

CATHERINE

Of the many mysteries that pervade Gene Wolfe's *New Sun* series, perhaps the one most interesting and central to the Book involves the pedigree of Severian.[1] Because the torturers refresh their membership with the male children of those they execute, Severian has come to the Order of the Seekers for Truth and Penitence as an orphan, never having known or being told who his parents are. This is not to say he is unable to riddle them out, for by the end of the *New Sun* quartet he's realized that his father is a man by the name of Ouen—a waiter at the Inn of Lost Loves—while his mother is Catherine, a runaway from the Pelerine sect, who also just happens to be the young woman who impersonates Saint Katharine in various Guild ceremonies. (Katharine is patron saint of the torturers).

It also turns out Severian has been keeping company, amorous and otherwise, with Ouen's mother, Dorcas, who's been resurrected by him from the Lake of Birds in the Botanic Gardens. Dorcas' husband—who's actually Severian's grandfather—has been encountered slightly earlier; he's the ancient boatman who spends his days on the Lake, seeking to retrieve his beloved Cas from the tannin-rich (and thus preservational) waters, having originally deposited her there upon her death many decades ago. (While not given, I suspect his name is meant to be *Caron*, recalling the obvious *Charon*—the Greek ferryman of the dead; providentially at least, such a saint exists, and this would adhere to Wolfe's naming stratagems.) And so we readers are given this much—we know who Severian's parents and paternal grandparents are. We're also told about a possible twin sister. (See *Severa*.) But what about the maternal side of the family? Are we meant to know nothing about the mysterious Catherine and who perhaps her parents are? Is the delineation of the Severian family tree meant to be lopsided and single-branched or are there clues in the text about Catherine and her bloodline?

Critic John Clute, of course, has already undertaken a stab at further unraveling Severian's maternal roots in his seminal book of essays, *Strokes*. But while his initial conclusions parallel those mentioned above, he also attempts to penetrate the identity of Catherine. Clute asserts—and not without marshaling his arguments from text—that Catherine and Severian's predecessor in office, the old Autarch, are one and the same. This approach is based almost entirely on the bold supposition that the old Autarch, whose androgyny is oft noted in the Book, is a woman. Argues the erudite Clute: since a woman could just as easily be unsexed by the Hierodules for failing to bring the New Sun, "he" might well be a "she; and since the old Autarch is never identified by name or soubriquet, certainly there's no reason it couldn't be Catherine the Wheel. These are not unreasonable conclusions, and to be fair, Clute wrote his essay before Wolfe's sequel, *The Urth of the New Sun*, was published; but it also ignores important evidence gleaned from "The Cat," an ancillary work of short fiction set in the Urth milieu, wherein we learn the old Autarch's name is Appian—which being male seems to vitiate much of Clute's argument. But another place he short circuits his thesis is in asserting a key piece of evidence to be the *only* phrase in Wolfe's quartet signally set off by ellipses, whereas there are actually at least 16 such phrases. And so it seems unlikely that Severian's mother and his predecessor are one and the same (although the essay in itself is still a fascinating read and has had more than subtle influence on my exegetical methods).

But then who *is* Catherine? Perhaps, before continuing, it's best to examine what little we do know about her, citing what we can from the quartet.

Saint Katharine

Long before he realizes what her relationship to him might be, Severian has seen Catherine a number of times, always in the guise of St. Katharine during Guild ceremonies. Comments he on her identity: "Of the maid I can tell you nothing. When I was very young, I did not even wonder about her; those are the earliest feasts I can remember." (*Shadow*, 106)

Later, however, when he is older, he has other, more developed, conceits:

> Perhaps she was a servant from some remote part of the Citadel. Perhaps she was a resident of the city, who for gain or because of some old connection with the guild consented to play the part; I do not know. I only know that each feast found her in her place, and so far as I could judge, unchanged. She was tall and slender, though not so tall nor slender as Thecla, dark of complexion, dark of eye, raven of hair. (*Shadow*, 106)

As for what happens to Catherine after the ceremony's conclusion, or where she goes, Severian informs us: "What became of the maid I do not know. She disappeared as she has each Katharine's day I can remember." (*Shadow*, 108–109)

Is there important information to be sieved from the above? Well, Catherine's height does seem to suggest she is either an armigette or an exultant, since there is a relationship between height and social class. And since we're also told later that "'Most of the Pelerines are either armigettes or exultants," it seems fairly reasonable to assume Catherine belongs to one or the other of these two upper classes. Yet another important detail may be her changelessness, at least as far as Severian perceives it. Granted, in his younger days, he may not have been especially perceptive about the effects of aging, but he also has redoubtable mnemonic skills. Given that he's probably seen Catherine over a range of at least fifteen years, it seems likely Catherine would have aged some and he would have eventually noticed. So perhaps this is a clue—as is a possible earlier connection to the guild and Catherine's steadfast disappearance after each ceremony, as well as her dark eyes, skin, and hair.

What little else we know about Catherine, however, comes from Ouen, Severian's father. After Severian seeks him out upon becoming Autarch, he's told by Ouen of their brief liaison, after which "There was trouble...She'd run off from some order of monials. The law got her, and I never saw her again." (*Citadel*, 306) This allows us to assume Catherine has been with the Pelerines, as mentioned earlier, and also helps to explain how Severian may have come to the torturers—apparently, he's born to Catherine while in their custody.[2] But look at the one other thing Ouen has to say and which leads into the admissions stated above. Severian, in soliciting information from Ouen about possible bedmates, asks: "A woman you loved—or perhaps only one who loved you—a dark woman—was taken once?" To which Ouen replies: "Once, Sieur...Catherine was her name. It was an old-fashioned name, they tell me." (*Citadel*, 306) An odd detail that: the old-fashionedness of her name—especially when, except for Robert and Marie of the jungle hut, all the names of the people we meet are old-fashioned. Can we otherwise relate this attribute to anything or anyone in the Book? Someone, say, with a special adherence to the past?

Sundials of Yesteryear

Curiously enough, the woman who eventually becomes Severian's wife, Valeria, comes closest to filling this description. A dweller within the Atrium of Time, she's first encountered by Severian when he comes up through a mazelike series of tunnels looking for his lost dog Triskele. Sensing he's being watched, Severian turns around and notices "a young woman dressed in furs standing before a door at the opposite side of the court." (*Shadow*, 43) Moreover, there's "an antique quality about her metal-trimmed dress and the shadow of her dark hair that made her seem older than Master Palaemon, a dweller in forgotten yesterdays." Valeria—as she's named—leads him inside, where there are "stiff, antique chairs." Here she regales Severian with her knowledge of dead languages (rendered in Latin by Wolfe) and tells him a little bit about her family, who at one time had wanted "to leave Urth with the autarch of their era, then had waited because there was nothing for them but waiting." (*Shadow*, 45) Currently, however, the family's prospects are poor and their tower is in ruins—although Valeria still seems, despite her impoverished circumstances, to retain her armigette status.

Part of Valeria's family's antique nature, of course, may be intrinsic to the Atrium of Time, which Michael Andre-Driussi, in his fine reference book, *Lexicon Urthus*, describes as "A time-traveling structure, like the Last House, located in the heart of the Old Citadel." Indeed, when Severian later searches for the Atrium on maps and from the air, he is unable to find it, suggesting it exists either outside or apart from Severian's temporality. As for other possible residents Andre-Driussi speculates the Atrium may indeed house Catherine, and Clute argues similarly. Is it therefore possible that Catherine ("an old-fashioned name") is somehow related to Valeria and her mired-in-the-past heritage,[3] and that it's she who emerges from the Atrium every Saint Katharine's day to portray her namesake at the torturer's guild, only to then return to its timeless courts and upended sundials?

Unfortunately, our hopes in this regard are not easy to support. After Valeria tells Severian that no one of her blood "carries a sword now against the enemies of the Commonwealth, or stands hostage for us at the Well of Orchids," Severian suggests one of her sisters might be called upon soon to do so. But apparently Valeria is the end of her line, for she says, "I am all the sisters we breed…And all the sons." (*Shadow*, 45) This seems to preclude Catherine being a blood relative, although it is still interesting to note the various similarities between Valeria and Catherine, from their armigette status to their dark hair to their connection with more halcyon times. And eventually, of course, Severian takes Valeria as his royal consort once he becomes Autarch.

Avia, Avus

But if you think we're now totally dead-ended in our exploration of Catherine's roots, you're wrong. Because in his sequel, *The Urth of the New Sun*, Gene Wolfe expands on the life histories of Severian and Valeria. She, as Autarchia, has remained behind on Urth while husband Severian has traveled to Yesod, the universe of the Hierogrammates, where he wins the White Fountain, which will bring about the New Sun. Through no fault of his own, Severian's epic journey takes him over forty years and routes him through various time loops, such that when he is finally able to return to the Commonwealth he discovers that Valeria is now a much older woman. Moreover, she's also remarried, Severian having been adjudged dead. But all this Severian finds out belatedly, the Urth having by this point flooded over due to tidal havoc wreaked by the White Fountain, and he is himself afloat, on first a raft and then a boat. It's from his fellow survivors that he first hears the startling news. And if this is not already difficult enough to deal with, when he attempts to gain more information about this mysterious second husband, Severian does so by maligning himself, saying "He was a hard man for all I know of him, and a cruel one too, at least by reputation, though perhaps he wouldn't have owned to that. Quite possibly Valeria wed him for his throne, though I believe she sometimes said otherwise. Her second husband made her happy, at least." To which Odilo, a former steward at the House Absolute, adds "Well put, sir. A distinct hit." (*Urth*, 315–316)

Given this, and later boat captain Eata's observation about how, in regards to Valeria and her new husband, "People said their marrying was good," surely it would not be overly speculative to imagine there being a child or children born from this union. Valeria, after all, is the last of her family and has already lost one husband. Apparently as well she and Severian never reproduced (Odilo again: "One would have heard of *that*, I imagine.") It's also not hard to imagine her being scared about losing Dux Caesidius, her second husband, who must regularly face death in his military dealings with the Ascians. Given either parent's demise, a child at least would insure neither line died completely out.

So let us imagine one, a girl, who's given an old-fashioned name by an old-fashioned mother. What characteristics might she pass on to a son in her chrononautical travails, courtesy of the Atrium of Time (for surely Valeria would show her daughter the old family stomping grounds)? Wouldn't there be some physical vestige of her father in Severian, his grandson? Indeed, this appears to be very much the case, for as Eata seeks to explain to Severian why Valeria has wed Caesidius, he states, "Some said it was because he looked like you…But he was handsomer, I think, and maybe a little taller." (*Urth*, 329) Eata, of course, has no knowledge that time may be contravened, and that the resemblance of Caesidius to Severian may be due more to simple genetics than latent wish fulfillment by Valeria. And even Severian himself may remain oblique to his own unique heritage—the unbeknownst grandson of his own wife, Valeria.[4]

So apparently there are two sides to the Severian family tree, and symmetrical ones at that (Severian having slept with both grandmothers). And lest one be too dismissive of Gene Wolfe's wickedness or perverse sense of humor in positing such quasi-Oedipal relationships, let us also remember the world he limns is every bit as wounded as Thebes or the medieval province of the Fisher King. Though it's unlikely Severian's "crimes against nature" are meant to be taken as the literal cause of the sun's dying, metaphorically the notion still adds resonance to the overall richness of Wolfe's wonder-filled magnum opus.

G & E

Just as certain events in the New Testament are symbolically prefigured in the Old, so too is there a similar typological correspondence between the events and personages of Dr. Talos' play, *Eschatology and Genesis*, and the larger work which contains it.

In this regard, let us now examine how certain passages in each help further elucidate the life and death of Severian's mother, Catherine.

In the play's fourth scene, the exultant character who has previously been introduced to us as the Contessa has just been granted audience to the Inquisitor. Upon asking him whether Meschia, who's assaulted her in Scene I (*Claw*, 228), has been captured yet, the Inquisitor answers negatively, whereupon the Contessa relates the following information:

"Scarcely a watch ago some soldiers found me moaning in the garden, where my maid sought to comfort me. Because I feared to be outside by dark, they carried me to my own suite by way of that gallery called the Road of Air. Do you know it?"

"Well," responds the Inquisitor.

Continues the Contessa:

"Then you know too that it is everywhere overhung with windows, so that all the chambers and corridors that abut on it may receive the benefit. As we passed by, I saw in one the figure of a man, tall and clean-limbed, wide of shoulder and slender of waist…In a little time, the same figure appeared in another window—and another. Then I appealed to the soldiers who carried me to fire upon it. They thought me mad and would not, but the party they sent to take that man returned with empty hands. Still he looked at me through the windows, and appeared to sway."

The Inquisitor asks the Contessa if she believes this man is the man who struck her, to which she replies: "Worse. I fear it was not he, though it resembled him…No, on this strange night, when we, who are the winter-killed stalks of man's old sprouting, find ourselves mixed with next year's seed, I fear that he is something more we do not know."

So ends the Contessa's little melodramatic speech. Now for the comparable "real-world" scene, which takes place in *Urth*. Severian at this stage has just returned to the world of his birth, emerging, via the Brook Madregot, from his own memorial. Entering the Secret House, he begins to look for a means to access the House Absolute. Narrates he:

> At last I came to an aperture closed by no door; a strong draft from it carried the sound of a woman's weeping, and I halted and stepped through.
>
> I found myself in a loggia, with arches on three sides. The woman's sobs seemed to come from my left; I went to one of the arches and peered out. It overlooked that wide and windy gallery we called the Path of Air—the loggia was one of those constructions that appear merely ornamental though they serve the needs of the Secret House.
>
> Shadows on the marble floor far below me showed that the woman was ringed by half a dozen scarcely visible Praetorians, one of whom supported her by the elbow. At first I could not see her eyes, which were bent toward the floor and lost in her raven-dark hair.
>
> Then (I cannot tell by what chance) she glanced up at me. Hers was a lovely face of that complexion called olive and as smoothly oval as an olive, too, with something in it that tore my heart; and though it was strange to me, I had the sensation of return once again. I felt that in some lost life I had stood just where I was standing then; and that in that life I had seen her beneath me in just that way.
>
> She and the shadows of the Praetorians were soon almost out of sight. I shifted from one arch to the next to keep them in view; and she stared back at me, until she was looking over the shoulder of her pale gown when I last glimpsed her. (*Urth*, 293)

Thus, obviously, we have the exact same scene as Dr. Talos' play, only expanded upon and with a change in viewpoint perspective (one of the Book's many recursive loops). But what about the woman Severian actually sees under arrest? Who, in other words, is the Contessa's real-life equivalent, and whatever will become of her when the looming tidal waters of the New Sun soon inundate the Urth?

Physically, of course, with her raven hair and olive complexion, Severian's "Contessa" resembles his mother Catherine rather well. Moreover, since Catherine is Valeria's daughter, we know she's alive during this time period. But in addition to Severian not recognizing her—a trademark character flaw repeatedly seen throughout New Sun—there's the following evidence. Though Wolfe only mentions it once, we learn in *Eschatology and Genesis* that the Contessa's name is Carina—a name, which like so many others in the quintet, has cryptonymic significance, being derivable from Catherine. (See *Appendix* for details.) Reinforcing this: the homonymic *Karina* is a Scandinavian variant for Katharine. It's therefore enormously difficult for not to see the woman being led by the Praetorians through the Path of Air as Severian's mother.

As for why she's under armed escort, this requires some extrapolation. Certainly, it seems unlikely that Valeria, her own mother, would have her arrested—or at least if she had that Valeria wouldn't mention something in the subsequent throne room scene. But what about the other bearer of power in the post-Severian autarchy—Father Inire? Knowing how close to doom the Urth is, he may well have had her arrested for her own safety—especially if, in her atemporal peregrinations, she has yet to encounter Ouen and become pregnant with Severian and Severa. (Otherwise, her imminent death would be of no consequence.) He subsequently has her ushered to the one locale where she'll be safe from the coming deluge—*approximately seventy years in the past*. Catherine then joins or is made to join the Pelerines—I favor the latter—perhaps even being placed under a sort of gentle house arrest by the scarlet priestesses' magna mater (see *Witches*). Eventually, however, she decides to flee the order for reasons unknown; there's an aside from Winnoc that suggests Catherine may have had abolitionist sentiments and thus she may have aroused the ire of the slave-heavy Pelerine organization, but I think it's much more likely she simply saw the opportunity to escape and fled. I categorically also do not believe that she's already with child and has therefore been forced to leave because her virgin status has been lost (the Pelerines are chaste by vow)—rather, that she becomes pregnant by Ouen only *after* she makes her escape. This, at least, is implied by Ouen's aforementioned, "There was trouble…She'd run off from some order of the monials. The law got her, and I never saw her again."[5] All this, of course, has been predestined—at least from the Hierodules' point of view, where our future is their past. Once Severian is conceived, however, Father Inire has Catherine rearrested, but this time brought to the Matachin Tower, where, eventually, in its dark hold, she gives birth to Severian and Severa. Once again, in regards to Catherine, the loop doubles back: we start with Urth's final days, we finish with the Nativity—by any other name, *eschatology and genesis*, the same as Talos's play.

But what about Catherine's fate after this point? Apparently, the Hierodules don't have her executed, but allow her to return annually to see her son during the Feast of Saint Katharine—perhaps as a reward for her eventual cooperation. Given her probable access to the Corridors of Time, she might also even become an itinerant of sorts. This, to me, is at least suggested by author Wolfe, who, in Dr. Talos' play, has the Contessa asks Meschia, "If my body held a part of yours—drops of liquescent tissue locked in my loins…" To which Meschia, who's portrayed by Severian, replies, "If you did, you might wander the Urth for a long time, a lost thing that could never find its way home." (*Claw*, 218) This, of course, is more Wolfean irony—Thomas Wolfe,[6] that is—since Severian/Meschia will be semi-present in Catherine's body as Ouen's male seed. (GW may also be attempting a hagiographic parallel here: upon her conversion Saint Katharine was mystically wed to the Infant Jesus, gold-ring and all.) On the other hand, since the character Meschia doesn't mate with Carina in the play, perhaps an alternate fate might be envisioned.

Given that her son eventually goes on to become the previous millennium's Conciliator, might she not, in her various time-tripping jaunts, wind up back in the Autarchy of Maxentius, where, as her own saintly namesake, she dies on the wheel that now bears her name—a fiery contrivance that in pyrotechnic form is also known to the French as *le soleil*—"the sun?" Or more prosaically does the skeleton that Severian finds at the very end of the Book in the tunnels beneath the Citadel belong to Catherine—unlike the mother of another messiah, there being no ascension to heaven for her, only underground anonymity?

2

AGIA AND AGILUS

From rather upfront evidence for a work by Gene Wolfe, it's relatively easy to conclude that Dorcas, Severian's waif-like traveling companion and lover, is his resurrected paternal grandmother. Even Severian himself, who can be rather thickheaded at times, figures this out by *New Sun*'s denouement. But what neither he nor many of his readers fully seem to grasp are the circumstances attending Dorcas's brief life as a mother. As Ouen, who is her son and Severian's father, tells Severian during their second meeting, teenage Dorcas has died giving birth. But at the same point it's more than clear from Ouen's testimony that *he* was not the difficult issue responsible. "I never knew her," he tells Severian in response to a question about his mother. "Cas they called her, but she died when I was young. In childbirth, my father said." (*Citadel*, 304) This, however, is a point most veteran readers of the Book fail to grasp: i.e., Cas has not died *giving birth* to Ouen, but rather *when he was young*—i.e., already born. Further evidence for Ouen's primogeniture is also given in *Sword* when Dorcas, who has begun to remember various bits and pieces of her previous existence, relates the following: "I lived with my husband above a little shop, and took care of our child." (*Sword*, 84) That child, of course, must be Ouen. It therefore follows that Dorcas died during the apparently much more difficult delivery of a second child.

But in the grand scheme of *New Sun*, is there a larger relevance to this tragic circumstance? Setting aside the question for the moment, let us instead posit that while Dorcas died giving birth, the child of that delivery did not. Certainly, we're never told anything of this explicitly (which, to be sure, is more like the cagey Wolfe most of us have come to expect). Ouen mentions nothing, and neither does Caron, the old boatman who is Severian's grandfather. Then again, as far as the latter is concerned, he tells us nothing about *any* offspring—only that he and Cas were married for nearly four years, and ran a shop in Oldgate that sold cloisonné and garments. It therefore seems possible that this second child may well have survived, but Dorcas's husband being unable to nurse it, or perhaps grief-stricken because of his wife's death, either rejects or abandons it, and so it is raised by others. Ouen, however, perhaps because he's older, he keeps, at least until the age of ten when Ouen is sent off to work as a potboy in an inn. If, as Dorcas tells us, she and her husband were together slightly under four years, Ouen could very easily have been born during the last part of their first year together, which would make him about three when she died. This is both consistent with his not remembering her—he's too young to retain memories—but yet being somewhat less dependent on grief-stricken Dad for his day-to-day wherewithal. It also means poor Cas was thirteen or fourteen when Ouen was brought forth into the world. (Agia, post-revival, judges her age to be sixteen or seventeen.)

But allowing for the survival into adulthood of Ouen's brother or sister, what becomes of him or her? Is there anyone in *New Sun* who might correspond to this lost aunt or uncle of Severian's? I believe there is, but before I discuss the individual in depth, let me indulge in an alternate bit of speculation. The tendency to produce twins is genetic, and so, if this person later married and reproduced, it's not unreasonable to assume twins might be born, just as Severian and Severa are to Catherine and Ouen. And if these twins were later to enter the same trade as their grandparents, selling garments, although they are used rather than new? By now, I hope you probably will have grasped I mean to suggest Agia and Agilus are the mystery twins in question—yes, of such fanciful stuff are not only dreams made, but exegetical woolliness. And yet if we can find support for the notion in *New Sun*'s text, who's not to marvel at the deviousness of Gene Wolfe, the Daedalean wordsmith of not only fine prose, but convoluted bloodlines? (In the latter regard Charles Dickens might well be Wolfe's emulatory model. Witness, for example, the secret paternities of Smike in *Nicholas Nickleby* or Estella in *Great Expectations,* or the extended family tree of Oliver Twist.)[1]

Kissing Cousins

I believe there are at least half a dozen areas where support can be marshaled to bolster the argument that Agia and Agilus are the grandchildren of Dorcas and Caron, and first cousins to Severian the Great.

The first involves Agia's saintly namesake. Saint Agia, as Andre-Driussi notes in *Lexicon Urthus*, was the mother of Saint Loup. It's long been my contention that many of the names Wolfe gives to Severian and his blood relatives belong in a special category, each having an additional valence, relating either to hagiographic or auctorial correspondences.[2] Ouen, for example, is a Welsh form of

Eugene; the expired *Saint* Dorcas was resurrected by Saint Peter. And, of course, Loup means wolf—another prime example of author Wolfe intromitting himself cameo-style, if subtextually.[3]

Agia itself also means saint in Greek—an association we might expect of blood relatives of the New Sun/Conciliator (though Agia is no saint).

The second area involves unlawful carnal knowledge. When Severian visits Agilus in his cell, he finds brother and sister Agia both naked together. Later, Agilus seems to confirm his worst fears: "Don't ask me about Agia. Everything you suspect is true—is that enough?" (*Shadow*, 255) This, as I will argue in *Severa*, parallels Severian's own incestuous relationship with his twin sister, as well as his having slept with both grandmothers.

The third area employs symbols: not once, twice or even thrice, but in four separate passages, Wolfe has the sun shining down on either Agia, Agilus, or both, and turning some facet of their features to emblematic gold—*something he does to no other characters in the Book*, but doubtlessly meant to emphasize their link to the New Sun:

> As I watched [Agia], the sun touched a rent just below her waist, turning the skin there to palest gold. (*Claw*, 152)

> Flecks of sunlight seemed to turn [Agia's] brown hair to dark gold.[4] (*Claw*, 193)

> There was a tiny window high up in the wall behind [Agia and Agilus], and from it, suddenly, as though the ridge of a roof, or a cloud, had now fallen below the sun, a beam of light came to bathe them both. I looked from one aureate face to the other. (*Claw*, 252)

> [Agilus] stared at his hands, slender and rather soft, where they lay in the narrow beam of sunlight that had given his head, and Agia's, an aureole a few moments before. (*Claw*, 255)

The fourth area involves Agia's acquired leg injury. "Now you'll have to carry me if you can," she tells Severian after their fiacre crash in the Cathedral of the Pelerines. "I don't think my right leg will bear the weight." (*Claw*, 166) Severian attempts to help, but as they seek to leave the burning tent (and foreshadowing his own injury) we learn the two can "manage nothing better than a limping walk." Later, once again Severian tells us how "[Agia] was limping, and I recalled how far she had walked today after wrenching her leg." The context here: as mentioned in *Catherine*, I believe that anyone who limps is related to Severian the Lame.

The fifth area involves a physical resemblance between Agia and Severian. Agia—whose "long, brown eyes" suggest a possible Asian heritage—is repeatedly described as having high cheekbones. Curiously, this is exactly how Cyriaca later describes Severian's hidden facial features at the masque held by Abdiesus: "You have high cheekbones—their outlines show a trifle through the mask, and your wide flat cheeks will make them look higher."[5] To be sure, Cyriaca is *guessing* what Severian looks like beneath his torturer's mask, but out of all the myriad attributes author Wolfe could pick for Cyriaca to use, why does he choose high cheekbones?

Finally, there are two linked passages in *Citadel*.

In the first of them Severian recalls a statement made by Dorcas: "Sitting in a window…trays and a rood. What would you do, summon up some Erinys to destroy me?"[6] To which Severian responds:

> "Yes. Yes, indeed, I would have if I could. If I had been Hethor, I would have drawn them from some horror behind the world, birds with the heads of hags and the tongues of vipers. At my order they would have threshed the forests like wheat and beaten cities flat with their great wings…" (*Citadel*, 19)

Notice how the language and sense of this passage are echoed later when indeed Hethor's birdlike, winged hags snatch Severian from his Ascian captors and carry him back to Vodalus' encampment, where vengeful Agia awaits him. "Once I had imagined such creatures threshing the forests of Urth and beating flat her cities," Severian reminds us. Then wonders: "Had my thoughts helped bring these?" (*Citadel*, 208)

But of course it's not his thoughts that have summoned the winged hags, it's his deeds. For in both name and physical description these posthistoric Erinys are derived from Classical Mythology, being the Erinyes of the Greeks and the Furiae of the Romans—remorseless spirits whose special dispensation it is to avenge violent crimes perpetrated against one's kin. Carnifex Severian, having taken Terminus Est's sharp edge to his male cousin's neck, has obviously committed one such violent crime, but like Orestes he too is exonerated by the gods—well, the Hierodules, anyway—and lives to ascend the throne.

Rood Mother

But what about Agia's missing parent? Who is this lost sibling of Ouen? Well, just as I've argued earlier that Caron may be the name of Dorcas's husband (there being a saint by that name, and Caron recalling Charon, the Greek ferryman of the dead), I'm tempted to call this second child Secunda, after the ancient Roman tradition of using numbers to label female offspring (if daughters, Tertia and Quaternia would be the next children in sequence). Appositely, of course, there's a Saint Secunda,[7] and she, like Saint Catherine, was beheaded. We're also told that the garment shop run by Agilus and Agia was bequeathed to them by their mother, while Dorcas, in another one of her recovered memories, remembers shopping for a child's doll—usually a girl's toy. But what yet still another recalled memory reveals is Dorcas's potent association with furniture. Dorcas and Severian are in Thrax at this point. Severian, out touring the city, sees Dorcas watching stevedores unloading boats in the wharf, but when he approaches her she will not speak to him. Only later does he find out why, that Dorcas has seen "An old chair. And a table, and several other things." (*Sword*, 81) As she then elaborates, "It seems that there is a shop in the Turners' Street that sells old furniture to the eclectics…There is no source here to supply the demand, and so two or three times a year the owner and his sons go to Nessus—to the abandoned quarters of the south—and fill their boat." But more to the point, it seems the salvaged chair has once belonged to Dorcas. As she attempts to explain to Severian, "I knew everything about it—the carving on the legs, and even the pattern in the grain of the arms. So much came back then." (*Sword*, 82) Dorcas, in short, is realizing that she may be the product of an earlier era (the implications of which are preoccupying her, hence her failure to talk to Severian), but what seems to stick in Severian's mind is her telling him about the looted furniture, as twice more before the Book concludes he mentions it[8]—a near extravagant amount given Wolfe's usual parsimonious clues.

Severian himself, however, fails to make any connection between Dorcas's painful recollections and the one other person in *New Sun* who exhibits an odd fascination with furniture—the female prisoner he visits in the Matachin Tower shortly after he returns to Nessus as Autarch. One of thirteen inmates he potentially screens for commutation of sentence, the woman has "stolen children and forced them to serve as articles of furniture in a room she had set aside for the purpose, in one instance nailing the hands of a little girl to the underside of a table so that she became in effect its pedestal." (*Citadel*, 274) This perversion of the crucifixion not only inverts traditional religious imagery (as indeed does the notion of a "Saint" Agia), but eerily recapitulates another of Dorcas's recalled memories, the already-mentioned "trays and a rood." (The table is the tray which the nailed girl supports, as well as a grisly cross or rood). The woman's eyes are also clear blue, the same as Dorcas's and Ouen's. Yet despite her outrageous crimes Severian does not believe her to be mad—a diagnosis confirmed by his attempted use of the Claw, which fails to heal the woman, just as it has with Baldanders and Jolenta. The implication we're left with is that the woman has forfeited her connection with humanity;[9] she's soul-rent, an imago of evil. In essence, as Severian says in the jungle hut, "If it is true that each of us has an anti-polaric brother somewhere, a bright twin if we are dark, a dark twin if we are bright," then surely the woman I call Secunda,[10] along with her children Agia and Agilus, represent that antipolarity.

"You are wearing a mask."

When Severian first meets Agilus at his rag shop, Agilus is wearing what Severian describes as a skeleton or death's-head-mask. Severian, however, in the dimness of the shop (Wolfe specifically mentions the lack of light), does not realize this until he sees "a narrow black ribbon that stretched forward a finger's length from the hair above his ears." (*Shadow*, 154)

"You are wearing a mask," he tells Agilus, and requests he remove it.

Agilus complies, but several paragraphs later, Severian says, "The ribbons that held your mask…They're still there."

But Agilus neither says nor does anything.

Later, at the Sanguinary Fields, when Severian faces his helmeted Septentrion opponent in monomachy, he makes this observation: "…in the shadow behind the cheekpiece I thought I saw a narrow band of black, and tried to recall where I had seen such a thing before." (*Shadow*, 237)

And then still later, after Severian leaves the arrested Agilus's cell, he notices the following immediately outside, where he's tossed an orichalk to starving Agia: "…the orichalk was gone. In its place…a design had been scratched on the filthy stones. It might have been the snarling face of Jurupari [a demon], or perhaps a map, and it was wreathed with letters I did not know." (*Shadow*, 255)

So what are we to make of these various incidents?

The answer, I believe, can be found in Chapter XX of *Sword*. Severian is work-ing his way down from the mountains where he's rescued his namesake, Little Severian, from both alzabo and zoanthrops. As they enter a high jungle, they find a fetish[11] that Severian believes is meant to prevent the coming of the New Sun, while suspended from trees are strips of red cloth written over "with symbols and ideographs of the sort those who pretend to more knowledge than they possess use in imitation of the writing of the astronomers." (*Sword*, 159) Not much later they're accosted, and Severian comments "…for a moment I thought the figures that stepped into the path were devils, huge-eyed and *striped* with black, white and scarlet; then I saw they were only naked men with painted bodies." (*Italics mine*) Severian later describes one of these painted faces as "expressionless as a mask."

Eventually, Severian is made to fight a sorcerer's duel with Decuman, whereupon, in response to a question by Little Severian about who their captors are, he opines: "I'm only guessing, but I would say this is an academy of magicians—of those cultists who practice what they believe are secret arts. They are supposed to have followers everywhere—though I choose to doubt that—and they are very cruel." (*Sword*, 173)

Agia and Agilus, I submit, are devotees of the academy cult.[12] This explains the so-called ribbon Agilus wears in his shop and on the Sanguinary Fields—it's *a stripe* of black paint—while the letters Agia scratches outside her brother's cell—*the letters Severian does not know*—correspond to the symbols and ideographs Severian sees in the jungle. In fact, if there's a witch anywhere in Severian's family, it's Agia, not Severa, and in many respects she's like Circe, only instead of turning men into swine, she commands the shape-changing Hethor. (See *Hethor*.) Unfortunately, neither of the twins seems much availed by their use of the dark arts, although at least Agia is not executed like her brother and eventually rises to command Vodalus's army. What ultimately happens to her, however, is anybody's guess;[12] perhaps, as Michael Andre-Driussi suggests in his *Lexicon*, she's meant to represent the Eternal Adversary, the implacable enemy who's always out there—thus Severian's guard must never be relaxed.

Pelagia Filia

On the other hand I believe there's evidence indicating that Agia may have had a daughter. After Severian brings the New Sun, and the Urth is flooded, he takes up with a trio of survivors, first on a makeshift raft, then on Eata's boat. One of the two women in the trio is named Pega and she claims to have been the servant of the armigette Pelagia. The name Pelagia, however, fairly screams its connection with the Megatherian Great Lords. Agia, being their ally, might well have named a daughter after them (a similar impulse must have motivated the Group of Seventeen). Also, in a slightly different context, there is a relatively famous seaside resort in Crete named Agia Pelagia, the area surrounding which is rife with significant archaeological findings—something Gene Wolfe would almost certainly know.

As for the male parent of Pelagia, who knows? Irrespective of paternity, she may have been held in the House Absolute more as a hostage than a guest, similar to the situation of the exultant concubines. Remember, Severian does not leave to bring back the New Sun until some ten years into his reign and only after he has dealt effectively with the Ascians. By holding Pelagia hostage Severian might therefore be attempting to ensure cousin Agia's continued pacificity.

Furthermore, it's possible that Pega and Pelagia are one and the same. Pega, of course, can be derived cryptonymically (see *Appendix*) from Pelagia, and there appears to be quite a bit going on between Odilo and Pega that Wolfe deliberately obscures. E.g., Pega, at one point, says she must have seen the Black Tarantines to which Severian claims he belongs marching in a procession (possibly the funeral procession of Dux Caesidius, who's died a year earlier):

"Odilo murmured. 'You went with your mistress, I take it?'"

"Pega made some response, but I gave it no heed." (*Urth*, 313)

Doubtless, this unheeded response contains vital information, but so too I warrant does Odilo's question. It's as if he's taunting her, possibly attempting to trip her up in her own skein of lies (Pega has earlier gone on and on about her usefulness to Pelagia). At any rate, Pega/Pelagia is thrice described as doll-faced,[13] which may link her back to Hethor, who first enters the *New Sun* narrative bemoaning the loss of his paracoital doll, and thus he may be her actual father.

3

ASCIANS

In *The Citadel of the Autarch*, the concluding volume of Gene Wolfe's *New Sun* quartet, a very strange scene takes place. A battle between the Ascians and the Commonwealth has been raging; during a temporary lull, however, Severian, our narrator and the novel's protagonist, notes the following:

> The savages seemed to have vanished. A new force appeared in their place, on the flank that had now become our front. At first I thought they were cavalry on centaurs, creatures whose pictures I had encountered in the brown book. I could see the heads and shoulders of the riders above the human heads of their mounts, and both appeared to bear arms. When they drew nearer, I saw they were nothing so romantic: merely small men—dwarfs, in fact—upon the shoulders of very tall ones. (*Citadel*, 180)

Only later, as Severian immerses himself in the fray, does he realize the even more bizarre aspect of these ridden tall men: "One of the tall men dashed forward…As he drew nearer he slowed, and I saw that his eyes were unfocused, and that he was in fact blind." (*Citadel*, 181)

Possibly, however, these passages may sound familiar to you in a *déjà lu* kind of way—especially if you've traveled the larger Wolfe universe. Because these blind tall men with their dwarf riders actually first appear in "'A Story,' by John Marsch,'" the middle novella of *The Fifth Head of Cerberus*. John Sandwalker, along with his newly-made allies, the Shadow children, is being stalked by four marshmen at this juncture in the narrative skein. Fortunately, Sandwalker and company are anything but defenseless:

> A man loomed in front of him and Sandwalker kicked him expertly, then drove the head down with his hands to meet his knees; he took a step backwards and a Shadow child was on the man's shoulders, his fleshless legs locked around the throat and his fingers plunged into the hair. "Come," Sandwalker said urgently, "we have to get away."

"Why?" The Shadow child sounded calm and happy. "We're winning."
The man he rode, who had been doubled over in agony, straightened up and
tried to free himself; the Shadow child's legs tightened, and as Sandwalker
watched, the marshman fell to his knees." (*Fifth Head*, 104)

Somewhat later, then:

The marshman who had dropped to his knees a moment before rose shakily,
and guided by the Shadow child on his shoulders staggered away [back
toward the pit]…The four men were there, three of them with riders on
their shoulders, the fourth moaning and swaying, scrubbing with bloodied
hands at the bleeding sockets of his eyes. (*Fifth Head*, 104–105)

Given that the Shadow children of *Fifth Head* are pygmy-sized, and the taller,
ridden marshmen have been blinded—the same particulars being recapitulated
with the tall men cavalry in *Citadel*—is Wolfe trying to tell us something about
the Ascians—that, in fact, they're Annese in origin? Surely, this is not that sub-
versive an idea; remember, according to Wolfe, the abos of Ste. Anne are actually
deracinated Adamic stock, having come to the green world in several earlier
migratory waves. Could not, at some future's remove, the Annese, aided and
abetted by the reintroduction of spacefaring, make their way back to the mother
planet? Indeed, Severian himself claims such returns are quite normal in The
Urth of the New Sun, as he's traveling from Briah to Yesod. "In ancient times,"
says he, "the peoples of Urth journeyed among the suns. [But] many came home
at last." (*Urth*, 73) So it's certainly well within the Wolfean range of ideaspace
that such a repatriation may have taken place. But other than the tall men riders,
is there any other evidence for this?

Well, consider the alzabo. Somehow, it manages to makes its way from Sainte
Anne to Urth (this, of course, presupposes that you accept Michael Andre-Driussi's notion about the ghoul bear of *Fifth Head* being the alzabo).[1] It's possible
the Annese may have brought it back with them as zoetic transport—imported
fauna from home to populate a vivarium and perhaps provide a study or nostalgia
base for future generations.

Then there's green Lune. Might not the original impulse behind its forestation
be to remind the displaced Annese of their home world? It's also been orbitally
shifted, if we're to believe old Rudesind, who describes a painting of a smaller,
grayer moon thusly: "Doesn't seem so big either, because it wasn't so close in."
(*Shadow*, 52) Again, by moving the moon in to make it appear larger—a faux sis-

ter world—could this have been done by the heartsick Annese, pining for Sainte Anne?[2]

Then there are several passages in *Citadel* that echo either implicitly or explicitly similar passages in *Fifth Head*. Witness, for example, Ava's remark to Severian in the lazaret where she is a Pelerine postulant and he a recovering patient: "Ascians are not human." (*Citadel*, 78) Compare this with the account of Mrs. Blount in *Fifth Head*, who describes the native Annese with similar dispassion: "We called them the abos or the wild people. They weren't really people, you know, just animals shaped like people." (*Fifth Head*, 146) And for something almost directly echoic, consider Dr. Hagsmith's remark about how the abos are "not…really human." (*Fifth Head*, 151)

Meanwhile, back on Urth and still in the thick of battle, Severian apprises us of yet another salient detail:

> I think I must have cut down half a dozen Ascians before I saw that they all looked the same—not that they all had the same face, but that the differences between them seemed accidental and trivial…All had large, brilliant, wild eyes, hair clipped nearly to the skull, starved faces, screaming mouths, and prominent teeth. (*Citadel*, 179).

This too has a parallel in *Fifth Head*, where, as we're told by Number Five, because of the small population base, "most of us have a kind of planetary face." How very much like some mad machination of Maitre, whose outsourced Wolfe clones, especially if they're allowed to reproduce, might well come to dominate the Sainte Croix gene pool. Indeed, though the words are the old Autarch's, the following might well summarize the end, if subconscious, result of Maitre's cloning experiments—even more so if they're continued by Number Five and his successors: "They [the Ascians] wish the race to become a single individual…the same, duplicated to the end of number." (*Citadel*, 206) Granted, the Wolfes of Sainte Croix are hardly Annese autochthons (unless, of course, Veil's Hypothesis is true—the central conundrum of the book); but even if refractive, I still maintain the parallels are germane.

But what about the abos' characteristic lack of manual dexterity? Is there anything in the New Sun books that seems to indicate the Ascians are any less impaired? In my opinion, there is little. From what Severian tells us the Ascian regulars are equipped with energy spears—not exactly weapons that appear to require a great deal of cheiral finesse. And while the dwarf tallriders also utilize bows-and-arrows, if the marshmen of Sainte Anne can weave and deploy fishing nets, it does not seem that big of a stretch to imagine them notching an arrow and pulling back a bowstring (recall as well Victor's expertise with ropes and knots—Dr. Marsch is most impressed with this if we're to believe his diary entries).

Even Severian the Great eventually seems to realize the Ascians are something other than simple battle foes. At least that's how I interpret his asking Appian, "Who are they?" Or as he elaborates in asking for yet further clarification from the old Autarch, "I asked who they are, sieur. I know they're our enemies, that they live to the north in the hot countries, and that they're said to be enslaved by Erebus. But who are they?" (*Citadel*, 202) What exactly, however, isn't covered by Severian's précis? Could it be planet of origin?[4] A not-so-much who are they, but what are they? At any rate he's told by Appian, "Who they are you will discover in due time," although we never hear Severian disclose any such result within the *New Sun* narrative frame. (And yet we're led to believe he does spend a year with them later, although Wolfe has never fleshed out the episode; perhaps if or when he does, we'll learn more details.)[5]

But if indeed the answer to Severian's triply-asked question is that the Ascians are the abos of Sainte Anne, let's consider the delicious irony of this. In classical mythology, because they live in the torrid zone, the Ascians have no meridian shadow twice yearly (Ascian actually means 'without shadow'). If we accept the notion that shadow represents soul—a popular motif in fairy tales—and that having souls makes us uniquely human,[6] it seems possible to connect the shadowlessness of the Ascians with their enslavement to Erebus, one of Urth's alien great monsters. Having apparently returned to their mother world in some glory (imagine the resources needed to terraform and shift the moon), for whatever reasons, the Annese/Ascians have chosen to cast their lots with megatherian Erebus, a being named after the underworld darkness beneath Hades through which all the dead must pass. In other words, now soulless, the former Shadow children have gone apenumbral, becoming in a completely different sense, well, yes, *shades*—and by so doing forfeit both humanity and future.

But then in many respects this is also what *The Fifth Head of Cerberus* is about: a descent through various levels of darkness, and ending in self-abnegation.

For surely, repatriated to Urth, but mocked by forested green Lune in the skies above them, this is where the Shadow children and their brethren have wound up—enslaved by an alien overseer, condemned to speak in stock phrases, shadowless in the dying, sun-impoverished inferno of home. In which case Severian's year-long sojourn among them might well represent not so much diplomatic niceties, but the harrowing of Hell itself.

4

DOMNICELLAE

Who is the Domnicellae, the high priestess of the Pelerines that Severian meets only once, the encounter taking place in the tent cathedral after he and Agia have crashed into and destroyed the altar of the Claw? Her name is never given (usually with Wolfe a sign we're meant to figure it out), and when Severian later convalesces in the lazaret of the Pelerines, she's conspicuously absent—simply "away," as Mannea, mistress of the postulants, tells us, with no reason given for her nonpresence. Does author Wolfe provide us with any clues as to whom she may really be?

I believe he does and suggest she's Thecla's childhood friend, Domnina, whose tale we first hear from Severian in the Jungle Garden. For starters there's her name, which can be extracted from the letters of Domnicellae; as I argue elsewhere and especially in the Appendix Wolfe uses this device over and over in the *Book of the New Sun*, where names are either nested inside larger names or derived via near anagrams from the parent word.[1] In addition, the witchy priestess has the stature of an exultant, the class to which we know Domnina belongs. And as for her being absent from the field hospital of the Pelerines, this is Wolfe cheating a bit; Severian, having incorporated Thecla's memories via the alzabo, would no doubt recognize her old childhood friend, and so Wolfe very conveniently has her missing. Finally then, we have young Domnina's experience with the numinous, a fish of light caught in the mirrors of Father Inire—about as potent a Christian symbol as you could hope for,[2] but also calling to mind Severian's eventual turn as the piscine Sleeper, the Oannes-like god of Ushas. The encounter apparently disturbs young Domnina quite a bit[3] and doubtless leads her to reevaluate her situation, nudging her toward a life spent among the Pelerines (almost certainly with some encouragement from Father Inire, whose favor she holds), and eventually culminating in her rise to the rank of Domnicellae.

5

FECHIN

✦

or
Psst: Have You Heard Severian Slept Here?

Who's the most famous offstage personage of the *New Sun* quartet? Someone we hear about over and over again, but never quite meet? Many readers might initially argue Father Inire, who's encountered only second hand, in the reminiscences of others or through passed-on communiqués. But at least he does appear to exist and draw breath during the main narrative frame of Wolfe's four books. (Indeed, he may be the Book's *major* character. See *Masks of the Father*.) The same, however, cannot be said of master painter Fechin. This is because by Severian's time he's dead—gone to that great artists' enclave in the sky, just down the celestial boulevard from Parnassus. Yet far from being a handicap, Fechin still seems to enjoy major celebrity status, especially among seniors.[1] The big question is why. Does Wolfe mean him to be the Mozart or Picasso of Urth, a talent so dazzling he's mesmerized society to the point that people who've spent time with him can't wait to tell others about their encounters? Human nature being what it is, we might expect a little anecdotal ear-bending by those eager to spin their own self-worth—but what about the grandiose, widespread fame that underpins such reminiscences? This, after all, is Wolfe's very stratified-and-low-tech Commonwealth we're talking about; despite some alien gadgetry, the primary means of disseminating information among the general populace appears to be neither print nor electronic, but word of mouth. Is it therefore likely that any artist, no matter how prodigious his or her gift, could even become well-known outside a small circle of patrons or aesthetes—let alone have such fame endure among the less educated or cultured? Or could it be that Fechin's name (which appears 17 times in the Book) has survived for alternate cause—reasons that transcend the merely artistic?

Let us examine the various instances where the legendary artist is mentioned and see what answers we might glean.

Fechin Rules!

The first time we hear anything of Fechin is when adolescent Severian is sent on a mission to fetch books from Master Ultan. Along the way Severian encounters the curator Rudesind, who is well along in years and hence somewhat addlepated. Severian mentions how he's never been to this particular part of the Citadel before, and Rudesind (who's cleaning paintings) immediately launches into a catalogue of its virtues:

> "Never been here? Why, this is the best part. Art, music and books. We've a Fechin here that shows three girls dressing another one with flowers that's so real you expect the bees[2] to come out of it. A Quartillosa, too. Not popular anymore, Quartillosa isn't, or we wouldn't have him here." (*Shadow*, 51)

Rudesind also vouchsafes that "We get what the House Absolute doesn't want, you see. That means we get the old ones, and they're the best, mostly." And then, two sentences later, he repeats, "We've got a Fechin here. It's the truth!"

Given that this is our first mention of Fechin, nothing much seems that unusual here. Rudesind being an elderly curator, we almost expect him to wax exuberant about the beloved artists of yesteryear, especially when compared to the current brood. ("Drippers and spitters," he deems them.) But there's also implicit in his words about Quartillosa the parallel, if somewhat contradictory, notion that Fechin the artist—*or at least his works*—may not be as popular as he once was ("…or we wouldn't have him here"). Rudesind also mentions how he learned to clean pictures as an apprentice and that the first canvas he's cleaned—a portrayal of forested Lune—is the very one he just happens to be working on, indicating a long tenure at his present situation.

When next Severian encounters Rudesind both are in the House Absolute, the Autarch's underground headquarters outside Nessus. Rudesind again is cleaning old pictures. But this time he one-ups his previous mention of Fechin and tells Severian he's been *painted* by the master artist:

> "An artist—a real one—came by where we lived. My mother, being so proud of me, showed him some of the things I'd done. It was Fechin, Fechin himself, and the portrait he made of me hangs here to this very day, looking out

at you with my brown eyes. I'm at a table with some brushes and a tangerine on it.[3] I'd been promised them when I was through sitting." (*Claw*, 180)

For what it's worth, Rudesind does not produce the apocryphal painting (though Severian is in a hurry and they do not look for it long), but he does imply that this meeting with Fechin, along with his own natural inclinations, have led him to became an artist himself, although most of his subsequent life seems to have been spent cleaning and restoring other artists' work. Still, let us take the old curator at his word. As a young boy he's met Fechin, who's already achieved some fame as a "real" artist. Rudesind almost certainly has not yet begun his journeyman phase in the curator's guild, although after he does and is apprenticed, it appears he's spent most of his career in various galleries nested within either the Citadel or House Absolute complexes. And in one or the other he stays, seemingly waiting to impress anyone he can with his tales of Fechin.

But when next we encounter the legendary artist, it is not through the testimony of Rudesind, but that of a nameless old man,[4] whom Severian encounters in the mountains between Thrax and Orithyia, far from Nessus. The dotard is the father of Becan,[5] Casdoe's dead pioneer husband, and in age appears to be a contemporary of Rudesind's (Severian himself notes this). Mistaking Severian for his son, the man begins to regale him with anecdotes about Fechin. In his account, however, Fechin is nowhere near to being the "real" artist of Rudesind's, but is, rather, an adolescent and somewhat of a rapscallion at that, "the worst of us all…a tall, wild boy, with red hair on his hands, on his arms,"[6] and who "could always get food or money from a woman." (*Sword*, 115) But as in Rudesind's tale, the old man has been sketched by Fechin, along with a young girl the artist's seduced, although Fechin keeps the drawing, despite the fact that the paper has been provided by Becan's father, who makes a big deal about having done so.[7] In addition, though the recalled childhood locale is never specified—about the only details we're given concern a nameless river (the Acis? the Gyoll?) and an old mill—we soon find out that Casdoe has been born in Thrax. This doesn't mean that Becan, her husband, couldn't have spent his more tender years in Nessus, as has apparently Rudesind, but it does allow us to speculate that he too may have grown up in Thrax, as might have his father. (Remember, the roads are closed, thereby discouraging travel.) Given this variance in location, plus the discrepancies about Fechin's age and public reputation—Rudesind's established, older artist versus Becan's father's adolescent rakehell—in concurrence with the inability of either gentleman to produce the portraits Fechin's made of them, make it hard to determine which account is more accurate or truthful. Or if both men are not simply senile and hence justifiably mixed up in their recall of salad days long past.

No, really: he RULES.

But where I think Wolfe finally clues us in as to what's going on with these various name-dropping episodes comes in the fourth and last time we hear about the oft-mentioned master. (*Note*: Wolfe very cagily spreads out his Fechin accounts so that there's one per book of the Quartet.) Once again curator Rudesind is our spokesperson, only now as he addresses Severian, our hero is no mere torturer's journeyman, but the new Autarch, having returned to Nessus and the Citadel, wherein he will preside. Curiously, however—and I think it's significant that Rudesind is the one to relay this—many people are now claiming to have known or met Severian previously—*just like Fechin!* Or as Rudesind puts it, in his longest speech in the Book:

> "Nobody here talks about anything else, seems like. How you was licked to shape right here. How they seen you this time and that time. How you looked, and what you said to them. There ain't one cook that didn't treat you to a pastry often. All them soldiers told you stories. Been a while now since I met a woman didn't kiss you and sew up a hole in your pants. You had a dog…and a bird and a coti that stole apples. And you climbed every wall in this place. And jumped off after, or else swung on a rope, or else hid and pretended you'd jumped. You're every boy that's ever been here, and I've heard stories put on you that belong to men that was old when I was just a boy, and I've heard about things I did myself,[8] seventy years ago." (*Citadel*, 284)

The fact that Rudesind relates this and not someone else (the pot calling the kettle black, I say), as well as the rich details he offers up as being part of these I-knew-Severian tales (notice how similar details underscore both his and Becan's father's anecdotes), coupled with the fact that Fechin's artwork has been consigned with Quartillosa's, lead me to speculate that Fechin himself was once Autarch—and that this is the source of his fame, not any artistic prowess. Where Fechin comes in terms of autarchal succession is not clear; certainly before Appian (which might make him the antepenultimate Autarch), but probably not before Maruthas. In fact, for all we know, Fechin may have been painting a portrait of the latter when Maruthas came to his earthly demise, making the Phoenix Throne a mere forebrain slurry away.

In any event, once Rudesind has narrated all of the above to Severian, he goes off once more—you guessed it—to clean his beloved, if perpetually dirty, Fechin.

6

GUARDIAN

Strange and wonderful tales abound in the *New Sun* quartet and its sequel, but not all of them are found in the brown book Severian carries in his sabertache. Some are told personally. Possibly the most interesting one of these is related by Cyriaca, the promiscuous armigette[1] Severian is sent to kill at Abdiesus' masquerade. Cyriaca's tale comes courtesy of her wine-drinking uncle, an avid bibliophile who's traveled far and wide seeking out old books.[2] "He's even gone to the lost archives," Cyriaca confides to Severian. "Have you heard of those?" Severian answers negatively, whereupon Cyriaca launches into a long, complex tale about the early days of starfaring man and the price that had to be paid to make such travel possible—no big deal really, *H. sapiens pangalacticae* simply bargained away the very things that made them human in the first place*,* soon "no longer [caring] for the taste of the pale wind, nor for love or lust, nor to make new songs nor to sing old ones, nor for any of the other animals things they believed they had brought with them out of the rain forests at the bottom of time." (*Sword*, 51) Eventually, however, the trustees of these surrendered goods—robots created by mankind—return the parcel, unleashing (not unlike Pandora) "a flood of artifacts of every kind, calculated by them to revive all those thoughts that people had put behind them." Millennia of machine-assisted rebuilding follows, but because the "faces and the maxims" of the original abdicators have been forgotten "the people...were delighted with the new things." Thus, according to Cyriaca, ends the First Empire, "which had been built only upon order." (*Sword*, 52)

But when the machines begin to die, Cyriaca tells Severian, the people despaired, not wanting to lose the knowledge embodied in them. Consequently, a great recording process is undertaken. "Each of them began to write down what he had learned in the long years when he had harkened to the teachings of the machines that spilled forth all the hidden knowledge of wild things." (*Sword*, 54) Untold centuries later, after these writings have either circulated freely or been hidden away for safekeeping, there comes a time "when some autarch (although they were not called autarchs then) hoped to recapture the dominion exercised by the first empire." Subsequently, he gathers up all these writings and the spoil is placed "into a great heap in the city of Nessus, which was then newly built, to be burned." But in his dreams that very night the Autarch sees "all the untamed worlds of life and death, stone and river, beast and tree, slipping away from his hands forever," and he decides not to burn the writings; instead, he intends to house them in a great vault, "For he thought that if the new empire he planned should fail him at last, he would retire to that vault and enter the worlds that, in imitation of the ancients, he was determined to cast aside."(*Sword*, 55) He also sets a guardian (or a series thereof) to watch over the archive, and to this day it remains faithful to him, eternally vigilant, awaiting his return.

So ends Cyriaca's tale of the lost archives, which Severian likens to a children's tale. Other readers, of course, have noted its resemblance to the intricate jeweled ficciónes wrought by Argentinean fabulist Jorge Luis Borges. Indeed, given the resemblance of Master Librarian Ultan to Borges (both are blind men of letters and Nessus is almost certainly Buenos Aires), it's tempting to identify the so-called guardian of the lost archives as Ultan himself and the library of Nessus (which may stretch well beyond the city limits all the way to the House Absolute) as the lost archives. Cyriaca's tale is also told within a chapter entitled "The Library of the Citadel," and after it's finished, Severian, who's met Ultan, concludes, "It is a wonderful story. I think that perhaps I know more of it than you." But is it actually Ultan that Severian believes is the guardian in question, with the great stacks of Nessus' library functioning as the lost archives? Or might he be thinking of someone or something else?

For a number of reasons I'd like to suggest the guardian is not Ultan,[3] but the thing awakened by Severian in the mine of the Saltus man-apes. This happens, as you recall, when Severian withdraws the Claw of the Conciliator; as he advances with it, the man-apes, mesmerized by its glow, halt in their attack. But when Severian begins to look for his lost *Terminus Est* by the same light, suddenly, even still further underground, giant footsteps began to sound. Severian flees the cave before whatever is making the footsteps manifests itself. But note his final commentary on the matter:

> What creature it was we had called from the roots of the continent I think I now know. But I did not know then, and I did not know whether it was the roaring of the man-apes, or the light of the Claw, or some other cause that had waked it. I only knew that there was something far beneath us before which the man-apes, with all the terror of their appearance and their numbers, scattered like sparks before a wind. (*Claw*, 55)

The important thing to highlight here is that Severian seems to lack the information necessary for him to make a proper identification of the footsteps-maker—*at
least at the time he heard them.* Later, however,[4] after he hears Cyriaca's tale, he's
able to connect the dots, even going so far as to imply that he knows more about
the story's true origins than Cyriaca.[5]

But more clues linking the lost archives to the Saltus mine can also be found
in Cyriaca's preamble to the tale. As she explains to Severian about the location of
the fortress containing the archives, "It stands upon a hill overlooking Gyoll, my
uncle told me, staring out over a field of ruined sepulchers, guarding nothing."
(*Sword*, 50) Saltus, of course, lies on the Gyoll, while the entrance to the mine is
accessed from a cliff. Moreover, as Severian and Jonas are led out of Saltus as prisoners of Vodalus' henchmen, witness what they see among the debris unearthed
by the miners:

> Everything foul lay in tumbled heaps ten times and more the height of the
> baluchither's lofty back—obscene statues, canted and crumbling, and
> human bones to which strips of dry flesh and hanks of hair still clung. And
> with them ten thousand men and women; those who, in seeking a private
> resurrection, had rendered their corpses forever imperishable lay there like
> drunkards after their debauch, their crystal sarcophagi broken,[6] their limbs
> relaxed in grotesque disarray, their clothing rotted or rotting, and their eyes
> blindly fixed upon the sky. (*Claw*, 73–74)

Clearly, if this doesn't constitute "a field of ruined sepulchers," nothing does. As
for Cyriaca's uncle's claim that the fortress lies *south* of Nessus—whereas Saltus is
situated north—I believe that this is her uncle deliberately attempting to mislead
Cyriaca. As Cyriaca herself has earlier explained, "It may be that he didn't tell me
everything, because as I talked to him I had the feeling he was a bit afraid I might
try to go myself." Hence his lie in this regard—to prevent his niece from traipsing
off in search of the lost archives.

The area code you have reached...

But is this the best we can do—identify the guardian of the lost archives as some
near-mythic sentinel slumbering away inside a deep dark mine—or can we make
further identification? Once more let's look to Cyriaca's narrative and see what
we can glean. Of immediate interest to us, I suggest, should be the various clues
pertaining to the *builder* of the archives. In other words, if we can figure out who
he is, we might be able to do similarly with the guardian. Not that there's all that

much challenge in the former regard—for clearly the Autarch who isn't actually an Autarch,[7] who wants to recapture the dominion held by the First Empire, but who fails in his quest—is Typhon the Great. We also know that Typhon has operated out of Nessus for a while and it appears quite probable he may even have had the city built for himself, to function as his new capital. As we're told by the physician attending Severian in the Matachin Tower,[8] "This coast is quake prone, as the old records indicate clearly enough—praise to our monarch, by the way, for having them brought here."[9] Additionally, Severian, before he's brought to Nessus in chains, has spent time previously in Saltus, where's he learned "that a shaft had been driven into a hillside about a year ago upon the advice of a hatif that had whispered in the ears of several of the principle citizens of the village, and that a few interesting and valuable items had been brought to the surface." (*Urth*, 245) *Hatif*, however, has a number of interesting meanings in Arabic; it originally meant "invisible caller" or "heavenly voice," belonging in mythology to dead poets who lead travelers astray in the desert with their song; but in modern Arabic *hatif* means telephone. What I'd therefore like to suggest is that this hatif is either one of the aforementioned artifacts calculated to revive all those thoughts that people had put behind; or is otherwise akin to the Matachin Tower's "unseen mouths[10] that spoke sometimes to human beings and sometimes to other mouths in other towers and keeps" (*Shadow*, 78) and which only Gurloes does not fear. In any event, it appears almost certain that the unnamed ruler in Cyriaca's tale is Typhon—just as it's he who's ordered the archives built.

But what about the guardian itself? Once again we need to remember that Wolfe continues the tale of Typhon in his *Long Sun* series. Here, on Whorl, when a particularly-vigilant sentinel or watchguard is needed, a talus is employed; we see, for example, the big robots guarding both Blood's estate and the tunnels beneath Viron.[11] But even though they're not identified as such, I also believe we encounter prototypical taluses much earlier, in *Urth of the New Sun*. When Severian is in the Cursed Town a second time, he notes the presence of "wains that rolled forward without oxen or slaves to draw them, no matter how steep the gradient, launching dense clouds of dust and smoke into the shining air and bellowing like bulls when we crossed their path." (*Urth*, 271–272) Certainly, these are some sort of robotic vehicle. And while most of their Vironese cousins appear to travel on caterpillar treads, like tanks, there's no reason that Typhon could not have had them modified, perhaps even fitting them out with the pedal equivalent of the telescoping arms they already bear. Being creatures of metal, with perhaps spin-down sleep cycles, they might well be perfectly-suited for the centuries-long task assigned them—guarding the lost archives, at least until Severian the Great wakes the last of their number.

7

HETHOR

The character known as Hethor has several mysteries attendant to him: (one) his real name, which Michael Andre-Driussi has neatly deduced to be Kim Lee Soong;[1] and (two) the means by which he's able to call up and transport his alien pets. Even Severian wonders about the latter, venturing that while the notules Hethor has unleashed upon Jonas and himself could be contained in a small cylinder, such could hardly be the case for the fire salamander and giant slug. Hethor is never seen hauling a large conveyance around, after all. Nor does Severian believe that vulcanal and limax have followed their master from a distance, waiting like dogs in the underbrush for his call. We readers, on the other hand, might speculate that Hethor's pets have been summoned up by apportional mirrors, such as Father Inire uses; but for Hethor to have carried them about on his person, they need to be rather small—perhaps too much so, if we credit the size of Inire's mirrors in the scene where Jonas returns to Tzadkiel's starship—and he almost certainly would have had them confiscated when he was arrested on the grounds of the House Absolute and thrown into the antechamber, just as Severian has had *Terminus Est* taken from him. And yet later inside that very locked antechamber, seemingly without specular redress, the slug makes its first appearance.[2] It also somehow makes its way to the remote, mountain jungle village of Decuman. But given the absence of Hethor in the village (whereas we know he shares lodgings with Severian in the antechamber), this seems more mysterious still. Could the beastmaster have simply directed the slug to follow Severian wherever he travels, including over chasm and cliff? This seems hardly likely for an entity both giant and protoplasmic. And so we're left wondering how Hethor, sans any visible sort of ark, is able to ferry his menagerie about—or even how he brought the subservient creatures to Urth in the first place.[3]

I do believe, however, a major clue can be glimpsed in Chapter XIII of *Sword*, "Into the Mountains." Severian, having fled Thrax, falls asleep atop a lee of naked rock, but only for about a watch, whereupon he wakes "with the impression—which was not a dream, but the sort of foundationless knowledge or pseudo-knowledge that comes to us when we are weary and fearful—that Hethor was leaning over me." (*Sword*, 99) The impression is very vivid at first: "I seemed to feel his breath, stinking and icy cold, upon my face; his eyes, no longer dull, blazed into mine." Later, however, when Severian is more fully awake, he rationalizes that the points of light he has taken to be Hethor's pupils have been "in fact two stars, large and very bright in the thin, clean air." Unable to fall back asleep, our hero attempts to pick out constellations in the night sky. He has little initial success, but soon begins to notice how many of the various stars differ in brightness and color.[4] "Then quite suddenly," Severian relates, "the shape of a peryton seemed to spring out as distinctly as if the bird's whole body had been powdered with the dust ground from diamonds." (*Sword*, 101) *Oh, my*, we go, impressed once more with Gene Wolfe's uncanny lyricism. But what the deuce is a peryton? None of the dictionaries I have access to contain it. Fortunately for us Andre-Driussi has traced the word's provenance back to Jorge Luis Borges' *Book of Imaginary Beings.* As he explains in *Lexicon Urthus*, "A peryton is said to be half deer and half bird, with the head and legs of a deer. [Only] Instead of casting its own shadow, it casts the shadow of a man." And while Andre-Driussi further describes the winged pteriopes that later rescue Severian and Appian from the Ascians as looking "somewhat like perytons," I'd like to go one step further. I believe that the winged creature carrying Agia in the very same rescue mission—Severian hears her voice above him as he's being lofted away—is actually Hethor; just as it's perytonic Hethor he sees from his mountain bed; and though we do not hear her, it seems equally likely he's carrying Agia here, which helps explain both how she manages to arrive at Casdoe's cabin ahead of Severian, as well as later escapes the alzabo. In other words, while Hethor casts the shadow of a man, he's actually a shapeshifter, or at least capable of assuming one other form—that of a peryton/pteriope.

Mother Slug

But how does this supposition help explain the various appearances of Hethor's dire creatures? Well, let's look at each of them individually, starting with the slug. As mentioned before, it makes its first appearance in the darkness of the antechamber, where both Severian and Hethor are confined. Possibly, we might conjecture, the slug could be Beuzec, who's been seen accompanying Hethor, yet manages to avoid confinement, escaping into the House Absolute. But this would mean that theriomorph Beuzec somehow had access from without to the antechamber—not an impossibility given the House Absolute's plethora of hidden passages, warrens, alcoves, etc., but how knowledgeable about these would the newly-introduced Beuzec be? On top of that, Severian, having himself escaped, later finds Beuzec hiding in a closet—most likely where he's been all along since evading his captors, and while there is a hole in the back of it, no telltale slime is anywhere evident. So in order for the Beuzec-As-Slug-Theory to work, the following has to occur: Beuzac escapes *into* the House Absolute, finds a way into the antechamber, protoplasmically explores it, then leaves by the same means he entered, ending up in a closet. Not an impossible journey; just an unlikely one. And so we're left wanting for a slug. Or are we? In other words, has there been any mention in the narrative of a slug-like creature before the antechamber incident?

I believe there has been, although it's very sly—just as you'd expect with Gene Wolfe. Shortly after Severian arrives in Saltus, you will recall, he's taken to the house of Barnoch the bandit, the door and single window of which have been sealed with rough masonry. According to the alcalde who accompanies Severian, this form of punishment—entombing someone in his or her own house—is traditional in Saltus. The alcalde then relates a tale about another miscreant so entombed. "A woman. I've forgotten her name, but we called her Mother Pyrexia.[5] The stones were put on her, just like what you see here, for it's largely the same ones doing it, and they did it in the same way." (*Claw*, 17) But when it comes time to unseal the house next year, the alcalde tells Severian, much to everyone's surprise, they do not find Mother Pyrexia dead. Explains the alcalde:

> "A woman sealed in the dark long enough can become something very strange, just like the strange things you find in rotted wood, back among the big trees.[6] We're miners, mostly, here in Saltus, and used to things found underground, but we took to our heels and came back with torches. It didn't like the light, or the fire either."

The alcalde never claims the creature is actually destroyed—hence I'd like to quibble with Mother Pyrexia's entry in *Lexicon Urthus* ("She had changed into something very strange when the house was opened, a nocturnal creature, and was quickly killed"), arguing that she may well have lived, taking to the woods about Saltus[7] until Hethor arrives, who is in the crowd at Morwenna's execution. Somehow, beastmaster Hethor is able to enlist/compel her aid and I believe it's the transmogrified Mother Pyrexia who attacks Severian in the antechamber, called by Hethor in whatever language shapeshifters share.

Comrade Sal

At any rate, since Severian leaves the secret door to the antechamber open,[8] it seems likely Hethor egresses via the same, eventually rendezvousing with Beuzec. Of course, Beuzec as Beuzec[9] is never seen again—Wolfe specifically has Severian mention this, but if ever there were a word I'd mistrust in GW's works, it's *never*, because I believe he uses it primarily to deceive. And so we flash forward to *Sword* and windowless Thrax. Severian the Lictor learns that five men have been burned to death, and not much later, after sparing Cyriaca's life, decides to flee the city, but not before he sees Dorcas one more time. He's on his way to the Duck's Nest, where Dorcas has been staying, when he encounters the inn's mistress, who relays dire news—Jurmin, her husband, has just been burned to death by a malefactor of fire, which, she surmises, is "looking for somebody." Severian rather quickly links its search to him, being almost certain it's one of Hethor's pets (one of the torturer's few valid deductions), and soon encounters it—"something dark and crooked and stooped" that grows into "a creature of glowing gauze, hot yet somehow reptilian." (*Sword*, 71–72) A similar change in size is noted by Severian later—"In the starlight it might have been only an old, hunched man in a black coat" (73)—suggesting (at least to me) the creature's dual nature as both man and vulcanal. Fortunately for Severian he's able to lead it to a dosshouse built over the edge of a precipice, where it burns a hole in the floor and falls to its death. End of Beuzec, end of fire salamander.

Winged Hethor, however, as mentioned above, probably transports Agia to Casdoe's cabin, just as Agia guides Hethor to Decuman's village. Remember, as I posit in *Agia and Agilus*, the twins belong to the same academy of magicians as Decuman and his cohorts—hence Agia's knowledge of the village's location. And it's here Severian re-encounters the slug (probably flown in as well), this time while confined in an underground holding cell; note, too, how it is dark. Once again Severian escapes it; then yet again in the log hall where he fights the sorcerer's duel with Decuman. The hall catches fire, but here evidently Mother Pyrexia dies—as perhaps befits someone named after a medical condition that mimics burning/heat. Hethor, meanwhile, disappears until near the end of *Citadel*, when, as winged peryton, he rescues Severian. And why doesn't he unleash another of his beast friends on Severian once he has his clutches on him? Circean Agia, his lover, doesn't wish him to, preferring, at least for the moment, to set Severian free. And so at last we part company from stammering Hethor, never to see him again.

Purns of a feather

Well, not quite.

Because in *Urth of the New Sun*, we meet a character aboard Tzadkiel's starship named Purn. Purn, who is younger than Hethor, has "the yellow hair of a southerner," but when asked if he hails from Urth, he replies, "Don't think I've ever been, but maybe I have. Big white moon?" (*Urth*, 27) Terraformed Lune, of course, is green, but the moon of Kim Lee Soong was almost certainly white.[10] Purn is also lying here; we learn later he's really from Urth, having boarded with Severian, intending to kill him, just as his older self has attempted to do in the past. This may seem a temporal paradox at first; but Wolfe very cagily provides us with the example of Gunnie/Burgundofara, each of whom is the same woman, just differently aged (Burgundofara is the younger version of Gunnie). Tzadkiel's starship, of course, can sail in and out of Time; and thus in a single round-trip journey may actually arrive before it departs. It's therefore possible young Purn has traveled to an older Urth where he already exists as Hethor;[11] it's also probable, as Andre-Driussi has suggested to me in private correspondence, that Purn and Hethor are *both* aboard the starship at the same time.[12] Gunnie, as well, may be responsible for Hethor/Purn's ultimate unhinging. (*Cherchez la femme, non*?) As Purn tells Severian, "I'd been hoping she'd kiss me…On this ship, every new hand's supposed to have an old one for a lover, to teach him ship's ways. The kiss is the sign." (*Urth*, 84) But in fact, Gunnie has chosen Severian, kissing him not once in front of Purn, but twice. Now recall the Hethor we first meet way back in *Shadow*, bemoaning the loss of his beloved paracoita, whose "great pupils" are "dark as wells" and whose "i-irises" are purple—are these the "wide dark eyes" of Gunnie?

As for the non-saintly name of Purn, I'd like to suggest it derives in the same fashion as Gunnie does from Burgundofara—being short, of course, for peryton.

8

MANDRAGORA

So, of a lone unhaunted place possesst,
Did this soul's second inn, built by the guest,
This living buried man, this quiet mandrake, rest.

John Donne, *Progress of the Soul*

Citadel of the Autarch concludes Gene Wolfe's *New Sun* quartet and it is to this titular edifice deep within Nessus that Severian retires very near the volume's end. Having consumed his predecessor's forebrain, Severian himself is now Autarch. Desiring quarters suitable to his position, he's assigned lodgings in the most ancient part of the Citadel, and it's here, among the more interesting effects in his dusty new environs, he encounters a mandragora in spirits—a mysterious bottled fetus that he inadvertently resuscitates and who engages him in conversation (although telepathically for its part). But who—or what—is this mandragora? In his *Encyclopedia of Science Fiction*, critic John Clute tentatively suggests it might be Severian's own long-lost sister, and in many respects, given that the mandragora at one point addresses Severian as "Brother," and that Severian describes the pickling fluid surrounding the homuncule in placental terms, this seems as potent a guess as any. But is it the only guess that warrants making or is there other evidence that suggests the mandragora may be something else? In lieu of deferring to Clute or decrying the general indeterminateness many readers seem to find in Wolfe, let us investigate the Something-Else-Theory.

In my opinion, author Wolfe, whose interest in etymology is well known, often draws upon a word's roots to provide essential clues in unriddling the deeper significance of much of his fiction. It therefore seems logical to take a closer look at *mandragora*—the Latin and more poetical version of mandrake. Almost at once, and without recourse to a single dictionary, we notice its *man* + *dragora* binomialness. *Man* requires little exegesis, the mandragora tuber being notoriously man-shaped (whence, in addition to its hallucinogenic properties, its use in folk medicine). *Dragora*, however, is slightly less evident, relating back to *draco*, the Latin word for *dragon* (as does *drake*). But while interesting, is this same hybridity manifest beyond an etymologic level in Wolfe's mandragora? Perhaps. His bottled imp does resemble a wizened foetal man, after all. Yet what about the draco moiety? Is there, on further reflection, anything or anyone in the *Book of the New Sun* that might relate to the notion of dragonness, whether symbolic or literal?

To answer this requires a bit of reappraisal and involves Typhon, Urth's grand Imperator—the Stalin-slash-Genghis Khan of Wolfe's posthistory. Typhon's namesake, of course, harkens back to classical Greek mythology, where he's the consort of Echidna and father of many monsters (a relationship Wolfe will perpetuate in his *Book of the Long Sun*). But while many readers may be familiar with Typhon's literal hotwindedness—our word typhoon derives in part from this—few may be aware he's often described as a hundred-headed dragon, with a body covered in serpents.[1] Now recall Wolfe's naming stratagems for the New Sun series—i.e., that while the human denizens of Urth are named after saints, *all extraterrestrials bear mythic names.* This is a point I seldom seem mentioned in connection with Typhon—that he's an alien, or at least at one time had an alien body.[2] For clearly by the time Severian first meets him, he appears human, if bizarrely so—his head having been grafted to the body of Piaton, a slave, whose head also remains. But surely this macabre arrangement has been undertaken only as a stopgap or intermediate measure, something that will allow the aging and mortal Typhon to continue living while he and his technicians devise something better than mere flesh to house him. And what might that alternative be? Well, how about an artificial, man-made body; an android, or to use the convention that Wolfe uses in his Long Sun books, a chem.

Chems, of course, play an important role in Wolfe's Whorl series. We're also given to understand that the majority of them were created before Pas launched his giant spaceship (Pas = Typhon's *nom de soleil long)*. But while for the most part these chems are programmed to be servitors or soldiers, several have in turn been co-opted for other purposes, not only by the so-called black mechanics of Patera Incus, but by members of the Ayuntamiento, Viron's ruling council. Indeed, Councilor Lemur of the latter seems to be mentally controlling a chem body while his decrepit physical body lies comatose, connected to life-sustaining machinery. Who's to say he might not eventually have been able to download his entire mind into the chem, completely unnecessitating the physical body? This, after all, is what Pas/Typhon has done, although the downloading in his case has not been to a mechanical proxy, but to Mainframe, the Whorl's supercomputer.

Lemur, for his part, dies under Lake Limna before any such advanced transference can take place. But given Typhon's success in a very similar area—sort of a reverse Pinocchio effect, where flesh becomes not wood, but metal and synthetics—it does not seem unreasonable to conclude such transformations are possible. Certainly Pas and the other "gods" of Mainframe can already subsume chem bodies should they so wish—we see this in Book 3 of the Whorl series, *Calde of the Long Sun*. Echidna, at this point, has taken over the mechanical sibyl, Maytera Marble, killing the brutal Musk. Protagonist Silk, however, is caught somewhat unawares by this ability. Says he: "I knew you gods could possess bios like us. I didn't know you could possess chems as well." Echidna, who has only seconds before revealed that Pas is dead, replies, "They are easier…My husband…" But the snake-wielding monstress never finishes her sentence (such aposiopeses are common in Wolfe), and this leads Silk to wonder if perhaps Pas may have killed his host during possession, thereby causing his own demise. Or at least that appears to be the context of Silk's follow-up question, as he asks: "Did Pas possess someone who died?"

No other citation is more crucial to the meat of this treatise than Echidna's terse response: "The prime calcula…" she says. "…His Citadel…" (*Calde*, 102) And that's all we're given by the parsimonious Wolfe—two fragments connected by ellipses, a mere five words between them, that we're left to wring some meaning from. But given that while on Urth Typhon has at least temporarily operated out of Nessus, what other citadel could Echidna be referring to than *the* Citadel—soon-to-be traditional home of the Autarchs? (Wolfe does capitalize citadel in each instance, removing them from the realm of the generic.) As for "prime calcula," it's not difficult to posit that *prime* means first; while *calcula* connotes both *calculato*r (read thinking machine or robot) and *calculus*, the Latin word for stone. The latter is more important than it may initially seem since all chems, by convention, are named after metals or minerals; e.g., Marble, Schist, Shale, etc.. Could the prime calcula therefore, built and housed in the Citadel, be the very first chem—who died when alien Typhon attempted to possess it? Is the mandragora, preserved in white brandy for purposes of either study or commemoration, this 1.0 chem prototype?

Let us return to the chapter wherein we meet the mandragora (*Citadel*, XXXV) and see if we can find any additional support for this notion. Here again we note that Severian's new quarters are in the *oldest* part of the Citadel, where the furniture we're told seems designed more for alien than human inhabitants. Comments Severian: "They did without chairs as we know them, having for seats only complex cushions; and their tables lacked drawers and that symmetry we have come to consider essential." Severian cites changes in fashion for the outré look, but exobiology might just as well account for the lack of convention; I submit that monocephalic Typhon would probably have felt quite at home here. Furthermore, in a connected laboratory, there's the fabled "emerald bench" of alchemy, one of the major goals of which was discovering the Philosopher's Stone, a magical artifact that will not only transmute base metals, but allow its possessor to achieve transcendence over all disease. Typhon, if nothing else, is obsessed with his own longevity. As Scylla, his daughter, puts it, "Daddy had this thing about a male heir, and this other thing about not dying." (*Lake*, 274)

But by far the most telling evidence for making my case is spoken by the mandragora itself. After first identifying Severian as "the heir"—i.e., not so much Typhon's literal son, but heir to the throne—it, in turn, is asked who it is. "A being without parents," it tells Severian, "whose life is passed immersed in blood." It has no parents, of course, because it's artificially made (this echoes a similar statement by Typhon about not having been born[3]). As for being immersed in blood, remember, the homuncule is preserved in white brandy—and alcohol is as much a fuel as gasoline or oil.[4] Just as we cannot function without life-sustaining blood, neither can androids without fuel (that energy source is primarily radioactive by the Whorl series, but it's also interesting to note that the taluses of Viron run on fish oil). Severian, drawing upon his status as both orphan and torturer, subsequently tells the mandragora how congruent their lives have been, saying, "We should be friends then, you and I, as two of similar background usually are." Also: "I think we are more alike than you believe." It's statements like these that lead the mandragora to address Severian as brother, not any putative genetic link, and even then the usage seems more cynical than fraternal. Or as the mandragora complains when Severian refuses to smash its imprisoning cucurbit, "So much for brotherhood." As for the latter's response to Severian's question about it dying, it says, "I have never lived. I will cease thinking." (Which is pretty much what a calculating machine does when the metaphorical plug is pulled.) "I neither grow, nor move, nor respond to any stimulus save thought, which is counted no response. I am incapable of propagating my kind, or any other." The *any other* here, I maintain, is Typhon, who, as I've argued, may have attempted to possess it, seeing himself, to use the Donne epigraph, as a guest hoping to check into alternate accommodations—"a second inn." Unfortunately, there appear to have been some bugs in the chem 1.0. programming. "I was deformed," the mandragora tells Severian, "and died before birth." That is, before Typhon could make his transference complete, or at least complete its trial run. Whereupon the mandragora is put into the pickling jar, until Severian comes along, reviving it.

Of course, rather than admit failure here and quit, Typhon and his technicians must have continued to work on new prototypes,[5] for more sophisticated and stable chems are readily available by the time of Whorl, including ones capable of breeding. Somewhere along the way Urth's Imperator also seems to have discovered how to scan himself directly into a computer, leading to yet another discard—this time not of a bottled man-dragon fetus, but a grotesque double-headed monster that Severian first resurrects, then kills—as if Jesus at dawn, but Heracles by twilight.

9

MASKS OF THE FATHER

Severian, despite being raised as an orphan, is eventually able to determine who his father is and meet with him twice. But even had he never encountered waiter Ouen or learned the truth about him, he would still have had a strong paternal surrogate in Master Palaemon, who rather nicely fills the bill in this regard. At the same time, however, torturer Palaemon is far from being the token representative of the male parent, for *New Sun* abounds with a number of important father figures—some real, some virtual, but all playing crucial roles in various ways, even if not entirely fathomable on first or second read. Indeed, while several enigmas may yet obtain to Ouen,[1] they are paltry when compared to the vast array of mysteries clouding the true particulars and motivations of his various *pères pareils*. Then again, perhaps this is be expected; each of them, unlike Ouen, typically wears a mask, and even this, in and of itself, may only represent the first level of duplicity. As we're prompted by the Hierodule Famulimus at another point, just before she removes a second mask, only then revealing her true countenance, "Did you not ever think that he who wore a mask might wear another?" (*Sword*, 273) In my opinion this double wearing of masks is not an isolated instance, but the rule—at least for the fatherly triumvirate that will be the subject of this essay. I also believe that no other plot element is more important to an understanding of *New Sun*'s narrative and thematic crux than the stripping away of these masks and revealing what is underneath, and that perhaps no other tenet in this book will be deemed as controversial.

Be that as it may, let us begin our discussion of the three fatherly figures involved—Palaemon, Inire and Ossipago.

The Robot

Unlike Master Palaemon and Father Inire, we initially encounter Ossipago rather late in the game—he makes his one and only quartet appearance near the end of

Sword, the third volume of the series—but I'd still like to begin with him, since his role, compared to the other two, is somewhat less substantial. Ossipago, of course, is the companion of the Hierodules Famulimus and Barbatus; when we first meet the trio, they're visiting Baldanders in his castle of terror, having dropped in on the giant via their sky ship, which can flit in and out of time as well as space. However, unlike Famulimus and Barbatus, who are taller than Severian, Ossipago is diminutive and stout, walks with "short, waddling steps," and appears to be made of metal. Indeed, Severian is later led to believe he's the robotic ex-babysitter of the two Hierodules. As he tells Ossipago, on re-encountering him aboard Tzadkiel's starship, "I know that Ossipago is a machine…[and that your name] means bone-grower. You took care of Barbatus and Famulimus when they were small, saw to it that they were fed and so on, and you've remained with them ever since." (*Urth*, 33) Obviously, this seems much more like privileged information than anything Severian could deduce on his own, and in fact, in his very next sentence, Severian confirms this to be so, telling us, "That's what Famulimus told me once." I'll come back to this later, when we have further context, but for now, suffice it to say that mendacity may not be a uniquely human trait. And yet, even without additional comment, the astute reader may have already noticed a discrepancy or two with Severian's statement. For starters, *Ossipago* is a mythic, not a saintly, name; by Wolfe's convention all such names belong exclusively to non-human characters—primarily alien. Robots, in the author's scheme, are named after metals; e.g., Sidero means 'iron' in Greek, while Hadid is Arabic for the same (both are android sailors aboard Tzadkiel's starship; plus there are the *Whorl* chems named after minerals). So why, then, doesn't Ossipago have a robot's name? Why is he named like Famulimus and Barbatus—two Hierodules? The obvious inference is that he's *not* a robot, but an alien—one wearing a metal suit of some sort. This might well explain several odd comments that Severian makes about Ossipago, but never provides additional gloss upon. For instance, when Severian first sees the three cacogens, he makes the following observation: "The masks all three wore gave them the faces of refined men of middle age, thoughtful and poised; but I was aware that the eyes that looked out through the slits in the masks of the two taller figures were larger than human eyes, and that the shorter figure had no eyes at all, so that only darkness was visible there." (*Sword*, 262) This, on first read, may not seem all that unusual, especially if we've temporarily forgotten Wolfe's naming conventions. Ossipago—ostensibly a robot—has no need for eyes, just some sort of built-in sensory apparatus that can process visual or equivalent information. And yet Severian still seems to believe Ossipago doesn't want him to notice his eyelessness; as he's shortly to state following a series of exchanges, "[Ossipago] turned and made a show of staring out the narrow window behind him, as though he feared I might see the empty eye slits of his mask." (*Sword*, 263) But why would a putative robot fear this? What might the empty eye slits betray? Something about the true nature of Ossipago's identity, but which he doesn't want revealed? Because unlike Famulimus and Barbatus, who will frequently remove their masks, Ossipago stubbornly retains his. Even thickheaded Severian seems to find this anecdysial behavior puzzling, noting how, in his penultimate encounter with the roboid child-sitter, "He had not removed his disguise. I suppose it did not render him less comfortable, and in fact I have never seen him do so." (*Urth*, 35) But again, what is Ossipago hoping to conceal by such behavior? At the very least that he's *not* a robot?—which therefore makes a liar of Famulimus, if an ever so curious one, since it's hard to envision what might be gained by misleading Severian in this direction. Or could it be something even more duplicitously sinister?

The Abraxas

To return to an earlier point, if from a slightly different perspective, part of the answer, I believe, can be found in the name *Ossipago*. Apparently, it, like *Famulimus* and *Barbatus*, is but one of many possible subsets of names the trio of alien travelers uses—nominal masks, if you will. Dr. Talos is the first to clue us to this, cautioning Severian just before he's introduced to the Hierodules, "You remember to be on your good behavior now. They don't like to be called cacogens, you know. Address them as *whatever it is they say their names are this time…*" (*Sword*, 261 [*Italics mine.*]) Talos' warning, however, gives rise to the very real possibility that the two Hierodules and their traveling companion have used different names in the past.[2] But when and where? Are there passages in the text that we can point to for possible corroboration? One of these occasions, I'd like to suggest, can be found in *Claw*, in the scene which takes place in the stone town. Merryn, at this point, is seeking to explain how the Cumaean is able to escape the confines of the present. "In sleep," she tells Severian, "the mind is encircled by its time, which is why we so often hear the voices of the dead there, and receive intelligence of things to come. Those, who, like the Mother, have learned to enter the same state while waking live surrounded by their own lives, even as the Abraxas perceives all of time as an eternal instant." (*Claw*, 289) Merryn's mention here of "the Abraxas" is ever so casual, which may be as good an indication as any as to Wolfe's subtlety, but it receives no further attention; we also never encounter it anywhere else in the five books of Urth. We're therefore left to guess or figure out who or what "the Abraxas" might be. Wolfe's use of the definite article, of course, might indicate mere ordinary distinctiveness, contrasting, say, Hierodules Famulimus and Barbatus with Ossipago *the* robot. But it might also be part of a title of some sort, akin to *the* Cumaean, or, maybe even in a loftier sense, the Lord God Almighty. Abraxas, after all, as a figure from Gnostic religion, has lots of history to draw on, and in point of fact, one 2nd-Century teacher, Basilides of Egypt, did call him the supreme deity. Ergo, perhaps Abraxas represents some god of the Hierodules, or one of the more powerful Hierogrammates. Then again, this also swings wide of our theory that Abraxas is simply another alien *nom de convenience*. So let me advance for now the notion that Wolfe is using *the* here to distinguish otherness—whether it's titular, supernal, or mundane—and that irrespective of the article that *Abraxas*—again, a mythic name—is one of Ossipago's nominal alter egos. But is there any textual evidence to support this? Well, in *Urth*, after Severian meets up with Famulimus, Barbatus and Ossipago again (as stated before, all are passengers aboard Tzadkiel's starship), he finally realizes that their sense of time runs counter to his own. Hence his initial meeting with the trio has actually been their last, taking place in their yet-to-occur future. Severian, then, in reminiscing a bit about that initial encounter, elicits the following comment from Famulimus: "Only Ossipago here has a memory like yours." (*Urth*, 33) But how curious a statement this is. Does it, for example, pertain to Severian's prodigal retention of all memories, or simply that he remembers time in a direction that is antithetical to the Hierodules' sense of recall? And why don't Famulimus and Barbatus have the same native abilities as their former childsitter? A robot, of course, might have total recall, but one gets the impression that Famulimus is talking here about being able to remember what is essentially the future. Could it be, however, that Ossipago—like *the Abraxas*—perceives all of time as a single instantaneous moment—hence is able to remember anything that has ever occurred over its lifetime? For such a being, obviously, there would be no past or future—only an omnipresent now. This, in many respects, recapitulates the situation with Lewis Carroll's White Queen, who is almost certainly Wolfe's paradigm in this case. It's she, we recall, who, similarly unconstricted by time, observes to Alice in *Through the Looking-Glass*, "[Living backwards] always makes one a little giddy at first, but there's one great advantage in it, that one's memory works both ways." Ossipago/Abraxas—perhaps singly for a Hierodule, perhaps not—may thus be Wolfe's *reine blanc* equivalent, and mnemonically able to retrieve anything that has ever happened to him, much like Severian—only his span is totipotent, whereas Severian's is limited to time lived.

The Isochronon

But this also gives rise to yet another series of linked speculations. What if we wished to convey in one word the sense that something "is able to perceive all of time as an eternal instant"? Wouldn't the Greek neologism *isochronon* fill the bill? Interestingly enough, the Autarch has a so-called isochronon. As Dr. Talos tells Severian:

> "I'm told that the Autarch has an isochronon in his sleeping chamber, a gift from another autarch from beyond the edge of the world. Perhaps it is the master of these gentlemen here. I don't know. Anyway, he fears a dagger at his throat and will let no one near him when he sleeps, so this device tells the watches of his night. When dawn comes, it rouses him. How then should he, the master of the Commonwealth, permit his sleep to be disturbed by a mere machine?" (*Sword*, 269)

Several things are worthy of attention here, I believe. The "it" in Talos' second sentence might actually refer to *isochronon* rather than *autarch*, making the sentence in its truer sense read, "Perhaps the isochronon is the master of these gentlemen here." Considering how Barbatus in the earlier castle encounter has made a deferential remark about how "Ossipago knows best," and that even Severian deems him "the servant and yet the master of Famulimus and Barbatus," this does not seem an unjustified conclusion. It's also possible that the isochronon—who's been deemed "a machine" just like Ossipago—is something else entirely, or at least more of a caretaker than a simple timekeeping mechanism. (One also imagines Ossipago standing watch over his two youthful charges and rousing them at dawn.) Perhaps as in Dr. Talos' typological play, "Eschatology and Genesis," there's a real life analogue for the isochronon—so much of Talos' little aside seems more ideally suited to a children's tale than anything else, and this has the effect of further blurring the lines between reality and fable. But for my money, there is almost certainly a link between the isochronon and the Abraxas, just as there is between Ossipago and the Abraxas, and no one of the three is likely to be a mere machine.

The Babysitter

But given all this talk of caretakers, perhaps it's time we discussed a parallel conceit—in his earlier rearing of Famulimus and Barbatus, for whom is Ossipago acting *in loco parentis*? Surely, the young Hierodules are not just two wayward orphans from Yesod, timeskipping about, imparting information to Baldanders one day, then saving Severian with a faux eclipse at the stone town on the next. Who, if anyone, has determined their mission? Who sanctions their activities? Perhaps, we might conjecture, it's some Hierogrammate potentate back on Yesod, who's relaying instructions through Ossipago. Yet if this is the case, why send juveniles, and short-lived ones at that? As we're told by Baldanders, "These things live only a score of years, like dogs." (*Sword*, 265) This brevity seems even more puzzling when you consider Father Inire has been around since the dawn of the Autarchy, which makes him at least 1,000 years old. Whence his longevity compared to his Hierodule counterparts? That being said I'd like now to offer a major speculation—that Famulimus and Barbatus are the children of *New Sun*'s other Hierodule pair, Father Inire and the Cumaean. This may seem a bit diffi-cult to swallow at first, but I believe that the evidence for such a line of descent is more than compelling. We know, for example, that "Father" Inire has supposedly built the Botanic Gardens just for the Cumaean. Certainly love, or its alien equiv-alent, might account for this. The Cumaean, in turn, has a matching, parentally-related honorific, i.e., "Mother," and out of all the characters in *New Sun*'s cast of hundreds, only she and female Famulimus speak in blank verse; surely, this is not just Wolfean happenstance, but a direct connection between the two. It also would not surprise me if the "hairless, crippled animals" Severian sees when visit-ing the Witches' Keep as a boy—recall that the Cumaean is watching them through "a glass tabletop," but which may be some sort of alien communications device—are actually Famulimus, Barbatus and Ossipago in transit aboard either their or Tzadkiel's spacecraft, just as I suspect it's the same trio Hildegrin has occasionally seen visiting her cave ("Sometimes I see somebody walkin' around up there, and metal or maybe a jewel or two flashin'." *Shadow*, 209). And in prac-tical terms, of course, having a single family unit headed by the patriarchal Inire, whose sole mission on Urth is to determine who will bring about the New Sun, makes much more sense than having rogue or independent elements attempting the same objective. As for the shortened "life spans" of Famulimus and Barbatus, this is figurative; it's much more likely they're intermediate forms, in transition between larvae and adult, and that it's only their current phase that's so short-lived. Tzadkiel, of course, evinces numerous metamorphoses, while Apheta is an admitted Hierogrammate larva; why should we not expect the Hierodules, who are Hierogrammate creations, to exhibit similar changes?

And so, then, the long roundabout answer to our question about the nature of Ossipago's stewardship is this: he's acting the surrogate parent for Father Inire and the Cumaean. Or is it still not quite that simple? Because while time and again Ossipago does his best to conceal his identity—or at least the facial portions thereof—from Severian, there's still one more character who does exactly the same, and that's Father Inire himself. This might strike you as surprising, but if you actually go back and read through Wolfe's entire five volume series, and look specifically at each instance where Father Inire is mentioned, you'll notice that, important though the alien is, he's never encountered in the flesh, only second hand and primarily in the reminiscences of others. In fact, we as readers never have any direct face-time with him. This may or may not make sense to you, depending on how you view Inire—as a powerful friend from the stars or a behind-the-scenes, alien Machiavelli, scheming to save Urth for his own selfish purposes. Either way, Wolfe may be attempting to portray not so much Inire's elusiveness, but his industriousness. Given as well that Severian spends the larger part of the chronicle wandering about the Commonwealth, seeking to either ply his trade or return the Claw of the Conciliator to the Pelerines, this may be another possible factor. Simply put, he just doesn't travel in the right circles, and since *New Sun* is his story, we can only expect to encounter Father Inire if or as Severian encounters him. But again this begs the truth, because there at least two occasions where Severian meets Father Inire, although each time the alien is in disguise, and Severian never comes close to guessing who he is.

The Monkey

First, however, before we examine those encounters in detail, let's attempt to co-ordinate what we do know about Father Inire's appearance, even though in each case our sources are secondary. Severian himself, trading stories with his fellow apprentices in the torturers' guild, offers an initial description, writing how "More fantastic still were the tales of [the Autarch's] vizier, the famous Father Inire, who looked like a monkey, and was the oldest man in the world." (*Shadow*, 82) Obviously, at this stage, Severian is simply repeating what he's heard from other guild members, but later he meets someone—the Stygian boatman who is both Dorcas' husband and his own grandfather—who's actually seen Inire in the flesh. According to the boatman, "Just a little man he is, with a wry neck and bow legs." (*Shadow*, 198) After this point, however, everything we're privy to about Father Inire's physical appearance is simply a variant on one of the above. Thus we hear of "Father Inire bent nearly double, like a gnome in a nursery book, with no more a nose than an alouatte" and "old, twisted Father Inire." Again, while probably accurate, these are not Severian's observations, but the testimony or hearsay of others, because in the course of *New Sun* we never see Severian and

Father Inire (or at least anyone who's expressly identified as such) together. However, after Severian escapes from the antechamber and stumbles upon the Autarch in the Secret House, he's eventually ushered from Appian's presence by "a bent little man [who] slipped silently into the room. He wore a cowled habit like a cenobite's. The Autarch spoke to him, something I was too distracted to understand." (*Claw*, 190) Whereupon the cowled figure conducts Severian to the Vatic Fountain, providing further instructions from there as to how to find his friends. But notice here how *bent* and *little* match what we know of Father Inire's appearance. Also, and mysteriously so, that the servitor wears a cowled habit—but for what purpose? Surely, this is not a custom at the House Absolute, where given the ever-present danger of assassination, no mere servant would be allowed to lurk about with his face concealed for long—to say nothing of the disrespect this presents to a figure of authority. And what exactly *doesn't* the distracted Severian hear the Autarch say—such lacunae are nearly always significant in Wolfe—something to the effect of *Ah, Father Inire, would you mind showing our young torturer friend the way to the thiasus grounds?* Father Inire is also probably the one person in the world who wouldn't have to make obeisances to the Autarch, and with quarters nearby could easily make a quick appearance whenever the Autarch deemed him necessary. Hence, with few doubts, my conclusions about the mysterious cowled figure: he's the elusive Father Inire himself.

But while such an encounter seems almost destined to happen given Inire's residency at the House Absolute, when Severian next meets him, it is not in or on the grounds of the Autarch's subterranean headquarters, but far to the north, in the remote jungle. Severian and Appian are both prisoners of Vodalus at this point, having been literally snatched by Hethor and his pteriopes from the clutches of the Ascians. Leading the entire party through the jungle are three savages, "a pair of young men who might have been brothers or even twins, and a much older one, twisted, I thought, by deformities as well as age, who perpetually wore a grotesque mask." (*Citadel*, 228) In addition, we're given this further detail about the latter: "The old man had a staff as crooked as himself, topped with the dried head of a monkey." Several days later, when the column beds down for the evening, Severian locates the Autarch (who, like himself, bears injuries incurred from the crash of their flying craft) in a nearby covered palanquin, then describes how Appian receives a late visitor.

> I saw the old guide (his bent figure and the impression of an immense head conferred by his mask were unmistakable) approach this palanquin and slip beneath it. Some time passed before he scuttled away. This old man was said

to be an *uturuncu*, a shaman capable of assuming the form of a tiger. (*Citadel*, 228)

Now to connect the necessary dots: the shaman is described in *exactly* the same terms as Father Inire—*old, twisted* and *bent*; moreover, his staff bears a dried monkey's head, which no doubt is meant to function for the head we cannot see, the one concealed behind the mask. Its simian qualities portend the obvious. As for the palanquin visit, later, when it becomes time for Severian to kill the Autarch and harvest his forebrain, Appian tells his imminent murderer/successor that "Father Inire is with the insurgents. He was to bring you what is necessary, then help you get away." Vodalus, of course, *heads up* the insurgents; subsequently, Appian reveals that he has, thrust into his waistband, "a hilt of silvery metal no thicker than a woman's finger, [with a blade that] was not half a span in length, but thick and strong, and of that deadly sharpness I had not felt since Baldander's mace had shattered *Terminus Est*." (*Citadel*, 235) Severian, who's been searched by his captors, has had a razor confiscated, but believes that the Autarch has simply managed to conceal the silver blade. I think, however, it's much more likely that it's been slipped to him by the *uturuncu*, and that this is one of the "necessary" things that Father Inire purportedly might be bringing. There's also in the shaman's alleged transformative abilities a possible link to the man-apes of Saltus, who, at one time are described by Severian as "firefly tiger-men;" the man-apes, remember, are specifically loyal to Father Inire, being perhaps his creation or even deracinated kin.[3] It therefore seems highly likely that the *uturuncu* is Inire, just as the cowled servitor is, and that Severian is completely oblivious to the true identity of either. Not that the clues are all that palpable; and to be fair, it's clear that Inire definitely does not want to be recognized. Perhaps, remembering the future, he knows that Severian will be the next Autarch, but is hoping to avoid any possible complications to his mission—who knows how the torturer might react once he finds out how manipulated his life has been? Hence one possible explanation for Inire's resorting to a series of disguises.

But in this demonstrated reluctance to reveal himself to Severian, whose behavior does Inire imitate? *None other than robotic Ossipago.* Is it therefore possible that Inire and Ossipago are one and the same? Certainly, if you accept the notion that Ossipago's outerwear is a metal suit of some sort, there's nothing that vitiates this supposition. In fact, the suit appears almost tailor-made for the wizened Inire, obviously having been made for someone of lesser stature. Remember too how Ossipago moves with "short, waddling steps"? Yet who builds a robot that locomotes like this? Whereas if the occupant's legs were bowlegged, this might be a natural consequence. Furthermore, it appears as if Ossipago may be using some sort of voice modulator, for he speaks "in a tone so deep that one felt rather than heard it." Considering that Severian has already heard Inire-the-cowled-servitor speak (to say nothing of the many times he will hear his undisguised vizier do so in the future), this adds yet another layer of concealment. And small wonder bashful Ossipago refuses to remove his mask—how could Severian not help but recognize the celebrated simian countenance of Father Inire himself? Perhaps as well this partially explains Father Inire's relative absence from the narrative main stage of *New Sun*. He's too busy shepherding around his children in their sky ship. The suit he wears may allow him to negotiate zero gravity or acceleration forces, and as for transportation from the House Absolute to the sky ship and back, he has his mirror devices.[4] It's also likely he could come and go as he pleases, without any one knowing, or even return at the exact same time he left (the sky ship can access the Corridors of Time). And by closely monitoring the activities of his children, in particular their relationship with Baldanders, he could more accurately judge who will better serve the Hierodules' long-term interests as future savior—the self-made giant or Severian—all the while attempting to wield multiple timelines from his unique vantage point.

Small wonder one of his sobriquets equates him with yet another prime mover.

Because whatever you choose to call him—Ossipago, Father Inire, or the Abraxas[5]—for all the heads he bears, he's as much a single entity as the titular beast of Wolfe's second novel. If not exactly Cerberus, still the god who wags the tale.

The Blind Torturer

Master Torturer Palaemon, of course, is *New Sun*'s other major father figure. Only instead of aliens or the larger figurative world, his putative child is Severian. This sort of bonding between master and apprentice is probably the norm in the Order of the Seekers for Truth and Penitence, I suspect, since torturers are forbidden to marry and the guild's young wards lack parents, but in Severian's case the arrangement seems to have worked out particularly well. When he betrays the guild, for example, it's Master Palaemon who intercedes on his behalf, arguing successfully that exile would be a more fitting punishment than death. It's also Palaemon who bestows upon Severian the carnifical *Terminus Est*—a sword expensive enough that Agia and Agilus will later attempt to murder their cousin to acquire it. But even had events worked themselves out differently and Severian never disgraced the guild, we would still have the sense that Palaemon and Severian enjoyed a special relationship. As Severian, when thrust into fatherly guise himself after Casdoe's family had been killed, and he becomes Little Severian's guardian, tells us: "I suddenly understood why Master Palaemon had enjoyed talking with me as a child." (*Sword*, 145) Implicit in this, of course, is much more than the standard master-apprentice relationship, and indeed Severian later avows, "I had always been his best pupil and his favorite." (*Citadel*, 267) The absence of Ouen from his life, therefore, may not have been as consequential as it might have, since in Master Palaemon Severian has had an adequate, loving, substitute father.

But again, as with the various figures discussed above, many mysteries still accrue to the person of Palaemon. For starters, there's the curious arrangement of lenses he wears. These seem less like common spectacles than "the protruding optical device" Severian mentions, although perhaps this reflects more on the lost art of glass-making than anything else, or that Palaemon's vision is so severely compromised he needs to wear something akin to bug-eyed goggles. He is, after all, somewhat advanced in years, and while most of the time he remains masked, on the few occasions he isn't, he's described as having an "aged face," "white hair" and "a few, crooked teeth." He never, however, removes the optical device—not in Severian's presence, anyway—and curiously enough, throughout all of Severian's travels, we meet no one else fitted out with anything similar, or even simple spectacles. Then there's the bifold cognomen *Palaemon*—unique because only it and one other character name draw upon *both* saintly and mythic exemplars. How, if we're to adhere to Wolfe's naming conventions—which, I maintain, are near inviolable—are we to reconcile this? Is he, as *Saint* Palaemon suggests, a man? Or is he, as *marine god* Palaemon implies, an alien? Obviously, the former—but how then, other than to attribute to Wolfe nomenclatural sloppiness, do we explain the mythic aspect?

Yet another problem is *Terminus Est*. As we're given to understand, it's Palaemon's personal sword, but how has he acquired the valuable blade? It seems well beyond the purse he's likely to draw as Master Torturer—especially when the guild itself seems so much in dire financial straits (Gurloes has subsequently been cooking the books, misrepresenting the numbers of clients dealt with by the guild). Of course, there's always the possibility that Palaemon may have picked up the precious sword during his own period of exile, either as long-term payment or a gratuity, but if so, there's no mention of such an acquisition, nor are we ever privy to the reasons why he too was once banished from the guild, learning of this development only late in *Citadel*, from Winnoc, one of the Pelerines' older slaves. Has Palaemon, like Severian, helped a client escape his or her due sentence, or has his transgression been in another area? In his peregrinations about the Commonwealth, is he also the silent man with a staff who visits the stone town? (*Terminus Est*, we discover, disassembles and can be used as a walking stick.) And lastly, why do we never hear of his ultimate fate? Is he still alive ten years later—not an impossibility, despite his advanced age—when Severian undertakes his journey to Yesod? Who's to say? Severian the Chronicler never tells us. In fact, in all of *Urth*, he sees fit to mention his kindly old mentor just once, and that very near the end, and the mention is a mere tangent to something else clearly more important—finding drinkable water. ("A client in a cell can endure three days or more without water, so Master Palaemon had taught us." *Urth*, 344) Master Gurloes, on the other hand, whom Severian professes to hate, is referenced as early as page 10, and several times thereafter (67, 123), while Master Malrubius, who's died when Severian was still a boy, plays a rather major role in the narrative itself, if as an aquastor. Meanwhile, poor, fatherly, life-saving Palaemon gets only the single token mention.

The Dead Torturer

But perhaps in the elevation of dead Malrubius to aquastor status, there's more than meets the eye and a clue to this marginalization. We know, after all, that aquastors must be true to one's recollections of them; in this respect they're like clones, only the blueprints are mnemonic, not genetic. Malrubius, therefore, cannot be anything that he wasn't in real life. So how then do we accord the considerable cachet that he has, especially with the Hierogrammates? It's he, after all, who writes the letter explaining how Severian is the legitimate Autarch of Urth, and which Severian so frantically fears may be stolen from his cabin aboard Tzadkiel's starship. In fact, Severian deems it his sole valuable possession. But again, considering its somewhat mundane authorship, why? Wouldn't Father Inire, as a Hierodule, be the much more likely choice to pen such a letter? (Or is he disqualified because of his nativity?) Wouldn't Palaemon, *who doesn't die before Severian ascends the Phoenix Throne*, and who's known him his entire life, be a better choice still? Apparently, not. Which thus gives rise to this array of questions: what is it that the real Malrubius has known that legitimizes him to act in this role? Wherein lies his validation? To what secrets and intrigues has he been privy?

The answers, I'm inclined to believe, can be found in a dream of Severian's—the one that occurs while he is racked with fever in the lazaret of the

Pelerines, early in *Citadel*. Dreams, of course, in the works of Gene Wolfe often have special significance, being either precognitive or possessing a core symbolic truth, despite elements of fantasy. This particular oneiric sequence begins with Severian's realization that the retrofitted towers of the Citadel have all been launched, like the rockets they were meant to be. Descending a flight of stairs, he stumbles into the sickroom of Master Malrubius. Here, however, he sees no fellow guild members administering to the dying man, but the Cumaean and Merryn, two witches. Eventually, after interludes in which Hethor and Thecla's maid appear, Severian is taken in hand by Master Malrubius and the Cumaean to the sickroom's two ports, which are actually the eyes of Mount Typhon. Only this time, instead of seeing the ordinary magnificence granted to mountain-top-vistas, and being offered stewardship over the world, he sees the Urth under a reborn sun.

> Shadows were alchemized to gold, and every green thing grew darker and stronger as I looked. I could see the grain ripening in the fields and even the myriad fish of the sea doubling and redoubling with the increase of the tiny surface plants that sustained them. Water from the room behind us poured from the eye and, catching the light, fell in a rainbow. (*Citadel*, 36)

Potent imagery, to be sure—especially in the latter suggestion that Master Malrubius and the Cumaean will lead Severian to a better tomorrow, where the New Sun will shine bountiful upon a renascent Urth. But doesn't this—plus the sickbed scene—also convey the notion that both torturer and witch are acquainted with one another, perhaps even having been working together all along? Certainly, this might not be a bad tactic for the Hierodules to have implemented; knowing Severian to be a legitimate candidate for the New Sun, they tell Master Malrubius, hoping he'll be able to divert whatever resources he can to ensuring that Severian will survive (remember, half or more of all apprentices die before they're raised to journeymen). Malrubius, because "Torturers obey" (a dictum of their Mysteries), subsequently does his best to honor the Hierodules' wishes, although there is at least at one point the suggestion that he may be co-operating more out of fear than altruism or sense of duty; he also maybe senses that he's being watched. Witness the following two passages, both as Severian recounts how constitutionally ill old Malrubius is just before he dies:

> "As he stood at his little table, one felt that he was conscious of someone standing behind him. He looked straight to the front, never turning his head

and hardly moving a shoulder, and he spoke as much for that unknown listener as for us."

"His trembling hand reached for the slate pencil, but it escaped his fingers and rolled over the edge of the table to clatter on the floor. He did not stoop to pick it up, fearful, I think, that in stooping he might glimpse the invisible presence." (*Citadel*, 188–189)

Severian, attempting to come to grips with this behavior, rules in favor of thanatopsis; Malrubius, sensing that he's not long for the world, is contemplating the presence of death—"the color that is darker than fuligin"—within him. But in my opinion this is wrangled metaphorical excess on Severian's part, who, for the most part, is not particularly astute. I believe that the *unknown listener/invisible presence* is an actual person and meant to make sure Malrubius toes the Hierodule line. At any rate, if you accept my suggestion that Malrubius has colluded with the Cumaean to watch over probable New Sun candidate Severian, this might help to explain his impress with the Hierogrammates, especially if Severian, after becoming Autarch, has heard the fuller details (something, however, I'm not quite sure ever happens).

But before we abandon Malrubius for good, I'd like to call attention to one last speech of his. It's part of the same scene as above, with the dying Master addressing Severian and his fellow apprentices in the classroom. "I have done my best to teach you boys the rudiments of learning," he begins. "They are the seeds of trees that should grow and blossom in your mind." Subsequently distracted by Severian's poorly lettered *Q*, Malrubius interweaves an anatomy lesson with penmanship, then attempts to pick up where he left off: "I have spent much of my life, boys, in trying to implant those seeds in the apprentices of our guild. I have had a few successes, but not many. There was a boy, but he—" Only here, instead of continuing and telling us who the particular student is, Malrubius goes to the window and spits out a clot of blood—another prime example of Wolfe using the aposiopesis to convey unrevealed information and which in this case may be dually significant. For starters, it appears possible that the very boy he's talking about is Palaemon—someone, who from context, was more than able to master "the rudiments of learning," and perhaps may have even been Malrubius' best student. But then apparently young Palaemon has done something seriously wrong—whatever it is that gets him expelled from the guild—hence Malrubius' bile. Or is the reason he never completes his sentence due to more than simple emotional pain? Might Malrubius actually fear naming the boy because the alleged unknown listener/invisible presence would hear him—perhaps even taking serious umbrage? Is it therefore possible that the spy upon his activities is Palaemon himself—*he whose name also suggests an alien heritage*? Could, as the other aspect of his name suggests, Palaemon simply be *portraying* a human being?

Honey and Swords

This suggestion, while iconoclastic and preliminary for now, might help resolve at least one of the mysteries centered about Palaemon: how he's acquired *Terminus Est*. As Michael Andre-Driussi very assiduously points out in *Lexicon Urthus*, there may be a connection between the sword and "the sacred thunder-stone of Terminus at Rome, [a meteor which stood beneath] a hole in the roof of Jupiter's temple." Andre-Driussi further cites Wolfe's *Castleview*, making a strong comparison between Arthur's Excalibur (which, *selon* Wolfe, may have been forged from meteoric iron) and *Terminus Est*. In addition, we know that the sword has been smithed by the famous craftsman Jovinian, whose name inferentially suggests Roman sky god Jove. It's therefore hard not to read some sort of heavenly connection with *Terminus Est*, as in "of or from the stars." Certainly, if anyone had the resources to acquire the valuable weapon, it would be Father Inire, who could then pass it on to Palaemon. I also believe it's possible that some sort of tracking device has been placed within the sword and that this may be the real reason it's bequeathed to Severian—so that he can be monitored by the Hierodules in his travels about the Commonwealth. Severian also keeps the hilt after the blade is shattered by Baldander's energy mace. This might help explain how the aquastors of Malrubius and Triskele are always able to find him.

Accepting this sort of scheme—where alien Palaemon, masquerading as a human, is able to exert a guardian-angel-style-relationship over the potential future messiah—also helps resolve another of *New Sun*'s nomenclatural conundrums. Remember how I said that Palaemon is only one of a pair of names that draws upon both mythic and saintly exemplars? Well, the other is Paeon, who, besides being a saint, is also a god of healing in Greek Mythology. Healing, of course, is associated with the torturers—all are trained in leechcraft, and the staff-like nature of *Terminus Est* may be an attempt by Wolfe to recall the staff frequently depicted with Asclepius in statuary. But notice also how the name *Paeon* is contained within *Palaemon*. In my opinion this is one of the central keys to understanding many of the mysteries in *New Sun*—that such names, extractable from a parent source either in whole or in part, are integrally related. This relationship may be truly familial, as it is with Severian/Severa; symbolic, as it is with Dorcas/Casdoe; or simply alter-egoish, as it is with Camoena—a name mentioned only once, by Famulimus—who is almost certainly the Cumaean. In the case under discussion I also firmly believe that the relationship is of the third nature; Palaemon, in other words, *is* Paeon, the honey steward who trained future Autarch Appian (both have been kitchen servants in the House Absolute), the same way Palaemon has trained Severian. Moreover, there's a further etymological link between the two. Palaemon, in Greek Mythology, was originally called Melicertes; *meli* in Greek, however, means 'honey,' which associates him with both senior honey steward Paeon and junior trainee Appian (*apis* = bee). The Palaemon-Paeon connection also helps to explain one of the old Autarch's more disjointed and confusing speeches, made subsequent to the crash-landing of his saucer, which has been shot down by the Ascians. As he tells Severian:

> "You remember everything, and so you must recall the night you came to my House Azure. That night someone else came to me. I was a servant once, in the House Absolute…That is why they hate me. As they will hate you. Paeon, who trained me, who was honey-steward fifty years gone by. I know what he was in truth, for I had met him before. He told me you were the one…the next. I did not think it would be quite so soon…" (*Citadel*, 206–207)

This explains, of course, how Appian has always known that Severian is to succeed him: he's been told so by the Hierodule known to him as Paeon, whom he recognizes from his servant days. "Paeon" may thus be wearing an associated human mask; or maybe has come in the guise of Palaemon, whom Appian has met before, but still knows what he is "in truth" (a phrase no doubt meant to echo the torturers' longer *Truth and Penitence* title). In either event, because of the Hierodule's unique temporal foresight, Palaemon/Paeon tells Appian that Severian will succeed him and the die is cast for all of their future transactions together.

Then again, as discussed earlier, how does any of this support my notion that a younger, hungry-for-knowledge Palaemon was once a student of Master Malrubius'? Am I now postulating that a suitably disguised Hierodule—possibly a larval type akin to Famulimus or Barbatus—has somehow been ferreted into the guild, where he then spends an indeterminate amount of time masquerading as a human child, learning the tricks of the trade, impressing Master Malrubius, only to one day be found out as a changeling and expelled? It's an interesting theory, and a staple in fantasy, but I see no evidence for such a scenario. Instead, I believe a more compelling case can be built around Palaemon's thirst for knowledge. Remember, as Malrubius implies, Palaemon, in the erudition department, may be one of his more successful students. We also know that someone who is possibly the exiled Palaemon—the silent man with the staff—has visited the stone town. The big question here, however, is why. Has he been drawn to the haunted ruins by Apu-Punchau, who, as a vivimancer, allegedly calls to those who can make the dead live again? Again, another interesting notion. But I think a better explanation can be found in what's told to us slightly earlier by Hildegrin the Badger, who's also been summoned to the stone town, although not by any genius loci, but the Cumaean. Asked by Dorcas what he's doing there, the Badger replies, "Bringin' back the past. Divin' back into the time of Urth's greatness. There was somebody who used to live in this here place we're sittin' on that knew things that could make a difference. I intend to have him up." (*Claw*, 288) In other words, laboring on behalf of the Cumaean, Hildegrin hopes to revive Apu-Punchau, *who knows things*—a system or arsenal of knowledge *that could make a difference*. What exactly that knowledge is isn't made clear, but at the same time doesn't it seem likely that this same esoteric lore, especially with its taint of the forbidden, would be equally appealing to someone like Palaemon? This might well explain why he's come to the stone town, then: he's hoping to salvage ancient lost secrets of the halcyon past.

The Pederast

But notice also how this same attribution of knowledge to previous generations is echoed in the following speech, the maker of which I'm initially not going to identify. Severian at this point has just accused the man of partaking in the cannibalistic ritual of the alzabo, by which memories of the dead can be chemically uploaded. Asserts the mystery man in response:

> "No, no. Learned men—particularly those of my profession—practice that everywhere, and usually with better effect, since we are most selective of our subjects and confine ourselves to the most retentive tissues. *The knowledge I seek cannot be learned in that way, since none of the recently dead possessed it,* and perhaps no one has ever possessed it." (*Citadel*, 215. *Italics mine.*)

Earlier, as well, the man, when asked by Severian why he has chosen to consort with the wicked people he has, tells him, "For knowledge. There is nowhere a man in my profession can learn as I learn here." If you haven't guessed his identity by now, however, let me drop the obfuscation: he's the old leech of Vodalus' jungle retinue, whose rather novel surgical techniques includes the linking up of Severian's vascular system to that of a thirteen year old boy. Mamas, the boy, is made livid by the exchange of blood, but the old leech still believes that "He'll recover quickly—just in time to warm my bed." (*Citadel*, 214) However, he also disavows homoerotic intentions, claiming: "I only sleep beside him because the night-breath of the young acts as a restorative to those of my years.[6] Youth, you see, is a disease, and we may hope to catch a mild case." Thus, perhaps, we see one possible line of investigation the old leech may be pursuing—the restoration of youth—although, as he claims, none of the recently dead seem to possess the knowledge he needs to advance his experiments. But also interestingly enough the old physician hails from Nessus,[7] and has the same sorts of skills taught to the torturers in their leechcraft sessions; just look at the work Severian does to man-gled Triskele, suturing and amputating a forelimb, and he is a bare novice. Imag-ine the refinement of those skills over decades, combined with a wide number of experiments, both anatomical and otherwise. Also keep in mind that while Mamas is identified, the old leech, whose own role is much more significant, is never named; almost always in Wolfe this is a sign we're meant to figure it out ourselves. My own personal belief—incredible as it sounds—is that it's Palae-mon. However, he's not the masked Hierodule look-alike we've all been led to believe is Palaemon, but the original, human Palaemon, who's been expelled as a young man from the all-male-torturers'-guild probably because of his pederastic leanings,[8] or perhaps because he indulged in one too many hits of the analeptic alzabo, or maybe even because of unorthodox experiments he's attempted upon the prisoners of the Matachin Tower; expelled, yes, and given to wandering, even going to the stone town, where, much to his disappointment, he does not learn the arcane secret he seeks from Apu Punchau's revenant (*perhaps no one possessed it*), only to wind up in the retinue of rebel-leader Vodalus, where he's allowed with impunity to seek whatever forbidden knowledge he needs, both sexual and intellectual. Meanwhile, back in the Torturer's Guild, either before or soon after Severian is born, the Hierodules replace the exiled Palaemon with one of their own—Paeon refurbished with a new mask—and it becomes his mission to subse-quently befriend and emotionally nourish the boy who will someday bring the New Sun. Master Malrubius is in on everything; so too—probably—is Gurloes,[9] which may perhaps explain Severian's truer hatred of the man. (Malrubius dies early, perhaps preventing his overt endorsement of the Big Lie). And eventually everything works out just the way the Hierodules want; Severian returns from Yesod with the New Sun and after a salvatory lavage/baptism, the Urth is born anew as Ushas, just like in his fever dream.

Eyes of the Torturer

But this still leaves one more angle to pursue. Remember Palaemon's optical prosthesis—the lenses which always obscure his eyes? Surely, they're not just the alien equivalent of designer shades. Perhaps then we might go back and compare them with Severian's earlier observation about how "the shorter [Ossipago] had no eyes at all, so that only darkness was visible there" and the roboid's similar evasiveness later, when he seeks to turn aside, "as though he feared I might see the empty eye slits of his mask." Don't both the wearing of an optical device and the turning aside accomplish the same thing—mask the eyes (or the lack thereof)? As Drotte at one point tells the tired Severian, who insists his fatigue is due more to Drotte's seeing him maskless than anything else: "I can see your eyes, and that's all I need to see. Can't you recognize all the brothers by their eyes, and tell whether they're angry, or in the mood for the joke?" Just as the old Biblical saw maintains, the eyes are the windows to the soul. And since Palaemon's eyes remain ever unglimpsed, perhaps this implies that he has no soul, or is not a brother, or even—to attempt a final bold synthesis—is not quite who we think, being actually the similarly eyeless Ossipago, aka you-know-who. But surely this is madness: Palaemon, Inire, Ossipago, Paeon and the Abraxas are all the same alien?[10] Well, again, Father Inire answers to no one, echoing Ossipago's words to the same effect in *Urth* (355): "I don't respond to commands from you, Severian. You learned that long ago." So not only would he never have to account for his long-term absences (if there even were any given his access to the Corridors of Time), but in all likelihood he could come and go as he pleased. Specular transport offers him avenue to his children, and maybe elsewhere. It also appears there may be an underground connection between the Matachin Tower and the House Absolute. As Severian at one point intimates, "There are parts of the Second House that are not unlike the blind corridors in which I searched for Triskele; perhaps they are the same corridors, though if they are, I ran a greater risk than I then knew." (*Claw*, 241) These tunnels, of course—as we remember from *Shadow*—debouch from the lowest level of the Matachin Tower, and may lead not only to Valeria's Atrium, but also the House Absolute, providing easy access between the two, especially for one privy to their layout (there are hints that Father Inire designed them). Palaemon's study also has a semi-secret door that allows him to descend within the tower. "I doubt those fellows out there know of the door that opens to the western stair," he tells Severian, when the latter, as Autarch, comes to pay his respects at the novel's end—a stairwell which is further described as the "least-used" and "perhaps the oldest," thus making it ideal for clandestine operations. (*Citadel*, 273) Masks, of course, provide still further cover; a Paeon guise in one case, a Palaemon in another—not that the latter would even have to be donned all that often, since Palaemon is usually wearing his gold-traced torturer's mask. ("*Did you not ever think that he who wore a mask might wear another?*") But apparently there's also something about Father Inire's eyes that requires disguising, although it may be nothing more than their telltale alien nature—hence both the prosthesis and Ossipago's evasiveness. And as I've argued before, a syncretic merging of all these divergent personalities and forces does allow for a more consistent, centralized effort—a single glowing cause headed up by a master figure of Renaissance proportions.

Remember how so many of the names in *New Sun* are nested within others, like Russian dolls?

Well, consider a final, further, reduction in form, one which constitutes a mere two letters, but still manages to exemplify the one thing Palaemon, Ossipago and Paeon all have in common.

I speak, of course, of *Pa,* as in *Father*, the alien known as Inire.

"Benjamin Button? Meet E.T."

Other than the two conceits about names in *New Sun*, I think there's one other grand concept that needs to be accepted in order to understand Wolfe's magnum opus completely, and that's the nature of time for the Hierodules. As Severian eventually figures out, their experience of it runs counter to our sense, and hence backwards. However, while some readers have further speculated that this is only so in Yesod and that the apparent anachronic trysts Famulimus, Barbatus and Ossipago have with Severian, where their last meeting with him is his first, and his last is their first, are actually due more to their flitting in and out of time than true reverse order, we have only to witness the testimony of undine Juturna at the end of *Urth*, where she too, after numerous previous encounters with Severian, remains oblique to them, having yet, in her backwards-living passage through life, to experience them. Such an argument also vitiates the notion of the Hierodules' foreknowledge about Severian, since it disallows their remembering the future. Furthermore, in his metafictional short story, "My Book"—which many readers believe to be about the writing of *New Sun*—Gene Wolfe constructs a very curious piece, telling us how the book he's been working on for so long has actually been devised in reverse order, from last word to first—as is, it turns out, "My Book." Surely, however, this is no mere stab at cleverness, but author Wolfe hinting at how he pieced together the narrative of *the* Book, at least for the contrapuntal strand that incorporates the life and times of Father Inire, the Cumaean, *et al.* And so in short let me reiterate: for the Hierodules of Yesod, in comparison to our point of view, time runs backwards. Or as Wolfe through Famulimus tells us, "Our clocks run widdershins round both your suns." (*Urth*, 360)

This, of course, presents some rather interesting implications. As has been mentioned numerous times before, it allows the future to be glimpsed, helping us to understand not only Father Inire's various machinations, but also the Cumaean's skills as a prophetess.[11] Yet another implication, however, is slightly less obvious, but much more devious: because of the disparities in frames of reference, what appear to us to be aged and wizened aliens are actually just the opposite—Hierodules in their prime. *If this were not so,* from the time of the very first Autarch, Ymar the Almost Just, when Father Inire "first" makes his appearance, *he would appear to get progressively younger*—something we know has not happened. This also explains why when we attempt to pinpoint the arrival of Father Inire on Urth, we need to take a contrary tack, looking not back to the time of Ymar (which represents, despite his more youthful appearance, the terminus of Inire's lifespan), but forward to the time of Severian, perhaps even right on up to the moment when the New Sun's tidal effects inundate the world. Again, given our own experience, these are slippery concepts: an "old" Inire who ages oppositely to us, becoming "younger," but geriatrically so—all the while seeming to live as a normal, if extraordinarily long-lived, human does. It's just plain doesn't make sense. Nevertheless, if we wish to plot Inire's trajectory through *New Sun*, this is what we need to accept—not exactly six impossible things before breakfast, but close enough.

Also, besides its prolixity, one of the things you may or may not have noticed about this essay has been my failure to address the etymology of *Inire*. Quite simply said, as a name, it has neither mythic nor saintly roots, but rather derives from Latin, being the infinitive for "to begin, to enter." This is quite singular, of course, and only other character shares the same distinction (Venant, son of Tzadkiel), although there are plenty of names that are Latinate in origin, largely due to the fact that their original bearers lived during times when Rome ruled the world. I also believe that *Inire* is a nom de convenience as much as Ossipago and Palaemon, and that Abraxas, because of his Gnostic identification with the Almighty, is the good Father's truest and real name. Still, Wolfe must have had some reason for using it, so let's see if we can figure out why or what it further tells us.

Start at the Beginning

Despite the initial observation that the sun has begun to fail as early as the time of Satanic-figure Typhon, the mission to find a candidate to repair it does not begin until Father Inire arrives on Urth. Hence in this sense he *begins* the instauration—the process by which the old sun will be renewed. Surely, this is the prime reason Wolfe chose to bestow "Inire" upon his number-one-alien. In much the same respect he appears to have chosen *Apheta*, which means "starting place" in the original Greek; it's she, we remember, who is Severian's larval Hierogrammate guide aboard the world-ship Yesod. Apheta, with whom Severian mates, is also popularly thought to somehow enable the New Sun to come into being, if not be its literal conceptress. So perhaps it's worth examining the passage from *Urth* which seems to indicate this, also noting that Apheta in English has come to mean "the giver of life in a nativity."

Severian, about to begin his love-making, writes:

> Lying upon my back, I entered Yesod. Or say, rather, Yesod closed about me. It was only then that I knew I had never been there. Stars in their billions spurted from me, fountains of suns, so that for an instant I felt I knew how universes were born. All folly.
>
> Reality displaced it, the kindling of the torch that whips shadows to their corners, and with them all the winged fays of fancy. There was something born between Yesod and Briah when I met with Apheta upon that divan in that circling room, something tiny yet immense that burned like a coal conveyed to the tongue by tongs.
>
> That something was myself. (*Urth*, 145)

But while colorfully metaphoric (if almost luridly so), are we actually to infer that Severian's mating with Apheta produces not a biological issue, but an astronomical one—the white fountain which will replenish the old sun? Even given the near God-like status of the Hierogrammates, and the astrological ramifications of Apheta's name, this seems a stretch. Much more likely, I'm therefore going to assert, is that the "something born between Yesod and Briah" is exactly what I first mentioned, a biological product; to be more precise, an intermediate form between Hierogrammate and human, the same way man is between angel and beast. No *sun*, but a *son*. And just as Mother Apheta has initiated a process, so too will her offspring, even to the extent of imitating her name.[12] She starts; he begins. And given the tendency for twins to be produced in Severian's bloodline, it's even possible that Apheta has borne two children, the other one being female, and that later the twins are further joined in marital union. Scoffers of this latter notion will kindly note that while almost certainly Barbatus and Famulimus are brother and sister, Severian, near the end of *Urth*, calls Famulimus the *wife* of Barbatus.[13] Also neatly resolved with a heritage of this sort: it helps to explain why Inire and the Cumaean can remember both past and future; as part-Hierogrammate, they experience tomorrow as yesterday; as part-human, today is yesterday's tomorrow. Time for them, in other words, has no direction, but is always eternally now.

Meanwhile, after their father, Severian, departs for Urth, arriving four decades after he left, his children, already aged adults (at least from our perspective), shortly follow suit. Witness the testimony now as Severian, having sneaked into the House Absolute, eavesdrops on his wife Valeria from a secret vantage point behind her throne. A junior officer has just reported the presence of another giant (Baldanders is already present), only this one is female. When asked if she would like to interrogate her, Valeria says, "We are tired. We will retire now. In the morning, tell us what you have learned." But already knowing, the officer blurts out, "Sh-she s-says that certain cacogens have landed a man and a woman from their ships." (*Urth*, 301) Would Juturna, however—the giant woman, as we learn shortly—risk her own life to relay this news if the man and woman mentioned were simple-seed-stock-humans—the real life equivalents of Meschia and Meschiane[14] from Dr. Talos' typological play *Eschatology and Genesis*—dropped off by the Hierodules to repopulate soon-to-be born Ushas? Surely, Abaia and the other Great Lords have deeper concerns; and how does this neo-primal couple escape the immanent flood, anyway? On the other hand, if the man and woman are actually Inire and Camoena, about to begin their centuries-long stint as Urth's stewards, the Megatherians have every reason to be concerned, since the Hierodules oppose their authority and further attempts at conquest. Here, too, the Inires are beginners. But experiencing time backwards they soon grow into their new roles, even diversifying their attempts when their own children arrive from Yesod.

Herald of the End

Finally, however, after a millennium or so, they retrogress to a point in time where Ymar the Almost Just (aka Reechy) has been born. Ymar, in turn, will be the first or last person to take the New Sun candidacy test, depending on your point of view. The Inires are now extremely old, perhaps even at the end of their own natural lifespans, although they appear anything but senescent. Suddenly, however, prodigal father Severian appears on the scene, having, because of Tzadkiel's sailing in and out of Time, been dropped off 1000 years before his own era. A few miracles later, Severian is soon being bruited about as the Conciliator, a healer and holy man. But when he and former ship-mate Burgundofara make their way to Os, he's challenged by the village's own wonder-worker, Ceryx, who, at first, seems a bit of a charlatan, predicting the obvious and so forth. Still, Severian seems to enjoy the show, telling us:

> I stayed in part because the mountebank's patter reminded me of Dr. Talos, and in larger part because something in his eyes recalled Abundantius. Yet there was another thing more fundamental than either, though I am not certain I can explain it. I sensed that this stranger had traveled as I had, that we had gone far and returned in a way that even Burgundofara had not; and that though we had not gone to the same place or returned with the same gain, we had both known strange roads. (*Urth*, 210)

Not much later, Ceryx challenges Severian to a trial of magic, but Severian refuses. This prompts Ceryx to ask, "You, my good man. Do you know what it is to train your will until it's like a bar of iron? To drive your spirit before you like a slave? To toil ceaselessly for an end that may never come, a prize so remote that it seems it will *never* come?" (*Urth*, 211) Severian and Burgundofara leave shortly after this point, but somehow from a distance Ceryx is able to snap Severian's staff.

That very night Ceryx pays a visit to the Chowder Pot, where Severian and Burgundofara have taken a room. Reanimating a dead man named Zama, he sends the walking corpse to attack Severian. Severian and Burgundofara manage to subdue Zama, but not without the aid of some strange allies; as Severian later recalls, "Certainly more guests came to our aid when Zama broke down our door than there was any reason to suspect, and I would like to think that maybe one or even several of them were myself. Indeed it sometimes seems to me that I caught a glimpse of my own face in the candlelight that night." (*Urth*, 227)

Finally, however, Severian is forced into a face-to-face confrontation with the sorcerer. Writes he:

> His iron-shod staff was topped with a rotting human head, his lean frame draped in raw manskin; but when I saw his eyes I wondered that he had bothered with such trumpery, as one wonders to see a lovely woman decked

with glass beads and gowned in false silk. I had not known him so great a mage. (*Urth*, 228)

Impelled by the training of his boyhood, Severian attempts to salute Ceryx with a knife, but before the two can further close, Ceryx is killed by Zama, who is himself subsequently impaled by a number of Os' citizens. Severian attempts to resurrect Zama, but is sickened as "the eyes of the head on Ceryx's fallen staff rolled in their putrid sockets to stare at [him.]" (*Urth*, 229)

Utilizing onomastics I now mean to make a case for Ceryx being Inire. *Os*, besides meaning 'bone' (cf. Ossipago, 'bone-grower'), can also mean 'source,' as well as "a represented head, a mask." *Source* as in *beginning place*; mask, as in, well, *mask*—what Ceryx wears to conceal his alien features.[15] The name Ceryx, in turn, is Greek for "herald",[16] *someone who presages what is to follow*—a diviner of the future, like the Cumaean; the instigator of the New Sun mission. Ceryx also has a mythic exemplar in Greek mythology, making the character, by Wolfe's naming convention, non-human.[17] This is how he's able to snap Severian's staff and resurrect Zama; he's privy to Father Inire's high-tech-gadgetry and no "real" magic is involved. (Perhaps even his iron-shod staff is an enabling tool.) As for the head adorning his staff, and Severian's look-alike rescuers, notice how these recapitulate similar elements in the earlier jungle scene where Vodalus' company is being led by a trio of savages—the old *uturuncu* (who's Inire) and his two younger accomplices, "a pair of young men who might have been brothers, or even twins." Gone, however, from Inire's staff this time is the dried monkey's head, replaced by a human's,[18] symbolizing Inire's retrograde youth; no longer wrinkled with extreme age, his face has lost its simian aspect, just as he is currently upright and ungnarled. As for Severian's rescuers—who are surely the same two young savages of Vodalus' retinue—I believe they're resurrected alternates of Severian. Remember, in his mausoleum, there are two empty coffins, while Hildegrin the Badger has mentioned he's done a couple of favors for the Cumaean. Given that his specialty is exhumation, it's very possible he's stolen the bodies, passed them off to Inire, who's then resurrected them the same way he did Zama. That way, should something go wrong, he still has other potential candidates for the New Sun. (Imagine the Three Wise Men cloning Jesus.) Severian doesn't recognize them the first time, of course; but his failure to divine either his or other people's familial relationships is one of *New Sun*'s leit-motifs. Notice as well how Wolfe keeps coming back to Ceryx' eyes; small wonder if they're so charged with obvious power Ossipago and Palaemon have done their best to conceal them. And finally there's Severian assessment of distance traveled, if by alternate means—from the Commonwealth to the stars, Yesod to Briah, tomorrow to yesterday; and no point-to-point transit always in the most straightforward of manners. Unfortunately for Ceryx, he's come to the end of the line.

The Monkey's Bride

But before we examine possible reasons for why Wolfe may have killed off Inire/Ceryx in this manner, let us quickly attempt to locate the Cumaean, for she too must figure in any would-be lethal valediction. Idealistically, as Inire's twin, Camoena should have an alternate Latinate name that is significant and possibly be killed by Severian (who at least catalyzes Inire's murder). Indeed, this is exactly what happens to the female torturer Prefect Prisca, whom Severian strikes with a lethal blow after he's taken prisoner to Nessus. While a saint of that name exists, *prisca* also means "old, ancient," something not only Wolfe's Cumaean is, but her mythic exemplar, who's 700 years old when Aeneas pays her a visit. Furthermore, Prisca's "martyrdom" ensures the separation of male and female children born to the torturers' clients, which may be vital to the long-term interests of the Hierodules. Women, it's observed, are crueler than men when it comes to inflicting punishment; so rather than take the chance a female Prefect might overly discipline a potential New Sun candidate, perhaps it's been decided to eliminate them. There's also evidence that the Cumaean heads up the Pelerines, in addition to the witches, and that both may be helping to prepare the way for the eventual return of the Conciliator. (See *Witches*.) And lest one think Prisca's grim nature does not jibe with the Cumaean's, consider Hildegrin's remark about how he's learned to avoid seeking out the Cumaean's advice. "People come sometimes hopin' to know when they'll be married, or about success in trade. But I've observed they don't often come back." (*Shadow*, 208) *Back* in this case, however, may mean *from* the cave, not *to*. In any event, Prisca dies at the hands of the very man she's devoted her entire life and career to succoring, just as her husband, if by proxy, does.

The big question now is why.

The Promised Land Denied

Besides its pseudo-Oedipal echo, where Severian unknowingly kills his own father substitute, I think part of the answer can be found in Ceryx's little speech about how he's struggled so long to attain a certain goal. *Do you know what it's like*, he's asked Severian, "to toil ceaselessly for an end that may never come, a prize so remote that it seems it will *never* come?" In many respects, this may be an expression of not only frustration, but also finally doubt, the fear that everything he and his wife have labored to accomplish will never come about. Some might equate this with Christ's famous seven last words on the cross, but I think a better parallel can be found in Deuteronomy. Moses, of course—another staff bearer and prophetic spokesman, who dies in his twelfth decade, showing no visible signs of age—eventually has doubts about his own mission and burden, and consequently, while shown the Promised Land, is never allowed to enter. Recall now the one Biblical passage in all of *New Sun* that Wolfe quotes, which is read by Marie to Isangoma (whose name is Zulu for 'sorcerer'), back in the jungle hut of the Botanic Gardens:

> "Then he went up from the plain to Mt. Nebo, the headland that faces the city, and the Compassionating showed him the whole country, all the land as far as the Western Sea. Then he said to him: 'This is the land I swore to your fathers I should give their sons. You have seen it, but you shall not set your feet upon it.' So there he died, and was buried in a ravine." (*Shadow*, 188)

The parallels are quite obvious, and plainly, Inire and Camoena are meant to be Mosaic figures, just as Severian is Christ the Redeemer.

But just as Moses had to contend with the artful duplication of his miracles by the Pharaoh's magicians, so too would any genuine wonder-worker in the Commonwealth be subject to imitation. These are precarious times, remember; the sun has noticeably begun to fail. Provided he could convince enough people his powers were genuine, a good mountebank could probably write his own ticket to prosperity, and maybe even spawn several cottage industries (notice how the owner of the Chowder Pot greedily believes more tourists will now flock to his establishment because the Conciliator has slept there). It's therefore likely that a number of thaumaturgic poseurs may be roaming about—perhaps even enough to dilute the Conciliator's current and future reputation. This, of course, could have serious, long-term, repercussions—one has only to imagine the existence of a Jesus, but no messianic tradition. So enter Father Inire in Ceryx guise. No common rod-into-serpent mummer, he; *this wonder-worker can actually raise the dead.* But when pitted against Severian, not even his potent skills can save him. And so this may be the real reason Ceryx/Inire must script his own death—to consolidate and amplify the legend of the Conciliator, the so-called New Sun, the one figure in Gene Wolfe's solar opus who will ultimately deliver us all.

Then again, let's look at that final tally and see if we can divorce ourselves from parochialism.

To sum things up: Severian, at a very high cost to humanity, but little to himself, saves a single world, which he's allowed to enter post-climatically. The Inires, who spend a millennium working diligently behind the scenes, die in their attempt, far from home, but ensure the birth of another universe.

Who's the greater Messiah?

10

MISSING IN ACTION

Very early in his relationship with Thecla, Severian is told by the imprisoned chatelaine that Master Gurloes has sent some of his charges to the House Absolute to fetch more clothing for her. The journeymen, however, are apparently unable to find the House Absolute. Later, back in the guild dormitory, Severian attempts to learn the names of the young torturers, but no one can tell him.

So who are these journeymen and what might have happened to them? Here's what I believe the text supports.

In Chapter III of *Shadow*, present at the excrucication of Thecla's handmaiden are Master Gurloes and three assistants—Odo, Mennas and Eigil. Later, we learn these three are indeed journeymen, as we might expect given the masterfulness of their technique, a full-boot skinning of Hunna. This also supports the notion that they're probably senior journeymen, and given the importance of Thecla (the first concubine Gurloes has ever had from the Autarch's inner circle), it stands to reason he may have sent his most experienced journeymen to the House Absolute. At the same time, however, Severian, believing the House Absolute to be the size of the Citadel, has difficulty accepting the notion it might be hard to find. To which Thecla responds: "On the contrary, it's quite easy. Since it can't be seen, you can be there and never know it if you're not lucky." (*Claw*, 81) Roche, pre-echoing Thecla's declaration, incorporates a distance factor, telling Severian the House Absolute is located not simply just beyond the Wall, but "Far past it. Weeks, if you walked." (*Claw*, 35)

We never hear mention of Odo, Mennas and Eigil again, and they are not present when Thecla is later placed in the revolutionary—something that seems awry given their senior status.

As for where they end up, when Roche and Severian are at the House Azure for their night of pleasure, the khaibit known as "Chatelaine Thecla" warns Severian about possibly hitting her when he raises his hand in anger. Says she: "There are people here to protect me…Three men." (*Claw*, 93)

Severian doubts her, but doesn't strike. He also taunts "Thecla" to scream and draw the three men. She refuses.

Later, however, just before they make love, the naked Severian is told by ersatz Thecla: "You must be clothed in favor, remember. Otherwise you will be given over to the torturers." (*Claw*, 94) The phrase itself may be part of the prostitute's religious instruction, since just before this they're talking about the theocenter; but the mention of torturers still seems a clue.

Could it be that, under impress of Master Palaemon, Odo, Mennas and Eigil have wound up at the House Azure? They might well have been represented to Appian as bouncers or security personnel. Torturers, after all, do seem to have the same sort of knowledge about nerve clusters that martial artists do. And who better to roust out malcontents than members of the Order of Seekers for Truth and Penitence, who are widely feared? Secretly, however, it's much more likely the three journeymen have been so placed to spy on Appian—hence no major hue and cry by either Palaemon or Gurloes when the trio never returns—and to make sure Severian neither comes to harm nor does anything rash.

Coincidentally, it's also possible that Ouen has served the old Autarch in a similar capacity. As he tells Severian during their second fateful meeting, he's purchased his father's locket, which contains a picture of Dorcas, from a pawnbroker. "I'd come into a bit of money then helping a certain optimate with his affairs—carrying messages to the ladies and standing watches outside doors and so on." (*Citadel*, 304) Appian, incognito, might well be taken for an optimate, and it's interesting to speculate how Ouen may have helped to round up stand-in "chatelaines" for those nights where inclement weather has made travel from the House Absolute difficult. (Possibly this is even how he and Catherine have met, although like real-life exemplars Owen Tudor and Katherine of Valois, perhaps we're never meant to know.)

11

NAVIGATOR

After Severian and Jonas are arrested on the grounds of the House Absolute, they're confined in an underground antechamber, where a large remnant prison population already exists. Unlike them, however, many of their fellow inmates have never known a single day of freedom. Quite a few, in fact, appear to have been born there, as have their ancestors before them, perhaps even as far back as eight generations.[1] Consequently—and this is small surprise, given such long-term isolation—prisoners' perspectives about the outside world tend toward the skewed, ludicrous side. Bees—"animals that made their own sugar"—carried "poisoned swords" and "were the size of rabbits."[2] So reports cyborg Jonas shortly, having in addition to say this about the oral, passed-on nature of such misapprehensions. "Family memories, I suppose, you could call them. Traditions from the outside world that have been handed to them, generation to generation, from the original prisoners from whom they are descended. They don't know what some of the words mean any longer, but they cling to the traditions, to the stories, because those are all they have; the stories and their names." (*Claw*, 130)

Another one of these stories is later relayed to Severian by a little girl whose name is never given, but which we later learn in *Urth* is Oringa.[3] Asked why he wears black clothes, Severian attempts to explain, prompting this response from the lass: "Burying people wear black. Do you bury people? When the navigator was buried there were black wagons and people in black clothes walking. Have you ever seen a burying like that?" (*Claw*, 134)

Severian, quite honestly for his experience, tells her that no one wears fuligin clothes at funerals because it would mark the wearer—and slanderously so for the deceased—as a torturer. He then attempts to change the subject. But we as readers are still left with several questions. Is there, first of all, any relevance to this tale of the navigator? Who, for example, might this mysterious figure be that details about his funeral have been transmitted down through the ages, from one generation of prisoners to the next? Is he a true navigator in the denotative sense?

Or is 'navigator' one of those words that the prisoners have lost all sense of, except perhaps metaphorically? Initially, given Jonas's history—he's the patched survivor of a spaceship crash—it's tempting to see the navigator as part and parcel of the same crash, only as a casualty. But how likely is it that the survivors of such a mishap could organize a funeral cortege like the one described, especially since it appears they've landed in extremis, not only in the future, but subject apparently to life-long arrest by the Autarch's representatives? And why does Wolfe seem to place such special emphasis on not only the blackness of the wagon, but the fact that people *walked* behind it?

The answer may not be that difficult if we think about it. Gene Wolfe, after all, is a staunch Catholic. And *The Book of New Sun* is filled with indelible memories. So it's seems only fair that author Wolfe be allowed to include one of his own—especially since it also comprises one of this nation's most searing. Ergo, for those of you not yet born, or too young to remember, let me reprise the circumstances of that dark weekend (while those of you who are of age try, try, try not to recall where you were when you first heard the horrible news).[4]

On November 22, 1963, in Dallas, Texas, Catholic President John Fitzgerald Kennedy—he who attempted to steer us through the perilous straits of the '60s[5]—was shot dead by an assassin's bullet. Three days later, in Washington, DC, Kennedy's coffin was transported to Saint Matthew's Cathedral atop a black horse-drawn caisson, followed by the rest of the funeral entourage on foot, because the widow of the slain president refused to ride in a "fat, black Cadillac."[6]

JFK, I therefore maintain, is the navigator. Assassinated to be sure, but never forgotten, even after untold millennia. Especially by present-day, Catholic sf writers.[7]

But now then, the curious reader asks—how is it possible that people from our time—the original generation that passed on the tale of the navigator—wound up aboard the universe-crossing ship of the Hierodules? I believe Wolfe attempts to address this in *Urth*. Gunnie, at one point, is discussing apports, the creatures occasionally caught in the ship's massive specular sails. Claims she:

> "Not all apports are animals, though there's a lot more of those than anything else. Sometimes they're people, and sometimes they live long enough to get inside the ship where there's air. You know, the others on their home worlds must wonder where they went when they were apported. Especially when it's somebody important." (*Urth*, 74)

So perhaps Wolfe is suggesting that the tale of the navigator originated with people who have been apported from the twentieth century—along with possibly such famous missing personages as Amelia Earhart, Madeline Murray O'Hare and Jimmy Hoffa.

12

PRISONERS

As we journey with Severian from the Matachin Tower to the House Absolute, and then to Yesod and back, we meet a variety of interesting prisoners along the way, from Lomer and Nicarete and Oringa in the antechamber of the Autarch, to Loyal to the Group of Seventeen in the lazaret of the Pelerines, to finally Canog of the Conciliator's era, who will write the first *Book of the New Sun.* But for me the prisoners I've spent the most time thinking about all reside in the retrofitted rocket ship that houses the Torturers' Guild. They include the unnamed man and woman Severian meets with when he returns to the Citadel as Autarch at the Book's conclusion—plus (on the polar side of the novel and nominal divide) the only other named prisoner we meet besides Thecla while Severian yet resides with the Torturers. This is because 1) a welter of details is provided about the nature of each prisoner's crime; 2) two are unnamed, which almost certainly means we're meant to figure out their names and if/when we've met them before); and 3) the resolution of their identities might provide another pathway into the labyrinth, adding further illumination to either the novel's plot, theme, or leit motifs.

The Ostler

I've already discussed the identity of the second unnamed prisoner Severian meets with when he returns with Palaemon to the holding cells beneath the Matachin—I believe she's Secunda/Pelagia, the mother of Agia and Agilus, the woman who's constructed her furniture from stolen children (See *Agia and Agilus*). Severian—to the best of our knowledge—has never met her before. Nor does he remember meeting the first prisoner he chats with, who as it happens is incarcerated in Thecla's old cell. Asked in turn if he recognizes Severian, the prisoner replies "No, exultant." This, however, is misleading; Severian, when he meets with Ouen a short while later, asks his father (and after prompting him whether he's ever served a torturer before, which should spring forth the memory, especially in someone also alleged to have powerful mnemonic skills) "You have never seen me before?" To which a negative response prompts this aside from Severian, "How strange it was to realize that I had changed so much. (*Citadel*, 303). So it's at least possible that Severian and the first prisoner have encountered or seen one another before, but Severian, due to the rigors of war, as well as all the downloaded personalities he now contains as Autarch,[1] appears so different he cannot be recognized. But perhaps more to the point, I believe the exchange between Severian and his father are part of a matched pair and that the mystery man who connects the two is Ouen's former cohort from the Inn of Lost Loves, Trudo the ostler.

Back while they're still working together, it's Trudo, of course, who's told Ouen that Severian is wearing the fuligin of a torturer and which Ouen mentions in his note meant for Dorcas.[2] But when later Severian asks Abban if he knows anyone named Trudo, the innkeeper gives Severian a bit of the runaround,[3] before finally admitting his ostler is named Trudo—almost as if he's trying to protect him. Severian asks to speak with Trudo at once, but a search soon reveals that Trudo has run off.[4] "Gone for good then," opines Abban. "He heard you were looking for him, sieur, that's what I'm afraid of." (*Shadow*, 233) Thus we now understand why Severian has never seen him before; also, apparently because he's been recognized wearing the garb of a torturer, Severian believes that Trudo has come from the district around the Citadel (most everyone else in Nessus is under the impression the torturers have been disbanded)—a supposition further supported by Abban who tells us that Trudo hails from the southern regions of the city and "across the river to boot." But what Severian never seems to wonder about is why Trudo has run off. Clearly, the ostler fears his imminent detention and arrest. What possible crime, however, has he committed? Can we find clues in the mystery prisoner's soon-to-be-heard protestations of innocence? New Autarch Severian, as we learn, will commute the sentences of those who admit their guilt, but who promise not to resume their wayward lives once released. But when asked to elaborate on what he has been accused of and how he came to be convicted, the prisoner in Thecla's cell delivers, according to Severian, "one of the most complex and confused accounts I have ever heard." This, however, matches perfectly what Abban has told us of Trudo: "You're not likely to get much sense from him, though he's a hard-working fellow." (*Shadow*, 230) More-over, his account seems filled with a certain amount of duplicity involving his sick wife and the money she may have inherited from her father; the prisoner claims the money never existed and yet at the same time asserts that his mother-in-law has used it to bribe the judge in his case. He's also accused of beating his wife and not knowing she was ill, but still insists he's hired a physician to treat her once he found out. Could perhaps—hoping to acquire her money, or at least not to be blamed for spending it—he have murdered his wife, either actively or by negligence? This, of course, is a much more serious crime deserving of punishment (especially if Trudo's beaten her so badly she eventually dies) and might explain why he goes running off when he sees Severian at the Inn of Lost Loves as well as the garbled account about his wife. And given that he lives in one of the more squalid sections of Nessus, we're left to ponder if his wife lays buried in the poorer sections of the necropolis Severian, Drotte, and Eata are taking a shortcut through after their midnight swim. Could, in fact, she be the dead woman exhumed by Hildegrin at the very beginning of *New Sun*? Remember, the prisoner is not incarcerated in just any cell, but in Thecla's[5]—almost certainly an important Wolfean clue—and as Thecla herself is later consumed and carnified via the analeptic alzabo, so might his wife undergo a similar posthumous return. Thus, given the resemblance of Trudo's name to Tudor[6]—and the historical figure Owen Tudor—perhaps we're meant to see the disinterred woman harvested by the corpse-eaters[7] as another Catherine[8]—unidentified, but one of a trio of similarly-named sisters[9] all playing an important and necessary role in the life of Severian the Great.

The Hooker

The day after Severian is elevated to journeyman status, a new prisoner is brought to the Matachin Tower. Her name, as we learn, is Marcellina and this is how she describes her crime: "I was affianced to an officer, and I found he was maintaining a jade. When he wouldn't give her up, I paid bravos to fire her thatch. She lost a featherbed, a few sticks of furniture, and some clothes. Is that a crime for which I should be tortured?" (*Shadow*, 112) Severian is enjoined by Gurloes to confine her and as it happens the cell next to Thecla is empty, so he puts there, reasoning the exultant may enjoy the company of another female. However, given a cryptonymic examination of Marcellina (see *Appendix*), we see it yields an interesting batch of names: Inire for starters—so is it possible she's working covertly for him—being planted as a spy next to Thecla to make sure Severian does not do anything stupid, such as either attempting to spring Thecla with violence or killing himself Romeo-style once Thecla has slit her wrists? It seems a plausible enough notion, and the only non-controllable element in the overall plan involves Severian's decision to put Marcellina next to Thecla. (Had he not done so, I believe Marcellina probably would have requested she be incarcerated next to the exultant.) That Marcellina may be something other than what she appears is further supported by the other two cryptonyms her name yields: Barbea and Gracia. Barbea and Gracia, we recall, are two of the prostitutes Severian and Roche encounter when they visit the House Azure.[10] Roche chooses Gracia to be his plaything, while Severian, in a moment of wish-fulfillment, chooses the prostitute introduced by Appian as "the Chatelaine Thecla"—not the real woman obviously, but a Thecla look-alike and later explained to be either a khaibit (i.e., a clone of the real thing) or a poor woman masquerading as Thecla. In point of fact I believe "the Chatelaine Thecla" is none other than Marcellina.[11] For starters, the clothes of each are described in very similar terms. Severian, undressing "khaibit" Thecla, is warned not to tear her clothing. Says he: "I would think that you, Chatelaine Thecla, would have plenty of clothes." Thecla, however, tells Severian that she "can't keep much in this place. Someone takes things when I'm gone." That, in turn, prompts the following observation and comment from Severian: "The stuff between my fingers, which had looked so bright and rich in the colonnaded room below, was thin and cheap. 'No satins, I suppose,' as I unfastened the next catch. 'No sables and no diamonds.'" (*Shadow*, 92) Compare this to the condition of Marcellina's clothing as she's handed over by the cataphracts: "The elaboration of her sateen[12] costume (somewhat dirty and torn now) showed that she was an optimate." (*Shadow*, 112) Additionally, as Severian conducts Marcellina to her cell, he writes: "She clung to my arm now as though I were her father or her lover." (*Shadow*, 112) All of these are clues, I warrant, that Marcellina is the "khaibit" Thecla—a connection further enhanced by the realization that both names have been conferred to butterflies: *Phoebis sennae marcellina* and the various hairstreak butterflies of the *Thecla* genus. Add in the subcryptonym—*ecla* (which I refuse to believe is a coincidence) and you can see how fiendishly clever Wolfe can be in his delegation of names. And then there's also the delicious irony:[13] false Thecla being imprisoned next to real Thecla, both of whom have yielded themselves carnally to Severian (indeed, they're his first two lovers), yet both oh-so-trapped in the spider web of power and deceit as practiced by the Machiavellian Inires.

13

MILES AND JONAS

Aquastors, according to Master Malrubius, are "beings created and sustained by the power of the imagination and the concentration of thought." Moreover, they're not phantasmal or ectoplasmic, like ghosts, but creatures of substantiality, "as solid as most truly false things are," being not only touchable, but able to touch. As for their nativity, Malrubius informs us they're drawn from the mind by alien technology, a machine of the Hierodules that looks among a person's memories and carnifies them with absolute fidelity. Aquastors must therefore be true to their mnemonic blueprints, the same way our eyes must remain blue if genetically coded so. Thus Severian's dog Triskele still has three legs (and will always have three, as long as Severian lives and the machine sustains his beloved pet's quiddity[1]), while Master Malrubius will never be anything but old, stern and wise. All this, of course, we learn rather late in *Citadel*, despite the fact that aquastors of Malrubius and Triskele have been appearing to Severian ever since *Shadow*. But are they the only aquastors to appear in the original quartet? Surely, it would not be above Gene Wolfe to sneak a few non-obvious, machine-fleshed eidola into the narrative. So let us investigate several potential cases and see if we can roust an aquastor or two.

Ghost Warriors

Starting on an epic scale, we proceed to the third battle of Orithyia, where, as Severian awaits the inevitable clash of armies, he notes among his comrades the following:

> To our right a mixture, as it were, of mounted men and infantry, the riders helmetless and naked to the waist, with red and blue blankets slung across their bronzed vests…I had no idea from what part of the Commonwealth these men might come; but for some reason, perhaps only because of their long hair and bare chests, I felt sure they were savages. (*Citadel*, 172)

Moreover, these savage riders are accompanied by "something lower still, brown and stooped and shaggy-haired. I had only glimpses through the broken trees, but I thought they dropped to all fours at times." This bifold nature of Severian's compatriots seems a partial clue (as does Wolfe's use of *I felt sure* in this context—almost certainly misdirection); but while the "savages" conjure up images of Native Americans (or at least their old-time cinematic equivalents), their shaggy cohorts are a little more puzzling; possibly, I thought, they're related to the dog-faced ape that runs in and examines Severian back in *Shadow* as he lies recovering from the avern's poison in the soldiers' lazaret. But then in *Urth of the New Sun*, Wolfe introduces us to shapechanging Zak, an avatar of the Hierogrammate Tzadkiel, and when we first meet him he's described in almost the exact same terms as the lycanthropic companions of the riders.[2] Wolfe's *Urth* is also where a more anthropomorphized Zak attempts to take Severian's place as the Epitome of Urth; being tall, muscled and naked, given a destrier and the proper accouterments, he might well approximate a savage rider. Is it therefore possible these two linked factions are aquastors, recruited perhaps by Father Inire from his own memories to fight in the army of the Commonwealth? We do, after all, see aquastors battling alongside Severian against the sailors of Tzadkiel's starship. And surely if any government had the ability to send in eidolonized, non-real soldiers to supplement its all-too-human-resources, it would do so. (Conversely, is it likely the Hierogrammates themselves would actually place their own lives in jeopardy to fight for Urth?) But to bolster this supposition, is there any textual evidence, overt or otherwise, that suggests such a process has taken place? Unfortunately, while there's a passage that suggests yet another link to Yesod,[3] and still another where Severian states "The savages seemed to have vanished,"[4] the notion, while intriguing, remains largely speculative.

Ghost Warrior

Scaling down our search now, we come to what I feel is the better case for a secret aquastor. Severian, tired, starving, and sorely wounded from his battle with Baldanders at Lake Diuturna, is attempting to find the Pelerines so he can return the Claw of the Conciliator when he notices an approaching column of soldiers. Uncertain how he'll be treated (Severian fears he might be accused of desertion, plus travel by road has been outlawed for ordinary citizens), he flees into the nearby woods, where, when the blood in his ears stops pounding, he hears a fly, eventually tracing it back to the boot of a dead soldier. Severian finds no wound on the soldier, but in his pack finds food and a handwritten letter[5] to the dead man's apparent paramour, which he reads, but only in part. Because by this time the soldier, perhaps through the agency of the Claw, is gradually returning to life. Not much later, and supporting each other, Severian and the soldier stagger off back to the road, where after a bit more travel and travail, they eventually locate the Pelerines' field hospital—almost certainly a journey neither man could have made on his own.

But who is this revived soldier? He himself cannot remember, and Severian's attempts to draw him out elicit typically Wolfean responses, being more ambiguous than concrete, but easily explained away nonetheless by Severian. Hence, when the soldier tells of "Music…and walking a long way; in sunshine at first but later through the dark," Severian equates this to their passage through the woods. The soldier elaborates further, remembering "Flying through the dark. Yes, I was with you, and we came to a place where the sun hung just above our heads. There was a light before us, but when I stepped into it, it became a kind of darkness." Once again Severian reduces this to mundanity—more journeying—whereupon the soldier utters his first Wellerism,[6] recalling old friend Jonas's sailor talk. Not much later, when needing a name to introduce him by, Severian picks Miles, "since I could think of nothing better." But *Miles*, of course, is Latin for *soldier*, which many readers of Wolfe will know.[7] At this point, Miles has also recovered enough so that he is thinking of leaving, telling Severian that "[I hope] when I go among the units of the army I will find someone there who knows me." But apart from who he is, Miles *has* begun to remember other things: "[Falling or flying through] a lot of darkness…Seeing my own face, multiplied again and again. A girl with hair like red gold and enormous eyes…The most beautiful [woman] in the world." (*Citadel*, 47) Recognizing the latter as a reference to Jolenta, with whom Jonas has been infatuated, Severian finally tells Miles his own theory about how he has come to be—that having previously expired in the woods, soldierly Miles has not only been revived by the Claw, but may, because Severian had been wishing for Jonas's return, also jointly be Jonas—neither soul displacing the other, but coexisting in the same body. Miles, skeptical, attempts to rebut Severian with his own prosaic explanation: "Possibly whenever a man loses his friend and gets another, he feels the old friend is with him again." (*Citadel*, 52) But when Severian subsequently tells Miles that Jolenta is dead and that he will have to seek another, Miles turns and leaves, and Severian never sees him again.[8]

But how does any of the above support the supposition that Miles is an aquastor? Well, first of all, there are Miles' extant memories. While few in number, they almost surely reprise events from Jonas's life. The "music" he remembers, for example, is most likely Famulimus' voice, which Wolfe typically describes as musical (pre-crash Jonas has been a servitor of the Hierodules). Then there's his frequent references to *flying or falling through the dark*—probably conjoined references to both Jonas's journey back to Tzadkiel's starship once he steps into Father Inire's bright mirrors *and* a remembered power failure aboard the same starship.[9] Seeing his face multiplied over and over obviously refers to Inire's specula again, and the girl with red gold hair and enormous eyes is clearly Jolenta. And so at least in part many of Miles' memories seem linked to Jonas. But why then doesn't Miles look like Jonas and how come he appears to be a soldier?

Schizoid Reflections

Let us again remember Severian's condition when he flees into the woods: he's hungry, he's exhausted, he's wounded. Also consider his later admission, "When I'm tired, and sometimes when I'm near sleep, I come near to becoming someone else." (*Citadel*, 28) This, of course, refers to *genius cerebri* Thecla, whose memories he sometimes shares so intensely she seems to take him over. This happens dozens of times in the Book, of course, not only resulting in Severian being physically mistaken for a woman,[10] but also in narrative dispossession. Severian, speaking or writing in the first person, actually at times does so as Thecla.[11] But imagine during one of these sessions, or when a mind meld between Severian and Thecla is more likely due to fatigue, that you are the machine of the Hierodules that scans the brain for memories. Isn't the mnemonic blueprint you retrieve almost certainly to be an amalgam of the two parent sources—a true brainchild of Severian and Thecla—and hence bear hybrid characteristics? Now if we consider the Jonas moiety of Miles to have come from Severian (this much seems obvious), we have only to account for Thecla's contribution—apparently, if we're to judge from Miles' military aspect, a soldier. But who is he?

I believe the answer can be found in the letter Severian finds among Miles' effects in Chapter I of *Citadel*. Addressed to "O my beloved," I'm positing the letter has been written by one of Thecla's lovers, having actually been completed and dispatched, reaching her back at the House Absolute before her arrest; hence its retrievability from her memories. Moreover, the writer is probably "that young man, the nephew of the chilliarch of the Companions"—a lover recalled by Thecla in the very next chapter, the title of which, "The Living Soldier" may thus have dual significance. Thecla, at some later point, must also have learned that the young man has died of fever; hence, when Severian first finds him and looks for a visible cause of death, he can find no wounds. This same strain of fever has apparently infected Miles' friend Makar, who's mentioned in his letter,[12] and may well be the source of the fever that strikes Severian in the lazaret. And even Miles himself at a still later stage seems to believe that pyrexia has been the source of his being found prostrate in the woods. "I had fever," he tells Severian, "and you found me." Miles here may be drawing on either a latent or a recovered memory, just as he might be when he finally does remember his name, telling it to Einhildis just before he leaves the lazaret: "Why, Miles, of course."[13] In other words, though Severian *thinks* he is naming Miles "Miles" because of the afore-said soldierly connection, he's actually doing so because Miles really *is* named Miles—a fact recalled for him, even if only subconsciously, by the abiding presence of Thecla. This is why Wolfe does not have Severian read the letter he finds in its entirety; because at its bottom it would have been signed Miles. Just as Wolfe cagily does not have Thecla recall the name of the young man who is the nephew of the chilliarch (though the proximal, if latent, recollection of his name seems to spur other associated memories). Nothing, of course, in *New Sun* comes that easy.

At any rate there's still at least one more bit of evidence in support of the Miles-as-aquastor theory. In Chapter I of *Citadel*, "The Dead Soldier," Severian sees mysterious lights in the sky just before dawn—flares of magenta that do not appear to change in frequency, coming on the average of every five hundredth beat of his heart. Somewhat later, just before he discovers Miles in the woods, he notices a number of damaged trees, torn in half and raggedly so at about eye level height. But aren't the lights and trees somehow connected to the nearby war? At first I thought so, but later in *Citadel*, when the Green Man takes his second leave of our hero, he steps off into "that direction I had never seen until I watched the [Hierodules'] ship vanish into it from the top of Baldanders's castle." Not simply gone, Severian notes, for "despite the dimness of the dawn sky," he can see the "running figure for a long time, illuminated by intermittent but regular flashes." (*Citadel*, 242) Hence the lights appear to be associated with either the Corridors of Time opening up or closing; what's more, out of that same "strangely angled tunnel" flits the flying craft that bears Malrubius, Triskele and the aquastor-creating machine, and when it takes off again, this time with Severian onboard, he hears "alongside [them], the crashing of great limbs"—yet another link back to the woods where Miles is first discovered. For sometime in the past, the craft, probably with Malrubius and Triskele aboard, has drawn from the joint mindset of Severian/Thecla the aquastor known as Miles, a schizoid personality like his progenitors, being part comrade and old boyfriend, but without whose help Severian might never have made it out of extremity to the lazaret of the Pelerines and further glory.

Gypsy Prime

Cyborg Jonas, like so many of the characters in *New Sun*, represents a composite figure, being in part based on Hans Christian Andersen's "The Tin Soldier,"[14] and in part on L. Frank Baum's Tin Woodsman. But what about Jonas's human side? Are there archetypes or literary forebears that Wolfe draws upon to amplify this aspect of his character? I believe there are, and that each, while incorporating the notion of wandering as expiation, plays off Severian's Christ-like persona. For in many respects, Jonas, who has been traveling up and down the seven continents of the world, looking to reconnect with the Hierodules, and "tinkering with clumsy mechanisms," embodies the figure of Ahasuerus, the Wandering Jew. Ahasuerus, we recall, was alleged to have mocked Christ on his journey to Calvary and was therefore condemned to wander the earth until the Second Coming. Severian, representing Christ, has not only come again, but been befriended by Ahasuerus/Jonas—an act of redemption by the latter that finally liberates him from exile; like Dorothy now, he can return home, and does so via Father Inire's mirrors.

But Jonas's admission about "*tinkering* with clumsy mechanisms" also recalls the Gypsies—aka *tinkers*—who according to legend have been condemned to eternal wandering because they provided the nails for Christ's crucifixion. Given as well the Gypsies' traditional association with metalworking, is it possible the grinder who at one time attempts to sharpen Terminus Est is somehow connected with Jonas? The grinder, who has been encountered by Severian and Dorcas on their journey to Thrax, is part of a "caravan of tinkers and peddlers," but becomes frightened when he lifts the mercury-filled blade. Now recall Severian's words when he first attempts to do the same: "She shifted as though I wrestled a serpent." Or to put it another way, *as if the metal were alive*. Could this then be Wolfe at his most ironic, hinting that this peripatetic tinker who's afraid of "living metal" is somehow related to cyborg Jonas, who himself embodies living metal? A further connection might be found in Miles's razor, which Severian describes as "one of those little blades that country people use, razors their smiths grind from the halves of worn oxshoes." It may even have been made by the aforesaid tinker and then later seen by Thecla. Yet another possibility still: the grinder may be the human killed when Jonas's landing ship crashes, and from whom he harvests his organic parts. But how can this be? Hasn't the crash in question taken place in the past, thereby vitiating this supposition? Not necessarily. Jonas, after all, is a former servitor of the Hierodules; ergo, his sense of time, like that of his creators, may run counter to ours. This would allow for Jonas to have crashed in our future, harvested what he needed from the killed tinker, and then lived his life backwards (at least from our frame of reference) until the point he encounters Severian. But again, aren't there moments in the antechamber where Jonas seems to be recalling the past, and a distant one at that? As he confides while imprisoned to Severian: "You told me once that you thought I had an unusual name. Kim Lee Soong would have been a very common kind of name when I was…a boy. A common name in places now sunk beneath the sea."

The problem here is that it's difficult to tell whose native memories Jonas is actually drawing upon: pre-crash Jonas, who's a metal servitor of the Hierodules; or post-crash Jonas, who as a cyborg is a mélange of metal and flesh. If the latter, this seems to assume that when Jonas harvested the eyes, larynx and "other parts" of the man killed in the crash, the man's memories came included with everything else—sort of a whole-package-deal, or that maybe cyborg Jonas is like the laboratory hydra whose sundered halves each retain a memory of a previously learned response when whole. Unless, of course, the "other parts" included brain tissue and that Jonas did the-alzabo-mind-slurry-cocktail-thing—for which there is no evidence. On the other hand, if these memories belong to pre-crash Jonas, there's less of a problem. They're part of the same mnemonic archive that Jonas draws upon when he tells Severian about the Wall and the black beans, which dates back to his long servitude with the Hierodules—not to a bunch of memories he's uploaded from his human biografts or picked up once Urth-bound. Also kindly note the ellipsis in Jonas's second sentence above—robots not having boyhoods, author Wolfe has Jonas searching for a mutually comprehensible term, one meaning an equivalently early time in his life as a sentient tin can, hence his eventual choice of "boy." The details about his donor (such as Pop being a craftsman) post-crash Jonas could have absorbed locally, especially if he takes up with his now fellow tinkers.[15] And finally: as a metal man, pre-crash Jonas may have already lived a long life before his accident, and thus may well have sailed with Asiatic spacers, back in the age of myth, when more than a few astronauts were named Kim Lee Soong.

14

BLACK HOLES AND GREEN MEN

The reason why Severian must become the New Sun, of course, is because the old sun is dying. Subsequently, temperatures are colder now, the world's ice is increasing, and brighter stars can be glimpsed by day. But while a reader of *Shadow* might reason this to be a natural consequence of late-stage stellar evolution, the reader of *Claw* would learn something else entirely. As the caloyer at Morwenna's execution calls upon the Increate in a final prayer, we hear him address the godhead as "You, the hero who will destroy the black worm that devours the sun" (*Claw*, 33). If meant to be taken as real—and it's certainly a surprise revelation at this point—possibly, we conjecture, the caloyer is talking about how a black hole is responsible for the sun's decline. This supposition, in fact, will be confirmed shortly later in Dr Talos's play, *Eschatology and Genesis*, as another holy man—the Prophet—proclaims: "Yet even you must know that cancer eats at the heart of the old sun. At its center, matter falls in upon itself, as though there were a pit without bottom, whose top surrounds it." (*Claw*, 222). What's more, as we learn in the next book of the series, the black hole has apparently been around since the time of Typhon the Great, roughly one thousand years earlier. As the revived two-headed tyrant will explain to Severian, "My astronomers had told me that this sun's activity would decay slowly. Far too slowly, in fact, for the change to be noticeable in a human lifetime. They were wrong. The heat of the world declined by nearly two parts in a thousand over a few years, then stabilized." (*Sword*, 206)

But how, we're left to wonder, has that black hole arrived where it has—and if not a natural process of the cosmos (the sun, in its heavenly gyre and gambol about the galaxy, moving into it rather than the other way around), who put it there? I've seen a variety of speculation about this over the years, but believe Wolfe provides the answer in his coda to the original tetralogy.

Severian, at this point, has come back from Yesod a millennium earlier than he left and is performing the various miracles that will soon become part of the Conciliator's legacy. At Vici, after a farmer has complained about how snow has come before the corn crop has ripened, Severian, in response to the farmer's "The sky people are angry with us," says, "The sky people—the Hierodules and Hierarchs—do not hate us. It is only that they are remote from us, and they fear us because of things we did before, long ago when our race was young." (*Urth*, 204) A little while later, Severian, now discoursing pearls of wisdom in his peripateticae, writes "I tried to tell [my audience] how the Hierodules feared us because we had spread through the worlds in the ancient times of Urth's glory,[1] extinguishing many other races and bringing our cruelty and our wars everywhere." (*Urth*, 207)

So the obvious implication is that the Hierogrammates via their "holy servants" have placed the black hole in the sun as both part punishment and part restraining device. The fact that Typhon's astronomers appear to be the first to realize the singularity exists is also perhaps significant, since Typhon, if successful in his attempts to recapture the glory of the First Empire, is most likely to repeat the excesses the Hierodules most fear.[2] But at the same time, if mankind doesn't return to the stars, the Hierogrammates, who owe their existence to humanlike ancestors, may be jeopardizing their own future. And so they must provide for a potential conciliation between the two—someone or something who can wash away the sun's stain in a baptismal-like lavage, and leave mankind not so much sin-free, but free to sin again—but this time with hopefully different results. That agency, of course: Severian of the fuligin-clad Torturers, whose story will become Wolfe's *Book of the New Sun*.

Green Genes

Met at the Saltus Fair, where's he a chained prisoner, but able to escape with the aid of Severian, who will give him half a whetstone, the green man later returns at the end of the series, where along with Agia he helps to liberate Severian from the Ascians. "We requite our benefactors," he tries to explain to Severian, who is recovering from the chemical effects of the Autarchy download. "I have been running up and down the corridors of Time, seeking for a moment in which you also were imprisoned, that I might help you." (*Citadel*, 241) Contrary to what the present moment seems to indicate, however, the green man still does not consider the debt repaid in full. Claims he: "You and I are not yet at a balance, for although I found you captive here, the woman found you also and would have freed you without my help. So I shall see you again." (*Citadel*, 242) The question for readers subsequently becomes when does the payback occur? Given the overall structure of the Book (we learn, for example, that Severian has a twin sibling long after brother and sister have met, while the first encounter Severian has with Ossipago, Barbatus and Famulimus is, from their frame of reference, the last), it's tempting to look for some sort of time inversion—that is, an intercession by the green man at a much earlier remove. And since Severian has to be captive at the time, we must look to those sections of his life where he's incarcerated or being held prisoner. Possibly, it's the green man who's looking for the opportunity to help in the antechamber of the Autarch; as Severian reports during the cruel attack by the jaded young exultants, "My eye was caught by a gleam of greenish light so faint that even in that darkness it was scarcely visible."[3] (*Claw*, 131) But when Severian via Thecla remembers where a secret door is, the green man's aid is unnecessitated. Similarly, the green man appears to be searching for a way to liberate Severian when he's being held prisoner by Vodalus and Agia in the jungles of the north. Writes Severian: "Though the leech came no more, as I have said, and Agia never visited me again, I frequently heard the sound of running feet in the corridor outside my door and occasionally a few shouted words." (*Citadel*, 218) Apparently, however, the occasion does not present itself for release, although the green man seems to follow the group as they continue to march through the jungle. ("Hardly a night passed without our hearing the sound of bones crushed by great jaws, and by night green and scarlet eyes, some of them two spans apart, shone outside our little circles of firelight.") And while it's tempting (or perhaps more of a last resort) to see the green man's aid in Severian's escape from the underground holding cell of Abundantius' coven—rather auspiciously Severian is able to perceive a semi-illuminated overhead hatch[4]—I have to admit that if this was the answer, it left me with rather an unsatisfactory feeling.

But then (and perhaps contrary to our expectations), in *Urth of the New Sun*, the green man is finally able to make good on his promise. Severian, at the juncture in question, has been buried alive in the stone town by the worshippers of Apu-Punchau. Attempting to dig his way free, he is not having much luck when suddenly:

> The immense stone above tilted ever so gently to the left. Dried mud cracked, sounding as loud as the breaking of river ice in the stillness, and came rattling down around me.
>
> I stepped back. There was a grinding, as of a mill, and a second shower of mud. I moved to one side and the great stone fell with a crash, leaving behind it a rough black circle of stars. (*Urth*, 365)

Severian does not explain the mechanism he believes responsible for the stone-moving but once he steps free of his tomb notices the Corridors of Time opening up all about him—where running along one branch next to Tzadkiel the Hiero-grammate is the green man, his long-standing promise now repaid. And given the latter's access to the Corridors, it seems the green man has been in league with the Hierarchs of Yesod all along, perhaps being tapped by them for the same mission as Father Inire—likewise ensuring the futurity of his own race, the Eloi-like green people.

15

SEVENTEEN

The number seventeen comes up a number of different times in the narrative of the New Sun, and each time it does it appears to carry a sinister valence.

The first time we encounter it is in the library of Master Ultan. One of the books shelved next to *The Book of the Wonders of Urth and Sky* is entitled *Lives of the Seventeen Megatherians*, and Blaithmaic is credited as its author. We're not privy to any of the book's passages, but given that at a later point Abaia, one of Urth's principal monsters and an enemy of the New Sun, is described as the "great beast Abaia," and knowing that megatherian means "great beast" in Greek, it seems safe to postulate the book concerns Abaia, Erebus, Arioch, and Scylla, along with their lesser counterparts. And how many of these malign alien beings have crossed the gulfs of space and taken up residence in the Urth's oceans or beneath its crust? Taking our clue from Blaithmaic, let us posit seventeen. Hence one possible context on its use as a number of charged sinisterness.

The second time we encounter seventeen is on the Field of Sanguinary Conflict. To announce their presence, the various combatants customarily shout out their names, and one such combatant identifies himself as "Cadroe of the Seventeen Stones." Seventeen Stones seems to refer to a place or a locale here, but we're given no further reference to any such place, so its use remains somewhat enigmatic, although I do note that the second syllable of Cadroe is "roe"—i.e., fish eggs—and that many of the Seventeen Megatherians appear to be aquatic. So perhaps Wolfe is merely seeking, however obliquely, to expand on this aspect of their nature.

The third time we encounter the number seventeen is in *Claw*, when Severian reveals there are seventeen cells per wing in the Matachin Tower. If you're a prisoner here, obviously you're in dire circumstances, and the retrofitter of the tower (the building is in actuality a rocket ship) may have picked seventeen to convey exactly this notion.

Lastly, in *Citadel*, we hear of the Group of Seventeen, the ruling polity of the Ascians. The Ascians are the longtime enemy of the Commonwealth and have aligned themselves with Abaia, Erebus, Arioch, *et al*—in other words, the Seventeen Megatherians. Their use of seventeen in both title and membership thus seems designed as an honorific to commemorate this alliance. As Michael Andre-Driussi also points out in his fine *Lexicon Urthus*, typical membership in the former Soviet politburo comprised seventeen, so there's this additional likely resonance, especially since the Ascians, lacking shadows/souls, come very close to the ideal godless practitioners of Communism.

But how is it that Wolfe-the-author has chosen seventeen to take on these various sinister shades? Why not some other number? Is it meant strictly to reflect the politburo connection? Wolfe, after all, as a man of deep religious convictions, might well have a particular horror of political systems that preach atheism.

The answer, I believe, can be found in *Genesis 7:11*:

"In the year when Noah was six hundred years old, on the *seventeenth* day of the second month, on that very day, all the springs of the great abyss broke through, the windows of the sky were opened, and rain fell on the earth for forty days and forty nights."

In other words, it's meant to signify the coming of the Megatherians, monstrous creatures of the abyss, Wolfe's posthistoric equivalent of Lucifer and the other Infernals.[1] And not only have the skies opened up figuratively, it seems, but literally, just as Genesis notes—there being a number of references in the Book to a great flood that's taken place in Urth's past. Severian, in describing the fourth and lowest level of the Citadel, mentions how "mud had seeped into the corridors until it lay to the thickness of one hand." (*Shadow*, 39) Two sentences later he tells us, "Yet the water had never been high here." Water, of course, always seeks the lowest level, so bad plumbing and a great leak (though never mentioned) might account for it, but how about mud several inches high four floors beneath the surface?[2]

Additionally, when Jonas and Severian are riding atop the baluchither bound for Vodalus's forest stronghold, Severian describes their jostling motion thusly: "I feel now that I'm traveling through the Citadel in a flood, solemnly rowed." (*Claw*, 76) Look, however, at the reaction this produces in Jonas: "At that Jonas looked so grave that I burst out laughing at the sight of his face." But why does Jonas appear so disturbed? Severian's remark hardly seems anything but casual. And yet, as we recall, Jonas seems to know quite a bit about the Megatherians; notably, about how, because of their behemoth-like nature, they've confined to pelagic waters. He's also attempted to explain why the Great Wall has been built with his tale of the black beans, which unfortunately for us he never concludes. But do the black beans, besides calling to mind the beans of Jack and the Beanstalk, also refer to black *beings*—i.e., the Megatherians? (Keep in mind the punning nature of these various little embedded tales; monitor for minotaur and thesis for Theseus, for example, in "The Tale of the Student and his Son.") Are the black beans meant to be sown like Aeëtes' dragon teeth and produce warriors to combat Typhon? Since all of the Brown Book's tales are conflational, combining a number of different myths and archetypes, Cadroe's stones might also represent not only the missile David slew Goliath with, but the stones Deucalion threw after the flood that Zeus sent, although in the Urth myth "great beasts" may have come forth from the waves, not men. Jonas, having been a servitor of the Hierodules, knows full well the facts behind his little tale, even if he doesn't share them, and this is why he reacts so gravely—if the creatures brought by the flood triumph, it means that he and his masters will have labored in vain, and that the New Sun will be guttered like a candle dropped into the sea.

16

ABDIESUS

Abdiesus, the archon of Thrax, is so concerned about losing his government appointment that he sends his lictor—the recently arrived Severian—to execute a woman for the mere political inexpedient of sleeping around. The woman, of course, is Cyriaca, and, like so many other significant people in his life, Severian meets the ex-Pelerine postulant quite by accident at a masked ball. (Severian has yet to be told she's his intended victim.) Her crime, however, she freely acknowledges once she realizes the situation: "[I've] loved too many men, men other than my husband." But even Severian (who's just made love to her himself) finds the notion that she's earned the death penalty for this a bit extreme, arguing "No woman is killed for being unfaithful, except by her husband." Only then does Cyriaca tell him the full details:

> "Among the landed armigers hereabout, [my husband] is one of the few who support the archon. The others hope that by disobeying him as much as they dare and fomenting trouble among the eclectics they can persuade the Autarch to replace him. I have made my husband a laughing stock—and by extension his friends and the archon." (*Sword*, 92)

But from a number of different contexts it's also apparent that Abdiesus is already fomenting his own notion of rebellion, and that Cyriaca is doing no worse than her husband—he's almost certainly the twice-met Racho. But first for Abdiesus's connection to the corpse-eaters. At one point, we're told by Severian that Abdiesus has a most unusual appearance: "His face was coarse, with a hook nose and large eyes rimmed with dark flesh, but it was not a masculine face; it might almost been the face of an ugly woman. (*Sword*, 34) Again, playing off of Abdiesus's female aspect, Severian later notes that "it was not until the door closed behind [Abdiesus] that I detected the faint odor of the musk that had perfumed his robe." But who are the two characters these traits most recall? The first is Severian, who's mistaken for a woman any number of times (Oringa, Emilian and Ava[1] all do it); and the second is Appian.[2] Their obvious commonality? They've each participated in corpse-eating via the analeptic alzabo and carry the abiding presence of internalized females. This, then, is probably the source of Abdiesus's femininity and perfume, and may help to explain the Archon's distraction when Severian first comes calling on him in *Citadel*.[4] As we're told by Ava the Pelerine, the corpse-eaters "talk to themselves…and they look at things that are not there. There's something lonely about it, and something selfish." (*Citadel*, 80)

Racho, on the other hand, we know has been associating with the Vodalarii or at least that's one inference we can make when we overhear him the first time he and the young torturer meet as Severian works his way to Ultan's library. "And so they all escaped," Racho tells his companion, another armiger dressed in bright clothes,[5] "Vodalus had what he came for, you see." (*Shadow*, 49) Racho is apparently talking about Vodalus's recent scrape with a citizen's brigade in the cemetery—the one where Hildegrin, Thea and Severian are all present when a woman's grave is violated.[6] But what's otherwise important to note here is Racho's social status as an armiger—something we learn from Cyriaca that her husband shares (he's also away in Nessus, which is why Severian never gets to meet him in Thrax). A year or so later then, after Severian has been exiled from the Torturers' Guild, once again we encounter Sieur Racho (such meetings of seemingly insignificant characters are almost always significant in Wolfe), only this time he's accompanied by a woman Agia deems a whore and he's driving a fiacre, and he wants to race Severian and Agia in their fiacre. The race between the two vehicles will end, of course, in the tent pavilion of the Pelerines, where Severian will find the Claw of the Conciliator (or vice versa). But we never hear what happens to Racho after this point. We do, however, hear quite a bit about the man to whom Cyriaca is married. "He was cruel to me," she says to Severian, attempting to explain her infidelity, "so cruel, after our marriage…and so I took a lover to spite him, and afterwards, another…" (*Sword*, 92) But apart from his social status and absenteeism, where we're ultimately able to connect Racho back to Cyriaca is in the type of vehicle suggested to Severian and Cyriaca to make their return to the masquerade. Severian, quoting a sentry's advice: "He said we might leave the boat at the Capulus if we wished and return in *a fiacre*."[7] (*Sword*, 94) Thus it appears Abdiesus's order to execute Cyriaca is predicated on his keeping Racho happy; Racho, in turn, when he's not whoring about or racing headstrong through the streets, will continue to publicly support the archon even as both work behind the scenes to undermine the Commonwealth.[8] And as for Cyriaca—well, she lives to see another day, as Severian changes his mind at the last minute and sets her adrift on the Acis under the green light of Lune.

17

SEVERA

Absentee or long-lost sisters are nothing new in the novels of Gene Wolfe.[1] David and Gene, the two cloned brothers who reside at 666 Saltimbanque on Sainte Croix, have one in *The Fifth Head of Cerberus*, while the prostitute Chenille is somewhat undramatically revealed to be Silk's sister in the Whorl series. But easily the most famous missing sister in all of Wolfe's work is Severa, the twin of Severian the Great, who artfully manages to avoid making her herself conspicuous through all four volumes of *New Sun* and its sequel, remaining to this day (at least in my opinion) unidentified. Many readers, of course, have attempted to pin down this elusive figure, and while there is a consensus opinion about who she may be, I think it's worth the effort to investigate a number of candidates, as well as seek to establish reasonable criteria we might use to quantify the search overall.

That Severian even has a sister is first intimated rather late, coming in the third volume of the series, *Sword of the Lictor*. Severian at this point has fled Thrax, hoping to rendezvous with the Pelerines so he can return the Claw of the Conciliator. Along the way he encounters the pioneer family of Casdoe and Becan. Having been gobbled up by an alzabo, Becan himself is dead, as is his daughter Severa, the girl twin of a boy also named Severian. The latter accompanies Severian-the-narrator when Casdoe is killed by zoanthrops and it's he who first asks his namesake if he has a sister. Big Severian's reply: "I don't know. My family is all dead." (*Sword*, 146) Later, after Severian reaches the field hospital of the Pelerines in *Citadel* (Little Severian having by now joined his family in the hereafter), he's asked by Ava the postulant if his name isn't part of a matched brother-sister pair, Severian and Severa—thus setting off one of the more complicated missing person searches in all of Gene Wolfe's fiction.

This being our goal as well, let us now establish some parameters for the search and see if we can rouse Severa from the mists of obscurity.

The first criterion we need to include plays off two of the more implicit aspects of twinship. Severa, as Severian's birth-mate, should be the same age as her brother. She might also share similar physical characteristics, though this is no guarantee in heterozygous twins, and even if true to a major degree, given the assortment of temporal paradoxes in *New Sun* and a predilection for mask-wearing by Wolfe's characters, such familial or isochronic resemblances may not be readily observable.

Secondly, we need to account for the fact that no one *named* Severa is ever actually encountered anywhere in the series. This seems to imply one of two things: that Severa is either one of the many unnamed characters Severian meets in his journey from torturer to Autarch or she's using a pseudonym. If the latter condition is true, we need to account for the change since Severian still bears his original birth name. We might also look to the pseudonym for hagiographical or auctorial correspondences, since there appears to be a pattern of this in Severian's next-of-kin. Ouen, for example—the name of Severian's father—is a Welsh form of Eugene, while *Saint* Dorcas was resurrected from the dead by Saint Peter—just as Severian's grandmother has been.

Thirdly, there's Severa's likely career choice. Or as Severian tells Pelerine Ava when asked if he has a sister, "If I do, she's a witch." This is because female children of the clients executed by the Commonwealth go to the Witches' Keep, where they're raised in the tradition of the weird sisters; boys, in turn, go to the Matachin Tower to become torturers. Most of the children so placed remain there for life, but not all; Eata, for example—one of Severian's childhood friends—doesn't, and even Severian himself briefly considers leaving the order before taking his final vows. ("I had known, as all apprentices know, that one was not firmly and finally a member of the guild until one consented as an adult to the connection." *Shadow*, 101) If one assumes all the guilds operate similarly, it's possible that Severa—though she's been raised as a witch—has opted to pursue alternate goals.

Fourthly, given the history of incest in Severian's family (he's slept with both grandmothers—see *Catherine*), as well as his promiscuity, it should not surprise us to learn that Severian has bedded his own sister—though he may be unaware of the endogamous act. Zeus, after all, tops sister Hera, and the parallel may be germane.

Lastly, there may be a number of symbolic associations—predominately of the solar variety—linking Severa to her brother, who embodies the New Sun, as well as a number of subtextual clues—Wolfe in my opinion is usually pretty good at interlarding these within the various mysteries he builds.

So much for establishing criteria. Now for the candidates.

The Witch

First and foremost among these must be Merryn, the young witch who partici-pates with the Cumaean in the séance at the stone town. Almost all attempts to pinpoint Severa have singled in on her as the most likely candidate for Severian's lost sister, and even Wolfe himself has quasi-endorsed this selection.[2] But let's see how Merryn fits the various categories of our profile and attempt to account for where she doesn't.

Does Merryn resemble Severian? Actually, it's hard to tell, given Severian's rather terse reportage. At one point he tells us she has "dark eyes and a serene face," while later, after she's collapsed during the séance, he compares her to "a black clad doll, so thin and dim that slender Dorcas seemed robust beside her." This constitutes most of what we know about Merryn's physical appearance at stone town—hardly details to which we can match fraternal similarities. How-ever, much to his surprise, Severian recollects having met Merryn before; this occurred many years previous, when, as a very young boy, he's asked to deliver a message to the Witches' Keep. Answering the door is someone he describes thusly:

> The face that looked into mine was hardly higher than my own. It was one of those that are at once suggestive of beauty and disease. The witch to whom it belonged seemed old to me and must actually have been about twenty or a little less; but she was not tall and carried herself in the bent-backed posture of extreme age. Her face was so lovely and so bloodless that it might have been a mask carved in ivory by some master sculptor. (*Claw*, 280)

This, of course, raises several immediate questions. If Severian and Merryn/Sev-era are supposed to be the exact same age, how can she exist as an adult when Severian is yet a boy? Also, is the face Severian describes as Merryn's her real countenance or a mask? In my opinion, the latter remains a distinct possibility, as witness Severian's remarks immediately after Merryn's aforementioned collapse: "Now that intelligence no longer animated that ivory mask, I saw it was no more than parchment over bone." (*Claw*, 291) We therefore have little way of deter-mining what Severa actually looks like. But as for her earlier adulthood, this is less a problem. Because in *New Sun* a number of methods for contravening time exist, and one might easily surmise the Cumaean could travel back into the past with her acolyte. This does not necessarily mean they have done so (what would be gained in the undertaking of such a jaunt?), any more than Merryn *must* resemble Severian under her mask. They are merely possibilities—as are their opposites. In conclusion, we have no way of ascertaining whether Merryn resembles Severian or if they're both the exact same age.

Similarly unable to determine is whether the name Merryn is a pseudonym. If it is, however, we need to account for why it's being utilized. There's no indication witches customarily change their names at any point in their lives (unless girl twins are automatically renamed to pre-empt their search for a possible brother among the torturers), nor does Merryn appear to be fleeing the authorities—hence requiring false identification. So why Severa would choose to call herself Merryn as opposed to her birth name remains a mystery. As for auctorial correspondences I've been unable to find any links between Saint Merryn and anything lupine, while hagiographical parallels also seem remote. (From Michael Andre-Driussi's *Lexicon Urthus*, 169: "Saint Merryn, or Meadhran, died c. 820, and was a disciple of Saint Congail at Benchor, venerated both in Scotland and Ireland.") In other words, nothing about the name Merryn seems to enhance the prospects that she's really Severian's long-lost sister.

Fortunately, however, with our next category—that of Severa's likely career—we score a direct hit, for Merryn is unequivocally a witch, the famula of the Cumaean. "Famula," of course, derives from the female form of *famulus*, "an attendant; esp. on a scholar or magician." (*OED*) I'd be a little more comfortable with the implications of this—i.e., that girl-child Severa was raised right next door to the Matachin Tower of her brother—if Merryn were somehow able to associate Severian's cloak of fuligin with the torturers' traditional garb; surely, she would have seen similarly-clad guild-members in the Old Yard. And yet when she first sees Severian in the stone town, she asks, "Who is this man in fuligin then, Mother?" To which the Cumaean replies, "He is but a torturer." Still, even with this slightly odd detail, there can be little doubt that Merryn is a weird-sister-in-training.

But as to whether Severian does or doesn't sleep with Merryn, again we're on slippery terrain. As the scene where the Cumaean explains how Dr. Talos worked his somaplastic techniques on Jolenta demonstrates, the witches are privy to even greater means of transformation. Comments Hildegrin: "I didn't know looks could be changed so much. That might be useful, that might. Can your mistress do that?" (*Claw*, 287) Merryn, in response: "She could do much more than this, if she willed it." It's therefore conceivable that any beautiful woman could be Merryn in disguise, transmogrified by the Cumaean's arcane skills. But when we consider the roster of women we know Severian has slept with—the prostitute-khaibit Thecla, the real Thecla, Dorcas, Jolenta, Cyriaca, Daria, Pia and Valeria—it's hard to imagine Merryn being any of them.[3] It therefore seems unlikely that Merryn fits the profile in this regard.

But maybe there is a plethora of solar or subtextual associations that could yet save Merryn's putative twinship. Unfortunately, if they exist, I haven't been able to find them. Yes, Merryn *is* described as having a face "immobile as an oread's in a picture," compared to a "black clad doll," and has mask imagery associated with her, but how these may sororally connect Merryn to Severian escapes me. Likewise, the total absence of anything emblematic of Severian's connection to the New Sun—golden or roseate imagery, for example—seems to signal a dead end.

Fortunately for us, however, early in the drafting of what would become GW's three-volume *Book of the Short Sun*, Wolfe acknowledged that he wanted to return to the world of Severian's boyhood, and that Severian and Merryn would probably appear.[4] Many people immediately seemed to assume this was Wolfe's way of confirming the consensus belief—that Merryn and Severa were one and the same. Now that the final volume of the series has been published, let us look to *Return to the Whorl* and see what additional evidence, if any, we can find to support this notion.

First of all, despite the build-up, Merryn's appearance is extremely brief and almost more of a cameo than anything else. She's never directly addressed by name, but recalled first by Jahlee—the adopted inhuma daughter of Incanto, *Short Sun*'s protagonist-writer—who says of her, "Merryn had troubles with animals, too," (*Return*, 266) and then subsequently by Incanto, who narrates the story of their meeting, which has taken place during one of his trips back to the Red Sun Whorl (i.e., Urth).

At the moment in question Incanto has been taken to a cell by a young torturer's apprentice where ill Jahlee is recuperating. Inside the cell, however, he sees not only Jahlee, but "an unhealthy-looking young woman…so pale and gaunt I feared that Jahlee had been feeding…" (The inhumi are vampiric and drink human blood.) Jahlee explains that Incanto is her father, while Merryn explains that the boy who's brought him to the cell—though never named, he's obviously Severian—is her brother. Exclaims she, as we already know: "We're brothers and sisters, we witches and the torturers." Severian then explains how he's brought Merryn to Jahlee's cell, thinking she might be able to help Jahlee, whom he reckons a fellow witch (the inhumi can not only shift shape, but fly, as well as oneirically transport others about the whorls of Wolfe's various *Sun* series). Merryn then renders her diagnosis of Jahlee's alleged witchiness, telling Severian and Incanto that she has no powers, after which she rises, "looking like a woman stiff with age."

The last we see of her is when Severian offers to show everyone his dog Triskele and Jahlee says, "I'd like to see it. I love dogs." Remarks Incanto then: "I followed her just in time to see the witch's gaping mouth and the utter blankness of her large dark eyes."

End of scene. So what do we have for congruent points? Well, there is Merryn's declaration that Severian is her brother; it's possible that one might see this as something other than what it probably is, i.e., Merryn talking about the *communal* nature of the witches and torturers, who are the children of those sent to the Matachin Tower—in other words that Gene Wolfe (wink, wink) is telling us that Merryn and Severian are indeed brother and sister in the truer biological sense. But this really cuts against the grain of Wolfe's fiendish talents, being far too unsubtle in my opinion, and it does nothing to explain either Merryn's "stiff with age" appearance or curiousier still, "her trouble with animals, too."

In conclusion, apart from the fact that Merryn is very definitely a witch, there appears to be little evidence to support the contention that she's Severian's long-lost sister. But then who exactly is she—simply the traveling companion and acolyte of the Cumaean? In my opinion she's *literally* the Cumaean's daughter—the same way Famulimus is. (Note that out of all the characters in *New Sun* only the Cumaean and Famulimus speak in blank verse.) *Famula* and *Famulimus*, of course, are also etymologically linked, both words sharing the common Latin root. Such cryptonymic pairs, where one word can be derived entirely or almost so from the parent word, are common in *New Sun*, and I believe are meant by Wolfe to suggest interrelatedness, either genuine or symbolic (see *Appendix*). It's also why, during the events in the stone town, Merryn addresses the Cumaean as "Mother" and the Cumaean addresses Merryn as "Child." The "bent-backed" witch Severian recalls as a boy, in turn, links her to Father Inire, who's typically described in similar terms (ditto for the "stiff with age" remark), just as the mask she is or is not wearing recalls Ossipago, Barbatus and Famulimus. Mother, Father, Daughter—all hail from Yesod, the universe of the Hierodules. Now we can also understand a little better Jahlee's comment about animal trouble, because one of the central conceits of *Short Sun* is that *animals can recognize the alienness in shape-shifted inhumi, despite their human appearance.* Merryn—an alien—can thus be recognized as Other by animals, just as Jahlee is. As for her saintly (as opposed to mythic) name, it might well be a pseudo-anagrammatized version of Myrine,[5] similar in formation to Camoena/Cumaean. This at least is how I see Merryn—as non-human—hence in no way can she be connected biologically to Severian the Great.

The Witch?

Obviously, this leaves us with a sizeable hole to fill, since Merryn has always been the odds-on favorite for potential-lost-sister-found. But several other candidates over the years have also been advanced. Critics Gregory Feeley and John Clute both cite the bottled mandragora in the Citadel as a possible candidate for Severa—not a bad choice overall and in part supportable, but ultimately erroneous. (See *Mandragora* for details.) On the other hand, in attempting to identify Severian's mother in *Strokes*, John Clute completely misses the boat when he fails to notice how well Morwenna of Saltus[6] matches up in the lost sister department. For starters, as Severian tells us in the very first sentence of *Claw of the Conciliator*, she has "hair dark as my cloak," providing an early potent link to the torturer. Morwenna—who will be executed for allegedly poisoning her husband and infant son—could be as young as Severian (remember, Dorcas has already borne a child in her early teens) and she may fancy herself a backwater witch, knowledgeable about poisons and potions; perhaps she's even learned her skills in the Witches' Keep, we reason, but opted to leave the weird sisters for a placid country life (cryptonymically, she and Merryn also match up). And in the process of performing his duties as carnifex, Severian brands Morwenna on one cheek and then breaks her legs, the latter being regularly done to victims of crucifixion and the former identifying her with both Dorcas and Severian.[7] Everywhere else, however, we find no match-ups. No hagiographic or lupine parallels; no sexual tryst with Severian; no roseate or solar imagery, etc., etc. But clearly there is enough other evidence to warrant consideration.

However, as much as I like the idea of Morwenna being Severa, and the delicious irony that Severian may have executed his own twin, in my opinion, Morwenna is one of several characters deliberately set-up by Wolfe *to appear as if she might be the missing sister*—a red herring, if you will. And like Merryn, on careful re-examination of the clues, she must be disqualified. Starting with her name, why is it Morwenna and not Severa? No reason I can think of; nor is she ever described as a recent arrival to Saltus—something Eusebia, her accuser and rival for her husband, is likely to have mentioned. Equally suspect, I believe, is Morwenna's alleged witchiness. Severian himself believes her husband and child have died from simply drinking bad water (although he later adjudges Morwenna responsible, perhaps to assuage his conscience) and it seems unlikely Morwenna could have poisoned Eusebia's threnodic roses from her position on the platform. Eusebia, too, eventually proclaims Morwenna innocent—only to die herself of poison.[8] But where the likelihood of Morwenna being Severa completely breaks down for me is in the fact that Severian breaks her legs; yes, this was done by the Romans to the poor wretches they crucified, but we are specifically told that the legs of Jesus Christ—another messiah—were not broken. To my mind this is Wolfe saying Morwenna is at best a false sister—especially when we shall see how much better the woman I really believe is Severa matches up in this regard.

The Wench

But before I introduce that person in both her avatars, we need to examine one last candidate—that of the slave girl Pia,[9] whom Severian encounters in the village of Murene. Physically, with "her long dark hair," she may resemble Severian; moreover, when Severian asks her how old she is, he tells us (without revealing that age) "I smiled to find her precisely the same age as myself." (*Sword*, 229) Pia and Severian later make love for another important match-up and once again the comparison to a known relative is invoked: "…for Pia with her hungry mouth and supple body recalled Dorcas." (*Sword*, 245) Pia also has "a slender waist, a thing seldom found in autocthon women (*Sword*, 228), hinting she may come from somewhere else; indeed, as suggested in "The Tale of the Boy Called Frog," which Big Severian has earlier read to Little Severian, perhaps, like the twin sons of Spring Wind and Bird of the Woods (Fish and Frog—Moses crossed with Romulus and Remus), little Severa has been placed into a basket by a kind matron in the Matachin Tower or Witches' Keep and sent downstream via the Gyoll to Lake Diurturna, where she, like each of the twins, is adopted by a poor woman and given the new name Pia.

The main problem with this theory is that the Gyoll runs downhill to the sea, not upstream to Lake Diurturna.[10] Also, Pia's non-native status is belied by the presence of a look-alike in Baldander's castle, a woman Severian claims could be her sister (if Pia is Frog, she may be Fish). And while Severian has compared Pia to Dorcas, he's equally quick to add, "But it was false too; Dorcas and Pia were alike in love as the faces of sisters are sometimes alike, but I would never have confused one with the other." (*Sword*, 245) Thus it appears hard, if not impossible, to identify Pia as Severa.

The Whore

Having dispensed with the four characters we're probably meant (at least by author Wolfe) to see as potential candidates for Severian's lost sister, I'd therefore like to introduce my own two nominees, state their particulars, and see how each fits the profile we've drawn up.

The first of these women is met at the House Azure on the night Severian is to receive his inaugural pleasures as a man. She's the "Chatelaine Barbea," one of the prostitutes trotted out by the old Autarch[11] for the consideration of clients Severian and Roche. Look, however, at the way she's initially described by Wolfe: "A tall woman entered. So poised was she, and so beautifully and daringly dressed, that it was several moments before I realized she could be no more than seventeen." (*Shadow*, 89) Severian, of course, is not only tall, but also approximately the same age. Both have straight noses[12] as well, but whether Barbea has dark hair like Severian's isn't immediately determinable, for she appears to be wearing a wig. Still, the age data looks promising, as do the height and nasal resemblances.

Another positive match is seen in the second category of our profile, for Barbea is obviously a pseudonym—the prostitute being a stand-in for the real Barbea, an exultant hostage held in faux concubinage back at the House Absolute. Ergo, there's no reason her real name *couldn't* be Severa. As for hagiographical correspondences, consider the following: Saint Barbea is always associated with her brother Sarbelius in martyrologic literature, while the -a/-lius endings of their names recall the similar endings of *New Sun's* other prominent twins, Agia/Agilus. Both brother and sister saints were also tortured before being executed, tangentially linking them to Severian's profession.

But doesn't Barbea's prostitute background conflict with her being a witch? Actually, I don't believe it does. Remember, according to Gurloes, witches often service the torturers in at least their first sexual encounters (this is how Gurloes lost his virginity) and they appear to be quite wanton. ("I learned much later that there was a good reason for selecting only boys well below the age of puberty to carry the messages our proximity to the witches required." *Claw*, 279)[13] Their patron saint is also Saint Mag, which may be short for Magdalen, the prostitute of the New Testament. So it's not that big a leap to connect Severa with prostitution—especially if she, unlike her brother, has chosen to leave the guild she was born into,[14] but subsequently couldn't find work, therefore being forced to fall back on the lustful ways of the weird sisters and earn her keep as a prostitute. Unfortunately, Severian has other plans than to make a witch, quondam or otherwise, his first sexual conquest. Because while he's attracted to Barbea/Gracia—they appear to be the same woman[15]—he picks another prostitute completely—the "Chatelaine Thecla"—thereby vitiating the incest angle. Still, this is the first time where a match of some sort isn't made.

However, any mismatches in the "crimes against nature" category, are more than made up for in the last area of consideration, the symbolic and subtextual associations. Prime among the nuggets here: Wolfe's description of Barbea's hair, wherein a certain key element is mentioned twice. "Her hair was so near to burnished gold that it might have been a wig of golden wires." (*Shadow*, 89) Gold, of course, is not only emblematic of Severian's role as the New Sun, but also foreshadows and bolsters the imagery Wolfe will later use in describing paternal grandmother Dorcas,[16] among other family members. This, in my opinion, is not a coincidence. Wolfe, a writer of endless circumspection, only uses the word *gold* as a character attribute to link the various members of Severian's bloodline, and out of nearly 300 named characters in *New Sun*, only six of them are so conjoined. (See *Agia and Agilus* and *Swimming with Undines* for additional information)

Then there's Barbea's sensual dancing, part of her attempt to entice the evening's customers: "She posed herself a step or two before us and slowly began to revolve, striking a hundred graceful attitudes." This may or may not be an attempt by Wolfe to associate Barbea with the tower of the torturers, where Severian has spent his youth: *matachin*, according to the *OED*, is "a sort of sword-dance in a fantastic costume." In addition, there's this marvelous passage from *Claw* that brilliantly conjoins witches, dancing *and* the Pelerines. "I recalled the witches, their madness and their wild dancing in the Old Court on nights of rain; the cool, virginal beauty of the red-robed Pelerines." (*Claw*, 258) Barbea, a dancer like the witches, is here linked via subclause to the Pelerines, from whose ranks Severa's mother Catherine has come. And lest one think that terpsichorean come-hithers are common in Severian's time, only Barbea, out of all the women he meets, dances for him.

But before I go all the way and anoint Barbea as Severian's long-lost sister—or at least as the most viable contender—let me discuss one possible impediment. Previous to Severian's first and only visit to the House Azure,[17] he's told by Gurloes that the prostitutes are all khaibits, "common girls that look like the chatelaines." (According to *Lexicon Urthus*, khaibit, in ancient Egyptian, means "shadow.") He admits to not knowing how they're recruited, but Severian later opines that they're drawn from the ranks of the poor. This remains the operant explanation until *Citadel*, when Appian implies they're actually clones, "grown from the body cells of exultant women so an exchange of blood will prolong the exultant's blood." But which of the two explanations is more credible? Seemingly, the Autarch would be more informed about the true nature of the prostitutes he employs; then again he lies at least once about them, telling Roche and Severian that "all the beauties of the court are here for you…by night flown from the walls of gold to find their dissipation in your pleasure." This, of course, is later shown to be hype by the "Chatelaine Thecla," who tells Severian, "Because of the snow…I came in a sleigh with Gracia." (*Shadow*, 91) In fact, the elements themselves seem to be directly conspiring against any sort of major journey that night, especially one that begins at the House Absolute, which lies leagues outside of Nessus.[18] Witness as well how Wolfe describes "Thecla's" reaction when Severian seeks to determine the current population of the House Azure. "I asked her how many of the court were here, and she paused, looking down at me obliquely." *Obliquely*, yes—as if to say, how naïve are you, young man? There's also a certain tackiness about the khaibits that doesn't quite befit their status as exultant knock-offs. They're shorter in stature for one thing, and their wardrobe appears constructed more from flimsy than finery. Comments Severian, as he examines Thecla's gown later in a private cubicle: "The stuff between my fingers, which had looked so bright and rich in the blue colonnaded room below, was thin and cheap." (*Shadow*, 92) Consequently, doubts begin to assail him. "I took a step away from her. There was nothing of Thecla about her. All that had been a chance resemblance, some gestures, a similarity in dress." Eventually he even declares, "'You are not the Chatelaine Thecla,'" only to have the prostitute seemingly reinforce the notion that she *is* playing a role: "I am Thecla. *If you want me to be.*" (Italics mine.) On top of all this, there's the suspicion that Severian is either drugged or drunk; he's been given wine upon his arrival, which he quickly gulps, and much of the scene where Appian brings forth potential bedmates for him seems imbued with a certain hallucinogenic quality. Indeed, Severian at one time describes himself as "half-hypnotized," and he's unable to remember choosing ersatz Thecla. ("'It is she you wish then,'" our host said. I could not remember speaking." *Shadow*, 90) Perhaps by drugging the visitors to his brothel, the old Autarch is thus more easily able to convince them of the khaibits "authenticity," especially on a night where he may have had to have called in local stand-ins because of the snow. In other words, at least on this particular occasion, I prefer Severian's explanation for where the khaibits have come from, rather than Appian's. Or as Wolfe has Severian say, "I was standing in a small, cold room looking at the neck and bare shoulders of some poor young woman whose parents, perhaps, accepted their share of Roche's meager silver gratefully and pretended not to know where their daughter went at night." (*Shadow*, 92.)

But even if none of the above is substantial enough to raise your suspicions about the true nature of Barbea and her bedfellows, let us further investigate the khaibits-as-clones theory. At one point, when Severian asks him why he doesn't use "real" exultant women at the House Azure, the Autarch replies, "Because I can't trust them, of course. A thing like this has to remain a secret…Think of the opportunities for assassination…There are few at my court I can trust, and none among the exultants." (*Citadel*, 195) But wouldn't this necessitate complete and total segregation of khaibits and exultants? For surely one or more of the former would be inclined to mention to the latter that they're spending their nights turning tricks for the Autarch—especially if as Gurloes claims they exchange roles (let alone blood) every once in a while. The exultant women, remember, are confined as hostages to the area about the Well of Orchids. Should we not assume the khaibits are confined similarly to their own seraglio elsewhere? Severian's seeing the khaibit Thea roaming about the backstairs of the House Absolute seems to argue otherwise—as does the notion of sleigh-traveling Gracia and Thecla. How has Appian therefore managed to keep his Azurean thralls from spilling the beans to their mirror images and engendering source?

Then there's the entire issue of cloning itself. Surely, if it's an option, it's not practiced widely outside of exultant circles. Thecla, for example—the *real* Thecla, she who shares Severian's skull—never mentions either having a clonal sib or undergoing any sort of rejuvenation by bloodsharing.[19] Nor is any mention of cloning ever made by the old leech who attends Severian when he's recaptured by Vodalus (his idea of rejuvenation, because "youth is contagious," is to sleep with a thirteen year old boy). Even star-traveling Typhon seems unaware of its potential. So apparently it's a quite limited technique, being practiced only by those with either extensive financial means or access to the proper technology. But wouldn't such an enterprise have to be conducted under the auspices of the Commonwealth—or at least its trustees—since the resultant clones appear to have little status other than as sexual chattel to be used or abused by the Autarch? And in that regard who is the most likely character to figure as clonemaster (especially since the technology involved may be extrasolar), but our old friend Father Inire? Such might provide an alternate explanation for the presence of "Thea" in his wing of the House Absolute, as well as provide him with a steady supply of the girl children whose company he so relishes.[20] Because if Inire in any way is able to connect with the fatherless khaibits as a paternal figure, he might be able to get them to do all sorts of things—from bedroom snooping to simple errand running. His association with them might also help to explain the Barbea-to-Gracia transformation, which smacks of the Cumaean's skills ("*I didn't know looks could be changed this much*"), and he may be using the journeymen who never returned from their errand to the House Absolute as muscle—all of this unbeknownst to

Appian, of course, who more and more looks the Claudius figure to his vizier's Caligula.

The Waitress

Now for my second candidate, who's also met in *Shadow*, but who plays a much larger role in the narrative than Barbea. She is, in fact, Jolenta,[21] the former café waitress who's given the ultimate makeover by Dr. Talos, transforming her from drab Norma Jean to voluptuous Marilyn. (Wolfe saw Monroe while stationed as a GI in Korea, so the parallel may be partially autobiographical.) Her particulars? Well, let's examine them the same way we did Barbea's.

In terms of age and appearance, once again Severian provides us with very little to work with, describing the ill-kempt waitress who waits on him, Baldanders, and Dr. Talos, as "a thin young woman with straggling hair." (*Shadow*, 147) Arguably, there's nothing here that immediately disqualifies her from being Severian's twin, but both "thin" and "young" are much too vague to connote anything of value. It's almost as if the woman is beneath Severian's notice—something that will be reversed once Talos completes his handiwork. But I also think that cardsharp Wolfe might be playing against our expectations here, anticipating our belief that missing sister Severa—whoever-she-may-be—will cast a much more magisterial shadow.

"Jolenta," however, *is* a stage name, crafted for her by Dr. Talos, and we never learn what the café drudge's real name is. No one ever asks Jolenta in our presence, so it may actually be Severa. Moreover, *Saint* Jolenta experienced Christ's stigmata and I don't believe that Gene Wolfe would waste such a blatant link to the New Son—paronomasia intended—on a mere waitress. This, in my opinion, is a very significant clue.

As for Jolenta's gig as a waitress, once again I'll cite the same possibility that I did with Barbea: Severa, not wishing to spend the rest of her life cooped up in a decrepit tower with a bunch of miserable howling witches, has opted to leave, found no employment, and wound up working in the world's second-oldest profession. Not that she's been there overlong; we're told she's only been waitressing for about a month, thereby prompting us to wonder (since it's the only clue we have to Jolenta's other life) what she's been doing previously. You'd think she might drop some hints in all the time we spend with her, but she never does, and this may reflect on the totality of Dr. Talos' makeover, for Jolenta seems the voluptuous sex kitten in ways that transcend the merely physical; she's transformed mentally as well. Ergo, if any residue of Norma Jean remains, it appears to be well submerged.

Big points, however, are once again scored in the next category. Severian, of course, *does* couple with Jolenta, shortly before he and his fellow troopers stage "Eschatology and Genesis" for the Autarch's thiasus, thereby fulfilling the incest prerequisite. But perhaps more significantly it turns out that *Dorcas* and *Jolenta* may have also made love. Certainly, Severian believes they have. As Severian tells us, "[Jolenta] had boasted that she made tribadists of women" (*Claw*, 207). Later then, in a dream, he reports that "Dorcas and Jolenta came hand in hand, smiling at each other, and did not see me. (*Sword*, 178) Only after Little Severian dies, however, does he voice his worst suspicions: "I knew then how Dorcas had felt when Jolenta died. There had been no sexual play between the boy and me, as I believe there had at some time between Dorcas and Jolenta." (*Sword*, 201). Thus Wolfe establishes a parallel to Severian's quasi-Oedipal relationship with his grandmother, having Dorcas sleep with not only her grandson, but also her granddaughter. Twin bonus points may therefore be in order.

There is as well a nice series of matches in the final category. Jolenta's hair, as we're told time and again, is red-*gold*, a character attribute I've argued is used only by Wolfe to emblematically link members of Severian's bloodline. But equally important is its red aspect—a color traditionally associated with witches ever since the Middle Ages.[22/23]

Jolenta also—because of the amplitude of her thighs—has difficulty walking, prompting Severian at one time to ask if she is lame, foreshadowing his own future condition and epithet.[24]

Then, in "Eschatology and Genesis," starlet Jolenta portrays the roles of both Jahi and Carina the Contessa; the former with its somewhat Cumaean-like character is a flashback to her youth (in addition to being able to tell the future and make it spontaneously snow, Jahi also accounts herself ancient beyond years; recall that the Cumaean of myth is seven hundred years old when Aeneas seeks her out); while the latter is a link even further back to mother Catherine (the homonymic *Karina* is a Swedish variant for Katherine).

And then last but not least: Jolenta, when we first meet her, is waiting on tables—the same thing *père* Ouen is doing when Severian visits the Inn of Lost Loves. Simply put: like father, like daughter.

Thus, with a nice quadruple slam, do I conclude the Jolenta-as-Severa thesis, and pronounce it an even stronger case than that of Barbea.

But if I had to pick between the two candidates and narrow it down to one? Well, let me attempt a final synthesis. Given what we know about each woman, is it possible that Barbea and Jolenta are actually the same person—lost sister Severa? No reason I can think of negates this potential unification. It's easily surmisable, after all, that Severa could be working as *both* prostitute and waitress, having taken up the latter after realizing her temp job at the House Azure will never pay the bills; or perhaps she's simply chafed at being grist for every Alto, Becan and Drotte who wants to lay a lookalike chatelaine. Severian's visit to the House Azure was so long ago, it's only natural she doesn't recognize him as a former would-be client—especially since both torturers have come garbed in their civilian clothes and she's bedded by Roche, not Severian—plus she may also have spread her loins for so many men they've all blurred together. Transformed by Dr. Talos, and in the dark of the stone town, she's then unrecognized herself by fellow witches Merryn and the Cumaean, who rather significantly are the two characters most knowledgeable about the high-tech means used to transform her. And both Barbea and Jolenta are clearly performers, although their venues and audiences are different, with the stage being the one area where drab Norma Jean can shine transcendent—the poor little orphan girl who's gone on to become a goddess, if not of love, at least of lust. Wolfe also seems to place an unusual amount of emphasis on both the wigs and provocative makeup of Barbea/Gracia, while virtually the only clue he relays about Jolenta's physical appearance is her straggling hair—a contrast I do not see as accidental, but one explaining the necessity for the other.

Lastly then we have two matched passages that attempt to describe Severian's difficulty in recognizing either Barbea or Jolenta. The first concerns how uncannily alike the prostitutes Barbea and Gracia look (again probably because they're the same person):

> There was something in the eyes of both women, in the expression of their mouths, their carriage and the fluidity of their gestures, that was one. It recalled something I had seen elsewhere (I could not remember where), and yet it was new, and I felt somehow that the other thing, that which I had known earlier, was to be preferred. (*Shadow*, 90)

Notice how this same sense of failure—the psychic dross of things half-remembered—is evoked in the second:

> Jolenta grew neither stronger nor weaker, so far as I could judge; but it seemed to me that hunger, and the fatigue of supporting her, and the pitiless glare of the sun were telling upon me, for once or twice, when I glimpsed her

from a corner of an eye, it seemed that I was not seeing Jolenta at all, but someone else, a woman I recalled, but could not identify. (*Claw*, 269)

Severian, who struggles throughout much of *New Sun* being unable to perceive either his or other familial relationships,[25] can hardly be faulted for his own persistent myopia. The familiar grace he sees earlier in Barbea/Gracia no doubt recalls similar qualities he's perceived in mother Catherine, who's visited the torturers' guild yearly on its feast day; while the woman he cannot quite identify, but whose half-remembered shadow still haunts him, is not just simply that of a former café drudge (she, too, echoing Catherine's physicality), but his own twin sister, who will die soon in the stone town from another form of stigmata—the bite on the wrist by a vampire bat.[26]

Poor lonely brother. It seems that without his ever knowing it Severa has been found and lost at the same time.

18

THAIS

One of the more mysterious personages met in Wolfe's sequel to the Book, *Urth of the New Sun*, is Thais the courtesan. She, along with two others from the House Absolute, the servants Pega and Odilo, has survived the flood brought about by the white fountain; and it's to the trio's makeshift raft that Severian himself swims to safety (though at this point he can breathe underwater. See *Swimming with Undines*).

Right from the beginning, however, Wolfe sets Thais apart from Pega and Odilo. She's described as fairly-young, "tall, dark, and hollow-cheeked" and to further distinguish her from Pega, who is short and cheery-faced like a doll, Severian usually refers to her as "the dark woman." Also, unlike Pega (who has been a lesser servant of the Chatelaine Pelagia) and master steward Odilo, Thais reveals (and has revealed) almost nothing about her previous circumstances—a fact that seems to irritate the pompous Odilo to no end—other than her name. But though we've never met her before as Thais, for veteran readers of the Book it is possible to place "the dark woman" within a larger context. The plain simple fact of the matter is we've met her several times before—and ironically it's Odilo who helps us provides the reference.

Somewhat given to garrulousness, shortly after Severian clambers aboard the raft, Odilo begins an anecdote about how his father (also named Odilo)[1] once encountered Severian the Great[2] in the secret passageways of the House Absolute. Severian, dressed in the fuligin of a carnifex, is thought by Odilo *père* to be on his way to a masque, "of which there are several in one part or another of the House Absolute on any given night. Yet," as Odilo *fils* continues to explain, his father "knew none was to take place in our Hypogeum Apotropaic, neither Father Inire nor the then Autarchy having much fondness for those diversions." (*Urth*, 314)

Notice however the reactions of Severian and Thais to this bit of information. As Severian notes, "I smiled, recalling the House Azure. The dark woman shot me a significant glance and ostentatiously covered her lips with her hand." Severian, however, thinks Thais merely wants him to cut Odilo's anecdote short, but I believe she's attempting to enjoin his silence, fearing he's recognized her. Hence the significance glance.

But there are also clues in the House Azure and Hypogeum Apotropaic references—these being the two places Severian and Thais have previously encountered each other.

The second of these has taken place in *Claw*. Severian, having escaped from the antechamber where he and Jonas have been imprisoned, is now looking for Terminus Est.

> I ascended some distance, reconnoitered the corridor there until I was certain I was still lower than the antechamber, then began to climb again when I saw a young woman hurrying down the stair toward me.
>
> Our eyes met.
>
> In that moment, I felt sure, she was as conscious as I that we had exchanged glances thus before. In memory I heard her say again, 'My dearest sister,' in that cooing voice, and the heartshaped face sprung into place. It was not Thea, the consort of Vodalus, but the woman who looked like her (and no doubt borrowed her name) whom I had passed on the stair in the House Azure—she descending and I climbing, just as we were now. (*Claw*, 170)

"Thea" and Severian each continue on their respective ways. But then who is the very next person Severian encounters? Odilo *père*—who will then pass on the anecdote of their meeting to Odilo *fils*, who will then tell the story to Severian on the raft fifty years hence. (Obviously, all the stairs in the House Absolute are designed by M. C. Escher.[3])

As for the first encounter in the House Azure, once again Severian is ascending a stairs, this time with his inamorata-of-choice, the Chatelaine Thecla,[4] who asks:

> "Aren't you coming?" She had already reached the top of the stair, nearly out of sight. Someone spoke to her, calling her "my dearest sister," and when I had gone up a few steps more I saw it was a woman very like the one who had been with Vodalus, she of the heart-shaped face and the black hood. This woman[5] paid no heed to me, and as soon as I gave her room to do so hurried down the stairs. (*Shadow*, 91)

Thus at the very least Thais/Thea appears to have spent time as a prostitute—a fact that later figures into Thais's apotheosis as a goddess by the post-climactic survivors of the New Sun. As Severian will learn when he returns from his stint as Apu-Punchau:[6]

> "Thais is the night goddess. All below the moon is hers. She loves the words of lovers and lovers' embraces. All who couple must beg her leave, speaking the words as one in the darkness. If they do not, Thais kindles a flame in a third heart and finds a knife for the hand. Aflame, she comes to children, announcing that they are to be children no longer. She is the seducer. Golden honey is the offering her woman brings her." (*Urth*, 367–368)

But is this the last meager deduction we can make about Thais—that she's simply a courtesan who's plied her trade at the Houses Azure and Absolute? First, I believe her "tall, dark and hollow-cheeks" attributes are meant by the mischief-maker Wolfe to suggest she could be Severa, Severian's missing twin sister.[7] And it's a neat conceit when you think about it—Severian, if unknowingly, reuniting with his sister at the very end of the Urth books. But ultimately I don't believe this is any more representational of the truth than are the various masks worn by the Hierodules; in fact, I believe Thais is *a* Hierodule—namely daughter Merryn. For starters, when Severian encounters her for the second time, she's in the Hypogeum Apotropaic, which belongs to Father Inire. Being aligned with Father Inire also helps to explain her agelessness; after all, when Severian re-encounters her on the raft, over fifty years have passed, and yet Thais still appears a young woman. Either she's had access to the Corridors of Time or she's wearing an elaborate mask/disguise. (Remember the Cumaean's "There are those who ride the night air who sometimes choose to borrow a human seeming"?) As for Merryn's failing to recognize Severian at the stone town, it may simply be due to Severian's wearing of regular clothes to the House Azure, the obscurity generated by nightfall, or, the reason I like best, simple prevarication. But again why would Merryn be working in the Autarch's whorehouse? Possibly she's conducting reconnaissance in much the same fashion as Crane's spies at Orchid's in the *Short Sun* series; but more likely she's there just this once to make sure Appian does not try to kill Severian when the Autarch is told by "Paeon" that Severian will survive him on the Phoenix Throne.

There is also a horde of cryptonymic interrelationships linking Josephina, Thais and Thea with Merryn (See *Appendix*) and it's hard to believe Wolfe would not try to sneak her into the sequel just as he did Inire and Camoena. But even with all of the subterfuge, we do actually get to see Merryn in her full glory at the end. As Severian tells the post-flood primitive who's filled him in on the world's latest religion:

> I said, "It seems you have two good gods and two evil gods, and that the evil gods are Thais and the Sleeper."
>
> "Oh, no! All gods are very good, particularly the Sleeper! Without the Sleeper, so many would starve. The Sleeper is very, very great! And when Thais does not come, her place is taken by a demon." (*Urth*, 368)

But it's not a demon, of course. It's Merryn, naked and undisguised—the only survivor of her race on the new island of Ushas.

19

THECLA

Out of all the characters in *New Sun*, I think the one who has the most complex bloodline to unravel is Thecla. This may seem odd given Severian's convoluted ancestry, his mother actually being wife Valeria's temporally-displaced daughter; but at least in regards to Severian Wolfe plants enough clues so we can eventually figure out (or at least argue from text) his pedigree. With Thecla, though, the author plays it more subtly, and this stands somewhat at contrast with Thecla's tacit admissions throughout the course of the Book, where, if anything, she's excessively candid—or perhaps it's just that she's honest, unlike her often prevaricating or duplicitous host. But while Thecla freely recalls her casual love affairs or how she's terrorized the prisoners in the antechamber, she's rather discrete about who her parents are, which is odd, because that lineage is so detrimental to what happens to her, both before and after death—especially as it co-involves half-sister Thea. Let us therefore see if we can glean anything about who Thecla's parents might be and what, in terms of thematic amplitude, this ancestry may add to Wolfe's *opus solis*.

Daughter of the Bull

Thecla, of course, is an exultant, a member of the Commonwealth's upper class. This much we learn early, in *Shadow*, from Master Gurloes. Just as we do the circumstances surrounding her arrest and deportment to the Matachin Tower: Thecla, whose aforementioned sister is the consort of Vodalus, has been given over to the torturers in hopes that Thea will betray her revolutionary heartthrob, thus saving Thecla.[1] Moreover, as a member of the Autarch's inner circle of concubines—in actuality, female hostages held to ensure the good behavior of the aristocratic Exulted Families—she's far from the ordinary exultant prisoner. (Gurloes again: "The client is highly placed. Quite highly connected. Not just an armiger family. High blood." *Shadow*, 74) This, in addition to a few possible important physical characteristics,[2] comprises much of what we are to learn about pre-sui-cide Thecla; but by far the majority of what we are to learn about the chate-laine—especially the more sordid autobiographical details—comes from *reconstituted* Thecla, whose alchemized memories are imbibed via the analeptic alzabo, whereupon physically dead Thecla becomes a sort of living secondary per-sonality within Severian. Indeed at times she even takes over the narration of *New Sun*, and while this usurping is usually somewhat obvious, at other times it's extremely difficult to tell who the author of a particular passage is, or even more complicatedly, which *words* in a particular passage are attributable to whom, for Wolfe hybridizes the two sets of resident memories at even this level. Adding still further to the problem: Wolfe's figurative use of almost all terms of kinship throughout much of the narrative; hence aliens known as *Father* Inire and *Mother* Cumaean; guild coevals called *brother* torturers; and a dream episode where The-cla is addressed as *sister* by Merryn.[3] Yet another complication involves Thea's half-sisterhood. Is she, we're given to wonder, older or younger than Thecla, and which parent do the siblings share—mother or father? And who might the non-common parent be? If Wolfe does not mean for us to puzzle these sorts of ques-tions out, why even make Thea and Thecla *half*-sisters?

It's a puzzle of labyrinthine complexity, to be sure, built by a master crafts-man, but unlike brave Theseus, I'm rather afraid of horned things in the dark. Nevertheless, as long as we've entered the maze, let's continue the Daedalean dis-course. Because it appears Thecla herself is literally familiar with at least one maze, for late in *Citadel* she recalls "games played in the hedge-walled maze behind my father's villa." But who is the most likely architect of any maze in *New Sun*? Clearly, Urth's version of Daedalus, Father Inire, right? And since Inire "serves" at the behest of the current Autarch, could Appian himself be the father of Thecla, as Minos is of Ariadne? This may seem implausible upon initial analy-sis, but before we delve into it further, let's pursue the mythological parallels a bit more. The name Appian, of course, derives from *apis*, the Latin word for bee. Given the numerous references to hymenoptera in *New Sun*, as well as knowing that the old Autarch was a honey steward before he ascended the Phoenix Throne, many readers were probably not too surprised when Wolfe finally dis-closed the old Autarch's name in an ancillary tale of Urth.[4] But what many read-ers may not realize is that *Apis* is also the name of an Egyptian god who took the form of an ox. This no doubt helps to explain the scene in *Citadel* when Severian, suffering from wounds incurred during the Third Battle of Orithyia, hallucinates, seeing not Appian above him, but "A man with the horns and muzzled face of a bull…a constellation sprung to life." Appian as Taurus, however, not only recalls the minotaur of Minos' labyrinth, but the wild bull of Marathon, which Theseus also slays. Now recall that Severian kills a charging bull with *Terminus Est* on the pampas in *Claw*, as well as takes Appian's life, and the circle is complete. That is to say, in *New Sun*, there are readily discernable analogues of Minos, Daedalus, Theseus and Ariadne.

But how can the first of these—a eunuch—be the father of the last? This isn't all that difficult to reconcile, really, for Appian has only been unmanned by the Hierodules *after* he's failed their test. Given his long reign—from evidence presented by Odilo in "The Cat" it can be deduced that he's reigned a *minimum* of 62 years[5]—he may have been biologically able to procreate for decades, right on up until the time he decides to go to Yesod.[6] And whom does he have, since we're told by Cyriaca that he has no consort, to serve his lustful needs? Why, his seraglio of concubines, of course, which if we're to believe Master Gurloes, consists not of hostage exultants, but their khaibits. And yet Gurloes also tells us that sometimes the concubines change places with their clones, standing in for them. Again, the odd detail; but if true, it could help to resolve certain matters of legitimacy since a daughter created in such circumstances would probably not be considered a true heir of Appian, but might well stand to inherit her mother's exultant status.[7] So let us make that our test hypothesis—that Thecla is the daughter of Appian and one of his exultant concubines—and see if we can find any textual evidence to support it.

Thecla's birth seems a reasonable place to start, so let us recall what she reveals about the circumstances attending it. Says she to Severian while still in the Matachin Tower, "When my mother was in labor, she had the servants carry her to the Vatic Fountain, whose virtue is to reveal what is to come. It prophesied I should sit a throne. Thea has always envied me that. Still, the Autarch..." (*Shadow*, 97) Such marvelous compression by Wolfe, who generates so many questions and implications in this sleight passage it's hard to know where to begin. But for starters why has Thecla's mother delivered her child at the House Absolute and not at the family's oft-mentioned country villa? Do her parents reside at the former? There's no mention that Thecla's father is somehow connected to a court post or that most exultant women have their children at the House Absolute because of its better medical facilities. Certainly, it's possible that Thecla's parents live in or are visiting the underground palace when the blessed event occurs. On the other hand, if Thecla's mother, as the Autarch's favored concubine, has been living there all along, a court-side delivery also makes sense. Even more so, we now see the wisdom of the Vatic Fountain's prophecy: how natural that a child of the Autarch might sit a throne someday (although most readers will assume this refers to Thecla's ascension via host Severian). And the part about Thea envying the prophecy may be Wolfe hinting that Thea is not the daughter of Appian, but someone else. Lastly, then, we reach the author's aposiopetic endcap. It reads simply, "Still, the Autarch…" And that's it. But, we wonder, "still the Autarch w*hat…?*" *Has never acknowledged me as his legitimate heir, so now I'll never sit a throne?* Severian, like we readers, would like to know, so he asks her to complete the sentence, but all Thecla will tell him is, "It would be better if I didn't say too much." We therefore never hear her finish her words, but I believe it's possible she may have been about to disclose the nature of Appian's relationship to her—that he is in fact her father. I also like the notion that in these mere three-and-a-half sentences Wolfe has neatly conjoined each member of Thecla's immediate family: herself, her mother, her half-sister and her father.

Moving on to Thecla's girlhood, several incidents appear to offer additional support to the supposition about her parentage. The first of these involves young Thecla in some sort of ornate dressing room. "Around me," she recalls, "were beautiful women twice my height or more, in various stages of undress. The air was thick with scent. I was searching for someone, but as I looked at the painted faces of the tall women, lovely and indeed perfect, I began to doubt I should know her. Tears rolled down my cheeks. Three women ran to me and I stared from one to another. As I did, their eyes narrowed to points of light, and a heart-shaped patch[8] beside the lips of the nearest spread web-fingered wings." (*Claw*, 257) It seems almost certain that the woman Thecla is searching for must be her mother, and that the women in the dressing room are members of the Autarch's seraglio, but why Thecla doesn't disclose the former seems odd, as does the homogeneousness of the concubines—does their makeup and dress simply render them alike or are they perhaps khaibits?[9] At any rate, Thecla's inability to distinguish her mother from the rest parallels Severian's similar problems towards most of his family. And perhaps, to some extent, as the child of a concubine, Thecla's been raised by all of these women—surely, some of them would find it painful to be locked away during their prime reproductive years, but denied the right to bear children (this assumes Appian fathered few children or at least confined himself to khaibits). It also appears that Thecla is still living within the House Absolute at this stage and it's hard not to see the tall women she's searching among as exultant hostages. If her parentage is other than I've speculated, however, said passage becomes much more difficult to interpret.

Similarly, when Thecla relates the story about Domnina, she again conveys the impression that she and her mother continue to reside at the House Absolute. Thecla is playing with her paper dolls at this point, waiting tremulously for the reappearance of Domnina, who's gone off with Father Inire. "At last my nurse called me to supper," she tells us. "By that time I thought Father Inire had killed Domnina, or that he had sent her back to her mother with an order that she must never visit us again." (*Shadow*, 182) Domnina, a guest, sent packing by Father Inire, ordered never to visit *whom* again? And yet while the kindly Hierodule probably has the authority to do anything he wants, this seems a strange act on his part, almost as if he himself is acting the surrogate parent, which perhaps he may be, especially if Appian is off conducting matters of state. *Us* in that yoking sense, if Thecla and her mother are assigned quarters in the Hypogeum Apotropaic, may well include him.[10] But I'd also like to point out Thecla's mention of a nurse in the above citation, for when Severian is carried off by Appian to his encampment, where he's given over to the Autarch's cat-nurses for mending, the latter recognize Thecla within Severian. This seems bizarrely coincidental. After all, how likely is it that the cat-nurses Appian has personally picked to attend him on the battlefield also just happen to know Thecla? She is at this point not only well past girlhood, but dead. Then again, if these feline women are longtime *family* nurses and have attended Thecla much of her life, this would go a long way in helping to explain why they recognize her now, even though deeply submerged within Severian.

Now for a little texture—one of those oblique passages I mentioned earlier where a blended sequence of memories is being recalled, but where it's difficult to tell whose memories at any given point are being accessed. Hence some confusion determining whom the narrative "I" is, Severian or Thecla. Not that distinctions can't be made; in fact, I believe it's possible to break down the passage by voice, so we can understand exactly who is saying what. I'm also going to run the end of one paragraph into the first sentence of the next, skipping the break between the two, because I think it establishes a connection. Therefore, if you'll indulge me, in the following citation, *italics* designate Thecla as the source, while ordinary text identifies Severian as the author.

> Again Drotte and Roche and I swam in the clammy cistern beneath the Bell Keep; *again I replaced Josepha's toy imp with the stolen frog;* again I stretched forth my hand to grasp the haft of the ax that would have slain the great Vodalus and so saved a Thecla not yet imprisoned; again I saw the ribbon of crimson creep from under Thecla's door, Malrubius bending over me, Jonas vanishing into the infinity between dimensions. I played again with pebbles in the courtyard beside the fallen curtain wall, as Thecla dodged *the hooves of my father's mounted guard.* Long after I had seen the last balustrade, I feared the soldiers of the Autarch…(*Claw*, 241)

Here, give or take a word, you can see how in the second to the last sentence Thecla takes over in the middle of a clause, while the forced enjambment of the two paragraphs seems to suggest that Thecla's "father's mounted guard" may indeed be "the soldiers of the Autarch." (In the latter regard, Wolfe may also be suggesting a parallel between "fallen curtain wall" and "balustrade.") It's an artificial reading, to be sure, but while I admit I've taken certain liberties, I think the results are valid.

But lest one think that everything is perfectly resolute with this genealogy, I would be remiss if I didn't admit there's at least one major obstacle. It crops up late in *Citadel*, being in fact a continuance of "the constellation sprung to life" quote cited above, as well as another hybridized dip in the well of memory. Here again wounded Severian is being attended by Taurus/Appian and once more the previous differentiation applies (i.e., ordinary text = Severian; italics = Thecla).

> I spoke to him and found myself telling him that I was unsure of the precise date of my birth, that if his benign spirit of meadow and unfeigning force had governed my life I thanked him for it; *then remembered that I knew the date, that my father had given a ball for me each year until his death, that it fell under the Swan. He listened intently, turning to watch me from one brown*[11] *eye.* (*Citadel*, 190)

Severian, obviously, wouldn't know the precise date of his birth given the circumstances attending it; but once Thecla takes over, she's able to recall the bit about the ball, the Swan and the death of her father. But since Appian is still alive, doesn't this vitiate the theory that he's Thecla's male parent? Perhaps. But at least two alternate explanations can be posited. (1) The father Thecla is talking about here is her stepparent, the father of half-sister Thea. Given how loosely Wolfe plays with all terms of kinship in *New Sun*, Thecla may well mean him—not her biological father. (2) Alternately (and the theory I like better) Thecla may be talking about her father's symbolic death—his unmanning by the Hierodules, whereupon his passage into androgyny (indeed, at one point, Wolfe describes him as looking like a forty-year-old woman.) This interpretation may seem a little too symbolic for some, but I do believe Wolfe has earlier attempted to set himself up for such a reading, if on a proleptically subtextual level. Recall in this regard Severian's journey with Dorcas and Jolenta across the pampas toward Stone Town; after killing one charging bull, however, Severian is able to bedazzle a second "fierce black bull" with the Claw, thereby placating it enough so that Jolenta can ride it. But when they reach the grass hut of Manahen's father, the herdsman describes the bull as an ox—i.e., castrated—although he initially believes he sees "something between the ox's legs." Once again Severian is cast in the role of Theseus, but the bull, having been shorn of its gender and potency, is now much less than any minotaur. The long and the short of this in human terms may be that Appian, as Apis, will father no more and is dead to Thecla as a paternal figure.

Queen of Pawns

Wolfe does not present the details about Thecla's arrest until late in the fourth volume of his quartet, but I think they're well worth looking into, especially as they reinforce certain aspects of both Thecla's paternity and earlier essays. Asked through Severian why he had Thecla arrested, Appian disavows all knowledge of the deed, claiming that she was "taken by certain officers, who had learned that you were conveying information to your half sister's lover. Taken secretly, because your family has so much influence in the north." Presumably, Appian is talking about Thecla's exultant relatives here,[12] who, if Thecla *is* the biological daughter of Appian, might be able to stir up a rebellion using her as a figurehead claimant to the throne; plus invoke the Vatic Fountain prophecy for further legitimacy. And Appian himself may well believe this is why Thecla has been spirited away from the House Absolute in the fashion that she has, smuggled out in a tapestry.[13] But all this hugger-muggery still seems a bit odd—as if someone were to see Thecla being led out of the House Absolute in chains it would be under exultant flames by morning. If, however, Thecla's heritage is generally known, and even if she's only acknowledged to be an illegitimate daughter, the arresting officers might be fearful that servitors loyal to the Autarch might prevent them from carrying out their task—or attempt to notify Appian himself, who because of his blood ties might be unable to recognize the potential threat his daughter poses to the Commonwealth. The officers might also justly fear incurring the wrath of Father Inire, who may be publicly perceived as her guardian. But this raises another interesting point. Because of the Palaemon connection, Father Inire would be among the first to know about Thecla's arrest. In fact, it would not be surprising were he to be the person who's engineered it, either covertly or directly. This might well give him the bargaining chip he needs to insure Appian does not seek to have Severian assassinated[14] or flee into exile, determined to save his forebrain for more mundane uses than a memory cocktail. (Remember his "So soon" plaint?) Appian, being unaware of Inire's double identity, would doubtlessly never suspect his closest advisor as the agent behind Thecla's arrest, just as Father Inire may not know beforehand that Thecla will commit suicide in the Matachin Tower.[15] Inire may also be attempting to neutralize any potential claims on the throne by Thecla's exultant relatives, or possibly be seeking (although this would require foreknowledge of Severian's complicity in Thecla's suicide) an excuse to send Severian into exile, where elements crucial to his development as the New Sun will have their chance to act upon him, shaping our hero for his final Promethean hour.[16]

In any event, poor Thecla, who goes from queen to pawn in rather short time, commits suicide, although the day will come when once again she is partnered with Severian.

Chrysalis

Throughout *New Sun*, as Thecla casts her memory over the past, she mentions various figures in her life, most of whom are given enough context so as not to remain totally ambiguous or anonymous. In short we know how they relate to the former chatelaine or where she's encountered them. Hence Midian, her uncle's huntsman; Emilian, a former gallant at court; Aphrodisius, her only named lover besides Severian; childhood friends Josepha[17] and Domnina; and Guibert and Lollian, fellow terrorists of the antechamber. But there is at least one person who stands apart from these figures, and he's mentioned early in *Shadow*. Thecla, imprisoned in the Matachin Tower, has just been addressed by book-bringing Severian as "Chatelaine"—a title she believes is much too formal for the present occasion, although her punishment at the hands of the torturers will almost certainly be less so. Hence her immediate speculations about who might attend her final travails: "There will be an exarch, I should think, if you should led him in. All in scarlet patches. Several others too—perhaps the starost Egino." The exarch in scarlet patches is almost certainly a higher church figure, an archbishop or ecclesiarch of the New Sun religion. But how about Egino, *the starost*—a term the OED defines as "a noble holding a castle and domain bestowed by the Crown in the former kingdom of Poland"? Could he be the father of Thea, someone who's married Thecla's mother after the term of her concubinage was over,[18] but whose honorary title and holdings are so meager he could never present a threat to the throne, even as Thecla's stepfather? This might also explain why he himself hasn't been arrested as a traitor; he, unlike Thecla, has no valuable information to relay to daughter Thea. He's never mentioned by name again, and it seems odd that Thecla believes no one else will attend her in extremis, but perhaps a father-daughter bond has developed between them, especially since Appian has never been able to recognize her as his legitimate child or has been too busy conducting the Autarchy to confer much love and attention.

But what about Thea and Thecla's common parent, then—their mother? Do we meet her in the Book? Can we put a name to her? Here I must admit to bafflement. I initially thought there might be a clue in the fact that Thea is a cryptonym of Thecla or that maybe knowing these same four shared letters mean *goddess.* Unfortunately, how any of these various items link up has so far eluded me. But I'm also intrigued by another possibility—one based more on gut instinct than any substantial skein of evidence—and it involves Nicarete. She's one of two elderly prisoners we meet in the antechamber (the other is Lomer), but whose incarceration is voluntary. As she explains to Severian, "Someone must make amends for the evil of Urth, or the New Sun will never come. And someone must call attention to this place and the others like it." (*Claw*, 126) Other details are rather scant: from the way she throws back her head Severian believes she was once beautiful; her hair is white, but she wears it "flowing about her shoulder as young women do;" she hails from an armiger family that may yet remember her, but will leave the antechamber only on her own terms, "which are that all those who have been here so long that they have forgotten their crimes be set free as well." She also appears knowledgeable about history, telling Severian: "Long ago—I believe before the reign of Ymar—it was the custom of the Autarch himself to judge anyone accused of a crime committed within the House Absolute." Perhaps the most intriguing thing about her, however, is revealed later, as Severian, now Autarch-turned-memoirist, writes, "I have also ordered that Nicarete be brought to me, and when I was writing of our capture, a moment ago, my chamberlain entered to say she waited my pleasure." (*Claw*, 165) But has Severian actually been so impressed by Nicarete's altruism that he now wishes to commend her personally or has he other reasons for wanting to see her again? The former, in my opinion, seems out of character for the gruff ex-torturer. If, on the other hand, Nicarete represents someone important to him/Thecla/Appian, this might account for his executive order. But could she be Thecla's mother?[19] If so, at least this might explain why Thecla does not expect to see her in the Matachin Tower along with Egino—she's already incarcerated herself, even if voluntarily. And there is in Gurloes' earlier description of Thecla's pedigree as "not *just* an armiger family" the implication that Thecla's family could have armiger roots,[20] meshing perfectly with Nicarete's remarks about her own clan. And perhaps Mother Nicarete merely wishes to atone for the sins perpetuated by her terrorist daughter upon the poor prisoners of the antechamber.[21] But why wouldn't Thecla recognize her own mother? This seems highly unorthodox. Then again, as a child, she has problems doing so, and in an earlier encounter with the Autarch, only when she first hears him laugh does she realize who he is. And yet while Severian is similarly encumbered when it comes to recognizing various members of his own family, I'm still not sure any of these observations would help explain Thecla's non-recognition of Nicarete. So obviously there are problems with this approach. The only other person I can find with possible hypothetical ties to the altruist may be Severian's wife Valeria. An armiger, she too knows much about history (as does daughter Catherine), and there is in the prisoners' clinging to scraps of the past and temporal isolation much that is similar to Valeria's home base in the Atrium of Time. So perhaps Nicarete is really Valeria's mother, or somehow even related to both Thecla and Valeria—there is, after all, rose imagery associated with each,[22] and for Wolfe she may be the figure who unites both families—the "Tudor rose" who blooms in the heart of the antechamber's dark.

20

SWIMMING WITH UNDINES

By far the largest narrative gap in Gene Wolfe's *Book of the New Sun* occurs between the end of *Shadow of the Torturer* and the beginning of *Claw of the Conciliator*. It's in the former that Severian is preparing to leave Nessus, the city of his youth, having been exiled from the Order of the Seekers for Truth and Penitence for allowing his lover, the imprisoned exultant Thecla, to take her own life rather than be tortured further. Traveling in the company of Dr. Talos' little theatrical troupe—besides playwright Talos, there is the giant Baldanders, Severian's resurrected grandmother Dorcas, and the former cafe waitress now known as Jolenta—and an even-more-newly-met man on a merychip, the cyborg Jonas—Severian has been caught up in the mill of traffic which is surging toward the Piteous Gate, one of four portals through the leagues-high wall which surrounds Nessus. Talk turns anon to the exotic creatures seen behind windows in the giant edifice, whereupon Jonas begins a fairy-tale-like-story about the origin of the Wall. But before he can finish, a sudden commotion breaks out. As Severian notes, "My attention was distracted by the sight of daylight ahead of us, and by the disturbance among the vehicles that clogged the road as many sought to turn back, flailing their teams and trying to clear a path with their whips." (*Shadow*, 300) Dorcas screams, "Why are they so frightened?" Then she's struck by the whip of a fleeing wagoner, whom Severian pulls down. "By that time," Severian tells us, "all the gate was ringing with bawling and swearing, and the cries of the injured, and the bellowing of frightened animals." The wagoner is trampled underfoot by the fleeing crowd before Severian can suitably punish him for lashing Dorcas, and so ends *Shadow* in chaos and confusion, with very little hint as to what has caused such widespread havoc.

But when Severian picks up the narrative again in *Claw*, he is in the bucolic village of Saltus, and just waking from a dream. Granted, there are references to the Piteous Gate incident in his dream—lance-bearing soldiers turn aside the tide of fleeing travelers, and Severian loses Dorcas in the pell-mell—but Wolfe via his

127

character provides no in-depth (or even superficial) explanation for what's happened, either in terms of catalysis or denouement. This reader was so intrigued by the cliffhanger ending of *Shadow* that he could barely wait for *Claw* to be published—only to have the matter so obliquely addressed and then dismissed in a mere half-a-dozen sentences…Well, I will not subject you to my disappointment. Still, as a longtime student of Gene Wolfe's fiction, I've learned to expect buried clues to mysterious events, and often widespread ones at that; for all I knew the events behind the mysterious gap would be explained in the third or fourth volumes of the narrative, and indeed, this does turn out to be the case.

Slippery Dreams

Back to the early pages of *Claw* then, as we begin to trace our way to some sort of understanding about the Piteous Gate incident: as we're shortly to learn from Severian, he has not been totally separated from his erstwhile companions; Jonas is with him in Saltus. Apparently, torturer and cyborg have gone one way during the commotion, and everyone else another; or at least this seems implicit by a statement Severian makes later when he describes "a forest much like the one through which Jonas and I had passed after being separated from Dorcas, Dr. Talos and the rest at the Piteous Gate." No mention is made of either Jolenta or Baldanders, so it's assumed they must comprise *the rest*. But then, after Severian eventually rendezvous with his lost companions on the thiasus grounds of the House Absolute (this after escaping the antechamber and dispatching Jonas home via Father Inire's mirrors), another detail is revealed: Baldanders has *not* been with Dr. Talos and "the rest" when the separation occurred, he's accompanied Severian, *but only temporarily*. Here's how the crafty Wolfe conveys that particular piece of information via his narrator: "I took Baldanders to one side, an hour or so after we were all awake, and asked him why he had left me in the forest beyond the Piteous Gate." (*Claw*, 194) Baldanders, however, plays dumb, in essence telling Severian that he has no recollection of the event; in fact, the only thing he claims to remember about Severian is the one night at an inn when they shared a bed together (not carnally, of course—just as two people forced to sleep on the same pallet). Still, given what's happened at the gate, is there any chance at all that it's related to Baldanders' sudden disappearance after exiting Nessus with the fuligin-clad torturer? Where, in other words, does the giant go after leaving Severian? And why?

Severian, getting no answers, must content himself with rejoining the troupe, and later that night goes on stage with them as they perform Dr. Talos' play,

Eschatology and Genesis. Only this time, when Baldanders in his role of the giant Nod appears to go berserk and attack the audience, he's fired upon by one of the beset. As Severian describes the action:

> Several exultants had drawn their swords, and someone—I could not see who—possessed that rarest of all weapons, a dream. It moved like tyrian smoke, but very much faster, and in an instant it had enveloped the giant. It seemed then that he stood wrapped in all that was past and much that had never been: a gray-haired woman sprouted from his side, a fishing boat hovered just over his head, and a cold wind whipped the flames that wreathed him. (*Claw*, 239)

Later, of course, we find out that Famulimus and Barbatus have been in the audience and that therefore, "that rarest of all weapons"—*a dream*—has been fired by one of them. But what a curious name for a weapon—especially since we already have some context for a *real* dream of Baldanders—the one which actually afflicts Severian when the two are bedmates upon the first occasion of their meeting. Could there somehow be a correlation between that dream and the Hierodule weapon of the same name? Well, in the sleep-wrought dream, which may, it seems, have been engendered in or transmitted to the wrong target, Severian meets the oneiric equivalents of Juturna, the undine who's previously saved him from drowning during his apprentice days—these are the so-called Brides of Abaia, who take Severian to a submarine puppet show wherein he previews his own eventual battle with a mace-wielding Baldanders. Severian at this point is wakened by the entrance of Dr. Talos, and action resumes in the real world. But later, toward the end of *Claw*, Severian has the opportunity once again to tryst with a Bride of Abaia—only this time it's genuine. Juturna, having swum a local tributary, subsequently makes him an offer every bit as Biblically resonant as the one Typhon offers him from the mountain top:

> "You will breathe—by our gift—as easily as you breathe the thin, weak wind here, and whenever you wish you shall return to the land and take up your crown. This river Cephissus flows to Gyoll, and Gyoll to the peaceful sea. There you may ride dolphin-back through current-swept fields of coral and pearl. My sisters and I will show you the forgotten cities built of old, where a hundred trapped generations of your kin bred and died when they had been forgotten by you above…All of this will be yours there, in the red and white parks where the lionfish school." (*Claw*, 262)

4

Severian, tempted (or more likely aroused by the undine's desirability), says, "Give me the power to breathe water, and let me test it on the other side of the sandbar. If I find you have told the truth, I will go with you." (*Claw*, 262)

But the undine immediately nixes this notion, claiming, "It is not so easily done as that. You must come with me, trusting, though it is only a moment. Come." (*Claw*, 263)

What, at this point, however, is Juturna's real intent? To murder Severian, the future New Sun? Or something else? Recall now the answer she's earlier given to Severian when he's asked her what it is she wants of him: "Only your love. Only your love." (*Claw*, 261) Is it therefore possible that, for whatever reasons, she hopes to mate with him? (We will not dwell here on the other potential meaning of *Come*.)

Severian, of course, is swayed from further temptation by Dorcas' screaming. But what if this same offer has also been extended earlier to that other possible candidate for the New Sun, Baldanders? Certainly, if we re-examine how Wolfe describes what happens to the giant after the Hierodules turn their weapon on him, a case can be made for this. The "gray-haired woman sprouted from his side" might actually represent sexual congress between Baldanders and an undine, while the fishing boat that's seen hovering over his head seems to indicate he's submerged, implying that he, having accepted a similar deal as the one offered to Severian by Juturna, can now breathe underwater—*just as we later learn that Baldanders is actually able to do.*[1] Indeed, might this not be his payback for mating with one of Abaia's Brides? Moreover, could not such a tryst have taken place beneath the Gyoll after Baldanders abandons Severian following the Piteous Gate incident?

I believe that the answer to both questions is yes.

Invasion

We know, after all, that undines have actually been spotted swimming within the confines of Nessus itself. Occurring very late in *Citadel*, this is the upshot of what Severian learns from the boat captain who is Maxellindis' uncle; Severian, at this juncture, has just returned to the Citadel as Autarch, and along with former companions, Drotte, Roche and Eata has rented a boat, intending to seek out Ouen, his once-met father. As the boat negotiates the Gyoll, however, Severian hears a strange tale from her captain. "There was things in the river up till first light," he begins. "There was mist, too, thick as cotton." (*Citadel*, 299) As a result of the poor visibility, when a large ship approaches, Max's uncle *hears* it first:

> "You can't count how many sweeps there is with a good crew pullin', because they all go in and come up together, but when a big vessel goes fast you can hear water breakin' under her bow, and this was a big one. I got up on top of the deckhouse tryin' to see her, but there still wasn't any lights, though I knew she had to be close. Just when I was climbin' down I caught sight of her—a galleass, four-masted and four-banked, no lights, comin' right up the channel…Of course I only saw her for a minute before she was gone in the mist again, but I heard her a long while after." (*Citadel*, 300–301)

But this is hardly the only mysterious thing that has occurred on the Gyoll the previous evening. As the boat captain continues to tell us:

> "There was things in this river *I* never saw before. Maxellindis, when she woke up and I told her about it, said it was the manatees. They're pale in moonlight and look human enough if you don't come too close. But I've seen 'em since I was a boy and have never been fooled once. And there was women's voices, not loud but big. And something else. I couldn't understand what any of 'em was sayin', but I could hear the tone of it. You know how it is when you're listenin' to people over the water? They would say *so-and-so-and-so*. Then the deeper voice—I can't call it a man's because I don't think it was one—the deeper voice'd say *go-and-do-that-and-this-and-that*. I heard the women's voices three times and the other voice twice. You won't believe it, optimates, but sometimes it sounded like the voices was coming up out of the river." (*Citadel*, 302)

This, of course, is because the voices *are* coming up out of the river. The female voices belong to the Brides of Abaia. The male voice is either Abaia's or Baldanders'. Moreover, the large vessel that Max's uncle has briefly glimpsed in the mist is almost certainly the Great Beast Abaia himself. (Compare the description we receive of this mysterious "ship" with that of the Monitor from *The Tale of the Student and His Son*: "His form is that of a naviscaput, which is to say that to men he appears a ship having upon its deck—which is in truth his shoulders—a single castle, which is his head, and in the castle a single eye." *Claw*, 146.) As for why Abaia and his minions have made the long hazardous journey from their undersea realm to Nessus, in all likelihood it's because of Severian's elevation to Autarch, which means he'll now be eligible to take the Hierodules' test; given, too, that this has probably already been anticipated, Abaia has earlier attempted to wage a final desperate assault with his Ascian legions. (As Master Ash has earlier speculated to Severian, "For some reason your foes have need of an immediate victory and are straining every limb.") Having failed to overrun the Commonwealth, however, the Great Lord now needs either to kill Severian or parley some sort of political deal, and indeed, when Severian returns from his quest to find Ouen, he finds "urgent messages from Father Inire and from the House Absolute" waiting for him. (Unfortunately, we never learn the import of those messages, making perhaps for a second large lacuna.)

But also notice how Abaia and the undines have come calling—not by the bright light of day; rather by mist-shrouded night. This is almost certainly because they would have been sighted by the pandours of the Autarch—the very soldiers Severian has seen earlier behind the glass enclosures built into the Wall, and whose mission, according to Dr. Talos, is "to defend [the Wall] just as termites defend their ox-high earthen nests on the pampas of the north." (*Shadow*, 299) Surely, given their sentinel-like-and-first-response nature, the pandours would never allow the Great Lord and his mermaids to access Nessus by its Piteous Gate conduit. (Wolfe never tells us how proximal the Gyoll is to the Piteous Gate, but since entrance to and egress from the city are monitored, it makes much more sense to combine checkpoint facilities than to maintain separate ones for water and pedestrian traffic. Certainly, we know the river is close; Severian, after leaving Nessus, travels directly to Saltus, which is situated on the Gyoll, but only some ten leagues distant. Therefore, if not directly channeled through Piteous, it must flow into Nessus at a point nearby.) Now for a bit of speculation: is it possible that on an earlier occasion Abaia has attempted to make the same journey up the Gyoll—say, for the ostensible purposes of meeting with Baldanders, the lone other legitimate candidate for the New Sun—only by day, where he's sighted by the Autarch's pandours, who, as they sally forth in defense of the Wall, frighten the living wits out of those waiting to exit by the Piteous Gate? This might well explain the sudden sense of panic and fright experienced by the crowd, compounded by the blue lancers' attempts to block the road on the other side. (It seems likely the lancers are deployed outside the gate to prevent those leaving Nessus from continuing by road once they are outside the city. Travel in such a manner has been banned since the Autarchy of Maruthas. The Cornet Mineas—who's first killed by a notule, then resurrected by Severian—is similarly clad and posted to a stretch of old road beside the Gyoll for seemingly the same purpose. This is not to suggest that the incident at the Piteous Gate has been started by the lancers; they have been merely caught up in its aftermath, attempting to keep the emerging exitus from accessing the forbidden road.)

Now consider the possible evidence from *Shadow* that seems to support this. As Severian, on his first night of exile, is told by the lochage on the bridge that overlooks the Water Way, "There's been some kind of trouble on the river, and they're telling each other too many ghost stories out there already." (*Shadow*, 134) This, of course, prefigures the later intimation of strange doings that we hear from Max's uncle. In addition, one day later, when Severian accidentally falls into the Lake of Birds, observe what happens when he attempts to retrieve *Terminus Est*—which he's dropped as he's attempted to right himself. Diving down, he locates and grasps his sword. But then

> At the same instant, my other hand touched an object of a completely different kind. It was another human hand, and its grasp (for it had seized my own the moment I touched it) coincided so perfectly with the recovery of *Terminus Est* that it seemed the hand's owner was returning my property to me, like the tall mistress of the Pelerines. I felt a surge of lunatic gratitude, then fear returned tenfold: the hand was pulling my own, drawing me down. (*Shadow*, 201)

Thus ends abruptly Chapter XXII; but notice how Chapter XXIII begins:

> With what must surely have been the last strength I possessed, I managed to throw *Terminus Est* onto the floating track of sedge and grasp its ragged margin before I sank again.
> Someone caught me by the wrist. I looked up expecting Agia; it was not she but a younger woman still, with streaming yellow hair." (*Shadow*, 202)

This, of course, is Dorcas—*who was not present when Severian first fell in*. Moreover, she's pulling him *up*, while the hand which seems to be returning *TE* to him has been pulling him *down*. This to me indicates the presence of two different personages—Dorcas above, and someone else below. Otherwise, we're required to believe that newly-resurrected Dorcas has at one point been pulling Severian down, but then after Severian breaks her hold and manages to rise to the surface, somehow outraces him to the top, climbs out of the water, and extracts the sodden torturer from the lake herself—all without Severian noting her passage. This is plainly difficult to believe. I'd therefore like to suggest that the hand pulling him down belongs to Juturna or a similar undine; her returning the sword to him also parallels an Arthurian episode—the Lady of the Lake performing a similar deed, handing Excalibur to the Once and Future King. And just as

Maxellindis attempts to explain her uncle's undine sightings as manatees, notice what Severian believes he sees in the very last sentence of Chapter XXIII: "For some time we rowed in silence; I saw geese…and once, like something in a dream, the nearly human face of a manatee looking into my own through a few spans of brownish water." (*Shadow*, 209) Again here, note the oneiric allusion—*like something in a dream*—and recall how Severian has intercepted the dream originally intended for Baldanders. (Baldanders claims he never dreams, which may be a result of his own self-tinkering, especially on his brain—this might help to explain his apparent dim-wittedness and memory lapses at times. It's equally possible Abaia may have used stellar-level technology to beam the "dream" Severian receives by mistake, missing the giant by a meter or so.) And so it appears that at least one other time the Brides of Abaia have managed to swim into Nessus undetected—perhaps to do reconnaissance for their Megatherian husband-father; perhaps to attempt to lure Baldanders into some sort of amorous tryst. This may also account for the giant's eventual leaving of Severian after the Piteous Gate incident—where just as the dream weapon of the Hierodules seems to hint, Baldanders mates with an undine, and the direct result may be the giant blond-haired child Severian finds in Baldanders' castle at the end of *Sword*. Severian first opines the child to be Baldanders' catamite, but by the end of *Urth* seems to have accepted that the child is more likely the union of Baldanders and a Bride. This child—in embryonic form—may even be with Baldanders and Dr. Talos when they part company with Severian and Dorcas at the end of *Claw*. As Dr. Talos notes about the abandoning of most of his stage props, "Baldanders is the only one of us with the strength to carry our baggage, and though we have discarded much of it, there remain certain items we must keep." (*Shadow*, 245) Perhaps, nestled in among the hologram projectors and rolled up scrims, there's an egg, bassinet or vivarium with Baldanders Jr. inside (depending on how you view the reproductive physiology of undines).

Son of the Sun

Then again, the child may not exactly be Baldanders', either. Look, after all, at how the child is described at length by author Wolfe.

> Indeed, he was a small child, though he stood nearly as tall as I, a naked boy so fat his distended paunch obscured his tiny generative organs. His arms were like pink pillows bound with cords of gold, and his ears had been pierced for golden hoops strung with tiny bells. His hair was golden too, and

curled; beneath it he looked at me with the wide, blue eyes of an infant. (*Sword*, 279–280)

Of signal importance here is the color of the child's hair—i.e., *gold*. As I argue in *Severa* and *Agia and Agilus*, Wolfe very circumspectly uses this attribute *only in conjunction with people related to Severian by blood*. I'd therefore like to speculate that the giant child Severian finds in Baldanders' bedchamber is *his*. (This does not mean there's no issue born to an undine by Baldanders. The "pandours" in Trason's boat may represent such offspring, and I've often wondered if Idas, who later attempts to assassinate Severian aboard Tzadkiel's starship, might not be the giant's daughter. Severian's first guess is that she's ten years old, which would make her the right age. She also proudly admits to burning the letter from Malrubius proclaiming Severian to be the true Autarch of Urth—something which may have especially grated upon her father, since he too was once in the running for the New Sun candidacy. And lastly, *Idas* is cryptonymic, being derivable from Baldander*s*—a pattern Wolfe uses over and over in *New Sun* to confer relatedness. See *Appendix*.) As for when the child was procreated, let's go back to the Botanic Garden scene where Severian is being pulled down deeper and deeper into the water by the mysterious hand. That he's gone a long time seems implicit in the fact that Dorcas is nowhere in sight where he first falls in. (Agia, of course, would be perfectly content if Severian drowned—then brother Agilus wouldn't have to face him in monomachy; once they subsequently hired a diver to salvage *Terminus Est* for them, they'd be set for life. This is why you don't see her attempting to haul Severian out of the water or screaming for help.) Also remember, as he's told later—although this is actually earlier for the imparter, given her reverse sense of time—Juturna wants *only his love*, in return for which she'll bestow upon him a certain gift. Is this why Severian doesn't drown when he's under the waters of the Lake of Birds so long—because he's mated/mating with Juturna? Possibly. But also consider what happens to Severian when much later, at the end of *Urth*, he attempts to commit suicide by jumping from Eata's boat. As Severian tells us, "Water closed over me, yet I did not drown. I felt I might breathe that water, yet I did not breathe." (*Urth*, 331) *This repeats almost exactly two sentences from the dream Severian has on the night he sleeps next to Baldanders.* "The water closed over me, yet I did not drown. I felt that I might breathe water, yet I did not breathe." (*Shadow*, 140) Fish, of course, do not breathe water, they derive their oxygen from the water via gills; hence Severian's asking Juturna for the ability to breathe water is likely the result of scientific naivety on his part. In other words, having done as the undine has wished—mated with her—Severian appears to have acquired the ability to respire underwater, whereupon he goes for an extended benthal tour of the world whose destruction he's wrought, adept as any merman.

Then again, as the soon-to-be piscine Sleeper god of new Ushas, he's perfectly at home—at least for a little while.

21

WITCHES

Very near the end of *Claw*, after the thunder and revelation at Stone Town,[1] Severian wakes from unconsciousness to the pelting of rain and Dorcas calling him. He starts to rise from the mud, but finds a cloth as he seeks purchase—"a long narrow strip of silk tipped with tassels"—which he then pulls free. Severian does not immediately explain what the cloth is, although the astute reader will almost certainly recognize it.[2] Nor does he mention keeping the garment, until *Sword*, the next volume in the series, when in a conversation with Cyriaca, who's dressed for Abdiesus's masque, he says, "'Most importantly when [Apu-Punchau] vanished, one of the scarlet capes of the Pelerines, like the one you're wearing now, was left behind in the mud.'" But how, we're left to wonder, did the cape wind up in Stone Town? Even Severian himself is unsure, commenting, after he leaves the cape in a shepherd's bothy in exchange for food, "I have never fully understood how it came to be where we found it, or even whether the strange individual who had called us to him so that he might have that brief period of renewed life left it behind intentionally or accidentally." (*Sword*, 219)

The mystery, then? Explain the provenance of the tasseled cloth.

Possibly, we might surmise, the cape has been left there previously by a Pelerine. As Manahen's father tells Severian earlier about the various people who've undertaken a trip or been drawn to the stone town, it is mostly virgins who do not return. If the Pelerines, who certainly qualify as virgins,[3] have come to view Apu Punchau as an aspect of the Conciliator, a pilgrimage of some sort might well be part of their religious rites. Stone Town might therefore be the Mecca or Jerusalem of the Pelerines. Hence no big mystery—the cloak was left behind by a visiting Pelerine, either abandoned in the dust or retrieved by Apu-Punchau, but ultimately found by Severian.

All this talk of Pelerines, however, in connection with the revivification of Stone Town by the Cumaean and Merryn, puts me in mind of a slightly more complex notion: while the two witches we meet in *New Sun* seem exemplary of weird sisters in general, almost equally so do the Pelerines. In fact, both groups are so similar in powers and disposition, I'd like to argue they're actually sacred and profane branches of the same religion, the Pelerines being the equivalent of Vestal Virgins, while the ecstatic witches typify Bacchantes. Furthermore, I believe a single person heads up both groups, and it's she who's left the scarlet cloak.

But first for the comparisons.

Scarlet Sisters

"Witches," we are told, "raised the dead." (*Shadow*, 211) This is paralleled by Severian's question of Cyriaca, "Do the Pelerines dabble in necromancy?" Severian waits for a response, then specifically mentions not receiving one (such unanswered questions are almost always significant in Wolfe). Be that as it may, eventually he does conclude that "the ancient sisterhood of priestesses beyond question possesses powers it seldom or never uses, and it is not absurd to suppose that such raising of the dead is among them." (*Sword*, 219)

Adding further texture to the argument is a remarkable passage by author Wolfe wherein both groups are framed within a single context; here GW's use of a semi-colon instead of a comma or a completely new sentence seems especially pertinent, conjoining rather than separating witch from priestess. Severian, in enumerating his lust, says: "I recalled the witches, their madness and their wild dancing in the Old Court on nights of rain; the cool, virginal beauty of the Pelerines." (*Claw*, 258) While seemingly consisting of antithetical clauses, contrasting the raw sensuality of the witches with the chasteness of the Pelerines, the sentence actually achieves just the opposite—a synthesis or unification of disparities. Notice as well how Severian's judgment of madness in the witches has already been echoed earlier by cousin Agia, who's declared that "the Pelerines are insane…and if I had had more time I would have told you so." (*Shadow*, 168)

Similarly, both groups appear privy to supernatural powers. Like her mythic namesake, the Cumaean is a seer, and people seek out her cave, according to Hildegrin, "hoping to know when they'll be married, or about success in trade." Of course, being a Hierodule, Camoena experiences time backwards, the same way her children Famulimus and Barbatus do; thus she actually *remembers* the future, so her gift of prophecy is somewhat less than impressive. In addition, she may have access to her husband's arsenal of potent devices, Inire being posthistory's alien equivalent of Daedalus. So again science may underwrite her alleged arcane abilities more than magic.

This, of course, is quite otherwise with the Pelerines, because the agency of their power—the Claw? adept-like training?—is less explainable. Nevertheless, they are still believed by the general public to possess mystical abilities. As Severian is told by Mannea, "We have not half the power ignorant people suppose—nevertheless, those who think us without power are more ignorant still." (*Citadel*, 115) She then proceeds to demonstrate by placing a hand on Severian's shoulder, whereupon he feels a slight shock.[4] But even earlier, when Severian and Agia crash into the altar of the Claw inside the tent cathedral of the Pelerines, they're subjected to the preternatural gaze of the Domnicellae, which apparently allows her to winnow truth from lie. Clairvoyance—an attribute also shared by the witches—means "clear seeing," and this may simply be the literal embodiment of it.[5]

And yet despite the slightly sinister aspect of these abilities, in addition to their employing slaves and regarding the Ascians as soulless, Wolfe clearly intends the Pelerines to be seen in benign terms, for they are far more than simply religious conventionals devoted to the Conciliator's worship, but also MASH-like nurses and providers of burial services,[6] very much akin to our own Red Cross. Thus the scarlet of their vestments, which Agia tells us, is for the descending light of the New Sun and possibly "the Wounds of the Claw," takes on additional resonance—the color of corporal mercy, of nursing. These two attributes—red, in conjunction with healing—also suggest another possibility—that what Severian calls the Tower of Healing may simply be an alternate name for the Red Tower. The latter, as *Lexicon Urthus*, tells us, stands between an ancient breach in the curtain wall and the Bear Tower. The former—well, there's only a single reference to it: "Torturers do not go to the Tower of Healing, no matter how ill; there is a belief—whether true or not I cannot say—that old scores are settled there"[7] (*Shadow*, 280) The obvious problem with this theory is that it seems likely Severian would be somewhat familiar with the Pelerines if they staffed the nearby Red Tower, whereas it's apparent from his first contact with them that he knows next to nothing about the order and has to be filled in by Agia.[8] Then again, since torturers don't go to the Tower of Healing, this might also explain the lacuna in question, and it may be that the Red Tower is the Pelerines' permanent headquarters, the base from which they launch their chatauquas and field hospitals.

Magna Mater

Lastly, we come to the parental head of each branch. Though we are never told explicitly so, it's hard to dismiss Camoena as the witches' *mater regina*. For starters, Merryn, the only other evident witch[9] we meet in *New Sun*, clearly defers to her, addressing her as Mother; Severian also recalls being ushered into her presence at the top floor of the Witches' Keep, when, as a child, he's asked to conduct a message to their tower. Again, we meet so few of the weird sisters, this may be a spurious conclusion, but if Wolfe intends another woman to be the equivalent of a Gurloes or Palaemon, he has disguised her singularly well. Contrast this with the Domnicellae of the Pelerines, who's clearly in charge of the monials; she too, of course, is addressed as Mother. Yet curiously, when Severian at the masque, asks Cyriaca if she knows where the Pelerines are currently bivouacked, she says, "No, I don't know where the Pelerines are now—I doubt if they do themselves, though perhaps the Mother does." The oddness of this statement—how can the Pelerines, most of whom seem well educated, not know where they are?—coupled with the guess about the privileged status of the Mother sets off my Wolfe Misdirection Alarm. Yes, doubtless, GW *intends* us to believe Cyriaca's speaking about the Domnicellae. But given the enormous similarities between the witches and the Pelerines, might she not actually be referring to the *other* Mother, whose guidance and authority perhaps unites both groups into a single sisterhood dedicated to ensuring the return of the Conciliator?[10] This would ultimately simplify the question about the scarlet cape's provenance in Stone Town, of course—as well as explain the diversionary delay by author Wolfe in both identifying the garment and telling us long after the fact that Severian has kept it—the first being obvious, the second obfuscation. For rather than having been left behind by some unknown Pelerine on a hypothetical pilgrimage, it seems almost certain the cloak has previously adorned Camoena.

22

WHITE WOLVES

After Severian manages to extricate himself from the antechamber where he and Jonas have been imprisoned, and goes looking for *Terminus Est*, he accidentally discovers Hethor's friend Beuzac hiding in a loft. Later, when he returns to the same closet, he discovers Beuzac has crawled out a hole in the back. That prompts this response: "It is said that in the House Absolute such recesses are inhabited by a species of white wolf that slunk in from the surrounding forests long ago. Perhaps he fell prey to these creatures." (*Claw*, 175)

Still later (and we must remember Severian is writing his memoirs at some future remove, so the time frame involved is much longer), Severian has this to say about apocryphal lupines lurking about: "In wandering [the Secret House's] narrow corridors, I have seen no white wolves."[1] (*Claw*, 240)

Gene Wolfe, of course, frequently inserts these sorts of punning references to "wolfes" in his works—they're the literary equivalent of cameos, and very similar to the appearances director Alfred Hitchcock made in his films. But other than this, and playing off a rather prominent urban legend (i.e., albino alligators in the sewers of New York), do the white wolves have any special significance? And why are they no longer present in the House Absolute? Thecla, at one point, remembers coursing them,[2] so apparently there is some truth to Severian's statement.

Two separate possibilities occur to me. Although interestingly, each plays to the same notion.

The first involves the alzabo. Source-wise, it is in Pliny's *Naturlis Historia* that we initially find mention of the fabulous beast called the leucrocotta, which translated from the Greek means "white dog-wolf." Pliny himself, however, has borrowed heavily from Ctesias the Cnidian's *Indica*, where the creature is known as a crocotta, kynolykos, or cynolycus, "dog-wolf."[3] In either event, both the cynolycus and the leucrocotta are likened to be a species of hyena with *a special facility of imitating the human voice*, just like Wolfe's alzabo. Does this mean that at one time there were alzabos running around the House Absolute? Possibly. Keep in mind that Wolfe has always portrayed himself as a *translator* of the New Sun manuscript, and that one of the perils of translating is choosing the right equivalent word in the second language.[4] One translator's leucrocotta might therefore be another's alzabo.[5] And to some extent having alzabos in the House Absolute, or access thereto, makes sense, because it would allow a steady and fresh supply of analeptic to be on hand, in case of dire event. As for why they are no longer around after Severian the Great takes office, there's no need for them—Severian is the last of Urth's Autarchs, the redemptive New Sun.

The second possible meaning of white wolf has its origins in alchemy. Antimony—which is brittle white in color—was known medievally as *lupus metallorum*, owing to its use in purifying gold. As Joannes Agricola in his *Treatise on Gold* puts it,[6] "The Grey Wolf must eat the Lion, which must be devoured by it three times, after first purifying itself and cleansing its eyes with the Wolf's blood, so that they shine brightly. The Wolf is the antimony; the Lion, however, the pure gold." Again, since Severian is the true New Sun—symbolically, pure gold—there's no need for any purifying reagents—hence no white wolves in the House Absolute.

NOTES

CHAPTER 1
CATHERINE

1. Indeed, the brilliant John Clute argues that figuring out who Severian's family members are may be central to a true understanding of the Book. As he writes in *Strokes*, "Most readers of the tetralogy will have been forced—forced indeed by Gene Wolfe himself, as he makes it clear that there is *some* mystery to be solved—into making some kinds of speculations about the nature of Severian's secret family, though perhaps not everyone will share my conviction that decipherment can have a stop, and the fuller task of interpretation begin, only when some sense of the identity of that family has been established." (*Strokes*, 163–164)

2. This is the custom, of course. As we're told by Severian, the guild's membership is "repaired solely from the children who fall into our hands. In our Matachin Tower a certain bar of iron thrusts from a bulkhead at the height of a man's groin. Male children small enough to stand upright beneath it are nurtured as our own; and when a woman big with child is sent to us we open her and if the babe draws breath engage a wet-nurse if it is a boy. The females are rendered to the witches." (*Shadow*, 20)

3. Added resonance here: Catherine may well be the woman Winnoc is talking about when he says "…we used to have a chatelaine in the order who knew a lot about history…" (*Citadel*, 93)

4. I am not convinced, however, that Dux Caesidius is the original figure Wolfe envisioned as Severian's maternal grandfather; rather I believe it's the old castellan who greets Severian when he first returns to the Citadel as Autarch (see *Citadel*, 265–266). For starters he's lame. As I will argue in a number of essays, one of the attributes that links various members of Severian's bloodline is a limp—an autobiographical element Wolfe frequently confers upon his major characters (Den Weer of *Peace* and Silk of *Long Sun*, for example), GW having had polio as a child. The old castellan also has silver hair—perhaps akin to tarnished gold (see *Severa* for hair details) and is unnamed in the text—just like Dorcas's husband (Severian's other grandfather). Moreover, his status as castellan

links him back to Valeria, whose family has "given many castellans to the Citadel." (*Shadow*, 45) He's also the first person to pay homage to the new Autarch, dropping to his knees and kissing Severian's hand, which seems apposite. But given his physical condition—he's described as old and battle-scarred—it seems most unlikely he would have survived the fifty years that transpires between this moment and Severian's return from Yesod, thus making it extremely suspect he is the Dux Caesidius of *Urth*. Rather, and for whatever reasons, it seems Wolfe has abandoned his original intentions and reinvented the maternal grandfather character at a later remove. If so, it represents the only example in the sequel I have been able to find where Wolfe violates previous continuity.

5. Catherine's being arrested by minions of Father Inire ("the law"), followed by her subsequent confinement in the Matachin Tower, also help to explain why Ouen believes he has no children. (To Severian's response about whether he's fathered children, Ouen proclaims vehemently, "No, sieur! Never, sieur!") He's only coupled once with Catherine and never realizes the result of that single action is pregnancy.

6. According to Gene Wolfe, he and Thomas Wolfe are distantly related.

CHAPTER 2
AGIA AND AGILUS

1. Consider also this very telling quote from Severian (italics mine): "*I*, who did not know my own mother's name, or my father's, *might very well be related* to this child whose name was my own, or for that matter *to anyone I met*." (*Sword*, 137–138) As we shall come to see, this statement is more than a little true.

2. Severian's bloodline also displays a fair amount of cryptonymic resonance. See *Appendix*.

3. For more details about Wolfe's connection to his signature beast, see my essay "Wolves in the Fold: Lupine Shadows in the Works of Gene Wolfe," *New York Review of Science Fiction*, Issue 155 (July 2001).

4. Agia's brown hair has also been described as chestnut—reddish brown. How this and the dark gold aspect further advance my case, see *Severa*.

5. Agia, at another point, is also described as having "wide, flat cheeks." (*Claw*, 23)

6. Dorcas' second sentence here is actually a quote from Dr. Talos' play, *Eschatology and Genesis*.

7. Secunda is also cryptonymically interesting. See *Appendix*.

8. "I remembered what Dorcas had told me about furniture from the abandoned houses of Nessus being brought north for eclectics who had adopted more cultivated fashions…" (*Sword*, 110); "It seemed that this could hardly be the quarter from which (as Dorcas had told me) furniture and utensils were taken…" (*Citadel*, 259)

9. This is the upshot of a somewhat philosophical discussion Severian has with Ava the Pelerine, while he's recovering at the lazaret. Asks Severian: "Do you think that if something—some arm of the Conciliator, let us say—could cure human beings, it might nevertheless fail with those who are not human?" (*Citadel*, 79)

10. It's equally possible the woman's name is meant to be Pelagia because of its various contexts (suggesting pelagic, yielding "agia"; plus Pelagia rendered into Latin is Marina, which has a Holy Family resonance to it); if so we have to wonder if Wolfe reappropriated the name for use in the *Urth* sequel.

11. And a gruesome fetish it is: "It was a cock's head; needles of some dark metal had been run through its eyes, and it held a strip of cast snakeskin in its bill." (*Sword*, 158)

12. It seems to me the cult should have a name, but I have been unable to discern what it might be—unless it's Seventeen Stones. (See *Seventeen*.)

13. "When I had clambered onto the back of a cabinet, I saw that the survivors comprised a fat, bald man and the two woman, both fairly young, one short and blessed with the merry, round face of a cheerful doll, the other tall, dark, and hollow-cheeked." (*Urth*, 311); "The doll-faced woman rescued me. 'I'm Pega, and I was the armagette's Pelagia's soubrette." (*Urth*, 312); "The doll-faced woman looked chastened, though I suspected the expression was entirely assumed." (*Urth*, 312)

CHAPTER 3
ASCIANS

1. See *Lexicon Urthus*, p. 11.

2. Michael Andre-Driussi also reminds me that all the inner planets of the solar system have Norse names—Urth, Skuld (Venus), Verthandi (Mars)—but the moon is called *Lune*, which is French—the same language spoken by the colonists of Sainte Anne, home planet of the abos. Given GW's circumspection, such is hardly likely to be a coincidence or the result of careless writing.

3. For my extended views on this, see "Queen of Shadows: Unveiling Aubrey Veil in Gene Wolfe's *The Fifth Head of Cerberus*," *The New York Review of Science Fiction*, Issue 168 (August 2002).

4. A cryptonymic clue, however, exists. See *Appendix*.

5. "Again I endured my imprisonment in the jungle ziggurat by Vodalus, *the year I spent among the Ascians*, my flight from the white wolves in the Secret House, and a thousand similar terrors…" (*Citadel*, 364) Wolfe also mentions the episode in his *Thrust* Interview, expressing regret that he could not include it in the final draft.

6. Wolfe as Master Ash seems to endorse this view when he has Ash relate the tale about how "a man sold his shadow and found himself driven out wherever he went. No one would believe that he was human." (*Citadel*, 125)

CHAPTER 4
DOMNINA

1. "Camoena"—i.e., the Cumaean—is also extractable from Domnicellae. See *Witches* for significance.

2. *Ichthys*, of course—the Greek word for fish—is an acronym for *Iesous Christos Theou Hyos Soter*—Jesus Christ, Son of God, Savior. And early Christians often used the fish as a secret sign to identify themselves.

3. Or so it seems from Severian's description of Domnina after the fact: "She found herself in another world, and even when she returned to Thecla she wasn't quite sure she had found her way back to her real point of origin." (*Shadow*, 193)

CHAPTER 5
FECHIN

1. It's possible, however, that Fechin's star has already begun to fade by Severian's time. Severian himself shows no recognition of the name, and even Dorcas (a possible contemporary of the man) seems to have difficulty recalling his name. At least that's one potential interpretation of the following remark, made by her in *Shadow*, after she's given an apple for breakfast: "Look at it, how round it is, how red. What is it they say? 'Red as the apples of…' I can't think of it." (288) If *Fechin* is the name she's struggling to recall here, could this be Wolfe's sly way of

suggesting how eminently forgettable Fechin is—an artist best known for the magnificence of his apples?

2. Father Inire, in a letter to Severian, addresses him formally as both Helios and Hyperion—titles that further link the position of Autarch with solar imagery. Bees, orienting themselves by the sun, are another aspect of this, so their association with Fechin might well be a clue to his Autarchal nature. (Also keep in mind that the old Autarch's name is Appian, after *apis*, the Latin word for bee.) Similarly, in the extended anecdote narrated by Becan's father, Fechin is identified with the New Sun (although we know he will not take the Hierodules' test): "They always say in prayers that the New Sun will be too bright to look at…But that day I learned it was all true, and the light of it on Fechin's face was more than I could stand." (*Sword*, 117)

3. Tangerines? Apples? Is it possible that Fechin has specialized in only the most trite and maudlin of tableaux—fruit, kids, clowns? If so, small wonder his work is now consigned with Quartillosa and other less popular artists, perhaps even sharing a wing with the black velvet Elvises.

4. Given the resemblance of 'Casdoe' to 'Dorcas,' and with grandchildren named Severa and Severian, is it possible the dotard's name is meant to be the same as Dorcas's husband, who also is never identified? Could Caron—after *Saint* Caron, but recalling the obvious Charon—be this name? Granted, Becan's father is no ferryman figure; but his son and granddaughter do wind up being eaten by the alzabo, a hound-like beast that in all probability has come to Urth from Sainte Anne, one of the sister worlds in Wolfe's *The Fifth Head of Cerberus*. So the Stygian connection, although different in context, is still preserved.

5. At least this is my belief. Severian, on the other hand, insists on identifying him as Casdoe's father. Later, however, when Casdoe reveals her mother is alive and living in Thrax, we're left to wonder why her parents are no longer together. Surely, Casdoe would not have brought her father into the hardscrabble environment of the mountains if she had other options. Whereas if he were Becan's father and had nowhere else to go, dutiful son Becan might well have had no choice. Doubtless, the confusion is meant to play off Severian's inability to parse familial relationships, whether it's his own, Casdoe's and Becan's, or Robert's and Marie's (Severian calls the jungle hut figures brother and sister, but Marie calls Robert her husband).

6. Becan's father continues his description of Fechin's hairy arms thusly: "Like a monkey's arms, so that if you saw them reaching around a corner to take something, you'd think, except, for the size, that it was a monkey taking it." Several paragraphs later, however, he asserts, "His face wasn't a monkey's face at all." But

could Becan's father be simply misremembering the details here and confusing Fechin with Father Inire—something we'd expect in a man of his advanced age—especially if he's never met either?

7. Technology has become so debased in the Commonwealth that even paper, apparently, is hard to come by. This further supports my observations about celebrity in Wolfe's futurity, i.e., there being no newspaper or pamphleteering for culture mavens to apprise the general public about up-and-coming or successful artists.

8. The implication here may account for the details in Becan's father's anecdote about Fechin—i.e., they've been borrowed from his own life.

CHAPTER 6
GUARDIAN

1. But perhaps no more promiscuous than her husband Racho. See *Abdiesus*.

2. It's very tempting to see this figure as Cyby, the frustrated assistant of Master Librarian Ultan who has yet to be raised to even journeyman's status; Cyby and Cyriaca are also cryptonymically related. (See *Appendix*.)

3. Or at least is not exclusively so since there's so much conflation and word-play in these various embedded fables of Wolfe, many of which have aggregate origins.

4. The arousal of the Saltus mine entity takes place in Chapter VI of *Claw*—the *exact same chapter* which in follow-up *Sword* contains the tale of the lost archives. I do not believe this is a coincidence, but is rather an attempt by Wolfe to link the two.

5. Readers still unwilling to accept this analysis must therefore attempt to come up with alternate reasons for why Severian is initially unable to identify the Saltus mine creature. What event triggers his realization if not Cyriaca's tale? Why have the tumblers of his mind not clicked home sooner—Severian having encountered Master Ultan and his library long before?

6. Could the mention here of crystal sarcophagi and private resurrections possibly refer to people cryogenically inhumed? If so, such would make the area around Saltus even more rife with "sleepers"—from the creature in the mine, to Mother Pyrexia, to the prematurely-wakened cryogenes. Severian also references the last of these one more time, writing, as he attempts to stay underwater upon escaping the hetman's boat, "I filled my mind…with the wonder of the color and the thought of the indestructible corpses I had seen littering the refuse heaps

about the mines of Saltus—corpses sinking forever in the blue gulf of time."
(*Sword*, 244)

7. Typhon is the last *monarch* of Urth. It's only after his reign concludes that
the Age of the Autarchs begins with the ascendancy of Ymar the Almost
Just—himself at one time a torturers' apprentice named Reechy.

8. This takes place in *Urth*, of course, after Severian has disembarked from
Tzadkiel's starship 1000 years earlier than his own time.

9. But from where have the records been brought—the old capital? I've always
wondered if this isn't Thrax, given that the Vincula there has, according to legend, been designed as a tomb. Could it have been Typhon's intended mausoleum
before he learned how to scan himself into a computer—the would-be, posthistoric, equivalent of a Taj Mahal or Great Pyramid?

10. "Unseen mouths" is almost a literal translation of *hatif* and seems to refer
here to some sort of communications device—perhaps how the Hierodules trans-
mit instructions to Master Gurloes when Palaemon is absent.

11. In Greek Mythology, of course, *Talos* was a huge bronze man designed by
Daedalus to guard the isle of Crete. Wolfe's taluses perform similarly.

CHAPTER 7
HETHOR

1. See *Lexicon Urthus*, p. 126.

2. Actually, only Oringa, the little girl, sees the slug, describing it as "a black
thing that snuffles in the dark." But apparently it's crawled over Jonas, for when
Severian picks the cyborg up he finds him coated with a thin coat of slime. (Is this
slime also the source of Hethor's greasy appearance?)

3. It's unclear whether Hethor is on the same crashed tender as Jonas. If he's
disembarked elsewhere, how have his creatures avoided detection?

4. This scene parallels in many respects a similar scene in Wolfe's *The Fifth
Head of Cerberus*, where Dr. Marsch attempts to find a constellation known as
The Shadow Children, which Victor Trenchard, his abo guide, has earlier
pointed out to him. Marsch, however, is unable to find "the two pairs of bright
eyes"—just as Severian initially has difficulty picking out the constellations
(though not the "bright eyes" of Hethor). Also worth nothing here is that the
Annese Shadow children are shapechangers.

5. Anyone willing to believe that the real name of the woman known as Mother Pyrexia is Febronia? There's a saint by that name, and *pyrex* means "fever" in Greek the same way *februs* does in Latin.

6. What else could these strange things be if not slugs or grubs or pupae? Certainly, all are found in organic detritus like this.

7. Apparently, the area around Saltus is rife with sleepers, from sluggish Mother Pyrexia to the guardian of the man-apes' mine to the disinterred cryogenes Severian sees when exiting the village.

8. The door has been revealed to him by mnemonic-ghost Thecla, being the means by which certain jaded members of the House Absolute access the antechamber on a nightly basis to terrorize the prisoners confined there.

9. According to Michael Andre-Driussi, *Beuzec* means "handsome prisoner" in Russian [*Lexicon Urthus: Additions, Errata, &cetera, Vol. 1*]—no doubt a reflection of Beuzec's obeisance to Hethor.

10. From *Lexicon Urthus* again: "In Severian's dream, Hethor mentions recognizable constellations—Aquarius, Pisces, and Aries—suggesting that Hethor comes from our time, the Age of Myth."

11. Observe the following additional evidence from *Urth* (26): Severian is telling Purn about how "Hethor had been a hand on a ship like this." He then comments, "That captured Purn's attention."

12. As Andre-Driussi comments, Severian, after being subdued in his skirmish with the muties, notes the presence of "a little man with dirty gray hair like Hethor's." (*Urth*, 90)

CHAPTER 8
MANDRAGORA

1. From *The Dictionary of Greek and Roman Mythology* (New England Library, London, 1975): "Typhon: Son of Typhoeus or the youngest son of Gaea. A powerful and destructive whirlwind which had one hundred dragon heads and a body covered with serpents…" This is *not* the only Typhon = dragon connection, however. Dragons, in Christian symbology, commonly represent Satan/Lucifer, and just as Satan once tempted Christ, offering him stewardship of the world from atop a high mountain, a similar scene takes place in *Sword* ("The Eyes of the World"), with draconic Typhon offering Severian the autarchy of Urth.

2. For those of you who have read Wolfe's *Short Sun* series, let me further assert that I believe Typhon hails from the Blue-Green system; i.e., that he's an expatriate Neighbor. For now, however, this is the subject for another book.

3. From *Sword* ("Typhon and Piaton"), with Typhon speaking: "No, I was not born as I am, or born at all, as you meant it."

4. Brandy, it should be noted, is also sometimes referred to as *aqua vitae*, "water of life."

5. If I therefore had to finish Echidna's sentence about chems, I would render it thusly: "My husband…designed them that way." I.e., to be easily assumable, like a metal suit of clothes.

CHAPTER 9
MASKS OF THE FATHER

1. How do Ouen and Catherine meet, for example? Critic Gregory Feeley speculates Ouen may have delivered family-made crucifixes—the rood of Dorcas' recovered memories—to the Pelerines, but by the time Ouen was a young man, he had long since left home, working first as a potboy at age ten, then possibly later as one of Appian's bouncers at the House Azure. So I'm somewhat skeptical. Given the Hierodules' knowledge about Severian, it's also possible they even arranged somehow for Catherine and Ouen to meet, but how and where and under what circumstances? Severian's mnemonic skills may also have been inherited from his father. ("I don't forget much," Ouen tells Severian on the occasion of their second meeting. *Citadel*, 303.)

2. This is further reinforced by an admission aboard Tzadkiel's starship. "You call us Hierodules, and that is your word and not ours, just as *Barbatus*, *Famulimus*, and *Ossipago* are your words, words we have chosen because they are not common and describe us better than your other words would." (*Urth*, 36)

3. There are, quite simply, a lot of apelike creatures in the Book. Besides those mentioned, there's the cynocephalus who checks out Severian's recovery in the lazaret after his duel with Agilus; another "monkey who might, save for his four hands, have been a wizened red-bearded man in fur" who spies upon Severian "from a fork as high as a spire;" the many alouattes of the Autarch's garden; plus, at the Third Battle of Orithyia, the infantry companions of the savage riders, who are described as brown, stooped, shaggy-haired, and at times quadripedal. Is this simply a Wolfean homage to Pierre Boulle? Or is there something else going on here? My inclination at first is to identify these creatures as being minions of

Father Inire, and secondly to speculate that they may be some sort of intermediate metamorphic stage in the Hierodule life-cycle (as might be the giant living statues of the House Absolute, which Severian keeps comparing to Famulimus and Barbatus—possibly oöcytes?).

4. Note also how Barbatus makes the following comment about the outréness of their quarters aboard Tzadkiel's starship. "We have seen the chambers your kind makes. They are as disturbing to us as this must be for you, and since there are three of us—" At which point Ossipago interrupts and says, "Two. It does not matter to me."—Indicating that he, as Inire, has perhaps gotten used to human-style dwellings and appurtenances.

5. Jesus Christ—another messiah like the Conciliator—is believed by the Basilidean Gnostics to have emanated from Abraxas. Also, in the tripartite scheme I propose, I prefer the following etymology: *Abraxas* being derived from *Ab Raza*, "Father of the Secret."

6. See Note 6, CHAPTER 21, WITCHES.

7. "I asked the old leech where he came from, and he, thinking me apparently a native of these parts, said, 'From the big city in the south, in the valley of the river that drains the cold lands. It is a longer river than yours, is the Gyoll, though its flood is not so fierce.'" (*Citadel*, 214)

8. "No, it's not what you think," the old leech avers after telling Severian about his sleeping with Mamas. Severian, however, has his doubts. "There was nothing—not even an admission, which might have been rooted in some perverse desire to maintain an appearance of potency—that could have convinced me so completely as his denial." (*Citadel*, 214) There may also be a significant double entendre in Winnoc's tale about his encounter with Palaemon. As he tells Severian, "I guess it seems *queer* to you that I'd talk so to a man that had whipped me?" (*Citadel*, 95)

9. Gurloes, it turns out, may also have been a spy for the Autarch. As Appian, referring to the council of torturers which has earlier debated Severian's fate after the Thecla transgression, tells Severian, "My agent reported that many of them wanted to kill you." (Although Palaemon seems a likelier choice—which again might play to the old Autarch's recognition of Paeon "in truth.") Meanwhile, the crazy person he talks to on the third level of the Matachin oubliette might be the only person Gurloes can unburden himself to—anyone else would think him insane, or worse, possibly report him to Palaemon. And, of course, as Severian notes, Gurloes drinks heavily and suffers from nightmares. Perhaps we know now why.

10. Let me also note for you the presence of three letters of cryptonymic significance in Palaemon and Paeon—a, p, e. (See *Appendix* for details.)

11. Or as Hildegrin puts it, "This that you see now is the Cave of the Cumaean—the woman that knows the future and the past and everything else." (*Shadow*, 208)

12. *Apheta*, when subjected to cryptonymic analysis, yields both *pa* and *ape*.

13. Severian does the exact same thing with Robert and Marie of the jungle hut—clearly Inire and Camoena analogues—at first deeming them husband and wife, then later brother and sister.

14. Meschiane also yields the cryptonyms Camoena and Inire. (See *Appendix*.)

15. Wolfe may also be playing off the notion of *Os* as *Oz*—the place we're supposed to recognize the wizard for who (or what) he really is.

16. The Basilidean Gnostics depicted Abraxas as a human with a fowl's head and snakes for limbs. Severian perhaps links this with Ceryx by reminding us, "The cock is the herald of the day." (*Sword*, 159)

17. Surely, Wolfe would not simply introduce a totally unknown and completely anonymous alien into the works at this late stage.

18. Its rotting nature, however, may adumbrate Ceryx's imminent demise.

CHAPTER 11
NAVIGATOR

1. The original figure is seven generations, but one of the women confinees claims her mother was a seventh-generation prisoner. This may help to date when the original crash occurred. Figuring three-and-a-half generations per century, and discounting generation #1 (since they're already adults), it appears the crash may have taken place approximately 200 years earlier. Are there any events in the Book that encapsulate this period? And who was Autarch? If we could answer either of these questions, we might be able to determine why the original prisoners were arrested. (Surely, immigration laws weren't that stringent in the Commonwealth.)

2. The giant insects, rabbit metaphor, and Jonas's recollection about a white knight sliding down the poker (he's describing a book he's read) are all part of Wolfe's homage to Lewis Carroll's *Through the Looking-Glass* (as are the mirrors that transport Jonas home).

3. The little girl, after first warning Severian about Hethor's slug, is told to go back to her mother. Writes Severian: "Then she released my hand and vanished,

but I am sure she did not do as I told her. Instead, she must have followed Jonas and me, for I have glimpsed her twice since I returned here to the House Absolute, where no doubt she exists on stolen food." *Claw*, 165) Many years later, after Severian returns to Urth from Yesod, he accesses the entrance to the Secret House, stating once within its narrow passageways, "Their suffocating constriction and padded, ladderlike steps summoned up a thousand memories of gambades and trysts: coursing the white wolves, scourging the prisoners of the antechamber, reencountering Oringa." (*Urth*, 291) Given that no character named Oringa is ever mentioned previously, it seems likely that she's the little girl from the antechamber.

4. I can still recall that day with terrible clarity more than four decades later and I'm willing to bet citizens of the UK will have similar unforgettable memories about where they were and what they were doing when they first heard the news about Diana Spenser.

5. John Kennedy, of course, was a highly decorated Navy PT-boat captain, which may relate to his "navigator" status. Serendipitously, perhaps, *navigator* also obeys the Second Rule of Names, being derivable from John Fitzgerald Kennedy. (See *Appendix*.)

6. This was seen as a bold, public, and humanizing move, and much to-do was made of it in both the electronic and print media. Hence why I believe Wolfe so diligently mentions "the people in black clothes *walking*."

7. For Catholics, JFK really was *their* President, his religion having been a hot electoral issue (just as it must have been with Al Smith in 1928), and doubtless, more than once, Wolfe heard arguments about how the US would wind up under the control of Vatican City if Kennedy were elected.

CHAPTER 12
PRISONERS

1. "When I was serving the food," Ava the Pelerine tells Severian in the lazaret, "I thought for a moment that one of the exultant sisters had come to help me…" Then shortly thereafter: "When you glance to one side sometimes you vanish, and there's a tall, pale woman using your face." (*Citadel*, 79–80) Now imagine the effect compounded by the memory-transferring drug of the Autarchs.

2. I.e., "The woman with you has been here before. Do not trust her. Trudo says the man is a torturer. You are my mother come again." (*Shadow*, 226)

3. Here's the deliberately-misleading exchange in full:

"I told the innkeeper no messenger would be required, and asked if he knew anyone named Trudo.

"Trudo, sieur?" He looked puzzled.

"Yes. It's a common enough name."

"Surely it is, sieur, I know that. It's just that I was trying to think of somebody that might be known to me and somebody, if you understand me, sieur, in your exalted position. Some armiger or—"

"Anyone," I said. "Anyone at all. It would not, for example, be the name of the waiter who served us, would it?"

"No, sieur. His name's Ouen. I had a neighbor once named Trudo, sieur, but that was years ago, before I bought this place. I don't suppose it would be him you're after? Then there's my ostler here—his name's Trudo." (*Shadow*, 229–230)

4. Says the boy who's gone to find Trudo: "Trudo's gone, cook says. She was out fetchin' water, 'cause the girl was gone, and seen him runnin' off, and his things is gone from the mews too." (*Shadow*, 233)

5. Another possible connection to Thecla may exist. Says she to Severian, "One can't talk to everyone because there are so many everyones, but the day before I was taken I talked for some time with the man who held my mount. I spoke to him because I had to wait, you see, and then he said something that interested me.' (*Shadow*, 72) Is Trudo—called "Reins" by Abban—the man who's held Thecla's mount? And if so what is it he says that Thecla finds interesting? (We're never told.) Also, if the exchange takes place at the Inn of Lost Love, has Thecla been spectating at the Sanguinary Field—or possibly rendezvousing with a lover?

6. John Clute was the first to highlight this relationship.

7. I've spent years trying to figure out who this woman might be and how she might be related to anyone present at the *Shadow* grave-robbing, but now believe she's merely a victim of circumstances, someone who's simply and freshly dead. The old leech in the jungle also seems to believe most of the corpse-eaters are far from discriminating when it comes to edible memories. As he tells Severian, "Learned men—particularly those of my profession—practice that everywhere, and usually with better effect, since we are more selective of our subjects and confine ourselves to the most retentive tissues." (*Citadel*, 215)

8. The historical analogue is Katherine of Valois, by whom Owen Tudor had at least four children.

9. The three are Holy Katharine, the patron saint of the Torturers' Guild; Severian's mother Catherine, who portrays Katharine; and Trudo's wife Catherine/Katharine whose exhumation will launch Severian in his journey from the Matachin Tower to the House Absolute.

10. Actually, they may be the same woman. See *Severa*.

11. This completely trashes the khaibit notion—which I've always maintained is false.

12. Besides the sateen/satin match-up, Marcellina's boyfriend has been maintaining a *jade*, while Severian will describe the Chatelaines Thecla and Gracia as "young, beautiful, *jaded* women." (*Shadow*, 91)

13. The irony and cleverness here may seem facile, however, when we re-examine Severian's visit to the House Azure and his encounters with the prostitutes there. As I maintain elsewhere (see *Severa*) Gracia/Barbea is his real sister Severa; the Chatelaine Thea encountered in the stairwell is Thais/Merryn, the woman popularly believed to be (but who is not) his sister (see *Thais*), while the Chatelaine Thecla (Thea's sister's alleged clonal twin) is portrayed by Marcellina. Given that we re-encounter both Gracia/Barbea and Thais elsewhere, it also seems appropriate that we should meet Marcellina one more time (hence the Matachin Tower scene), and the duplication and duplicity involved where one set of characters portrays another set of characters (or actually their look-alikes) will be paralleled in part later with the old leech and Father Inire in the jungles of the north.

CHAPTER 13
MILES AND JONAS

1. This could be a very long time. According to Malrubius, the alien technology involved has a range of "but a few thousand years." *But* used in this fashion may also suggest that a few thousand years is a rather limited period of time—a clue perhaps to the Hierodules' life spans?

2. Severian frequently refers to this version of Zak as "the shaggy creature"—Zak having "a covering of flattened, brownish-gray hairs."

3. The Hierogrammates (or at least their larvae) speak by shaping ambient noises. This may or may not explain the following passage: "Having hit us, the enemy gunners diverted their fire to the savages on our right. Their shambling infantry shrieked and gibbered as the bolts fell among them, but the riders reacted, so it appeared, by calling on magic to protect them. Often their chants

sounded so clearly I could make out the words, though they were in no language I had ever heard." (*Citadel*, 174)

4. Severian does re-encounter at least one more set of rider and hairy companion somewhat later in the battle.

5. Since Malrubius does not appear naked, I assume he steps forth from the Hierodules' materializing machine whole cloth: i.e., wearing whatever garments Severian remembers him wearing. So at least to some degree objects are reified. This may help to explain Miles's boots, sword and backpack.

6. Named after Sam Weller of Charles Dickens' *The Posthumous Papers of the Pickwick Club*, whose characteristic diction included the type of proverbs uttered by Jonas, Miles and Maxellindis' uncle.

7. Miles Gloriosis—"the Swaggering Soldier"—is an old stock character from Roman comedy and if not familiar from various original works might be so from either stage or film versions of "A Funny Thing Happened To Me On The Way To The Forum"—Larry Gelbart's modern and delicious recasting of Plautus.

8. Well, at least, not that we're told. I do think he's aboard Tzadkiel's starship in the form of a Sidero-like android (who once patched with organic parts becomes the Jonas we know). It's also possible he's the assassin Severian resurrects in the Secret House at the end of *Urth*: (a) the assassin, like Miles, is seemingly brought back from the dead by the Claw; (b) both he and dead Miles are found with swords near their hands; and (c) flies initially buzz about both cadavers. Severian, who typically has difficulty recognizing many people, might be forgiven his failure to recognize his old friend. As to why Miles (who as an aquastor is probably ageless) might be seeking to assassinate Valeria, he's probably been originally dispatched by the Hierodules to kill Dux Caesidius a year earlier ("[The assassin] lay, as he had surely lain for a year at least, upon his back"), but in the interim between his dying (Severian believes he's been nicked by his own poison sword—another aspect that links back to Jonas, the antechamber, and the prisoners' notions about giant bees) and his being resurrected, Caesidius himself has died. This removes Valeria's husband from being any sort of obstacle once Severian returns, but perhaps the assassin has been programmed to kill whomever sits atop the Phoenix Throne.

9. At one stage during their incarceration in the antechamber, delirious Jonas says, "We must get power to the compressors before the air goes bad." Not much later, however, he clarifies the situation: "I feel weight. It must only be the lights." Wolfe almost certainly reprises the actual event Jonas is recalling in Chapter VI of *Urth*, where we learn that Severian himself has caused it—his attempted use of the Claw having drained the starship's power supply.

10. E.g., Oringa, the little girl in the antechamber, sees this manifestation as "a tall lady," while Emilian, a soldier in the Pelerines' lazaret, actually recognizes Thecla, knowing her from court.

11. Later, after Severian kills Appian, and imbibes his forebrain, we have even more memories to sieve through, and trying to determine whose are whose is often crucial to determining certain plot threads.

12. From the soldier's letter: "Makar, of whom I told you, has fallen sick and was permitted to remain behind." (*Citadel*, 15)

13. Actually, Einhildis is speaking at this point, relaying what she's been told by Miles. But it's also worth noting that a *Saint* Miles does exist—thus adhering to Wolfe's naming conventions.

14. In Anderson's tale, the tin soldier is missing a leg (he's the last of twenty-five soldiers to be cast and there's not enough tin) and he falls in love with a paper ballerina (who can balance herself on one leg). Like Jonas's namesake, he's swallowed by a fish after various adventures, but eventually makes it back to rendezvous with his fellow toys. Unfortunately, both he and the paper doll wind up incinerated in the stove. Wolfe's short story, "It's Very Clean," reprises the tale and also features a character named Miles.

15. The entirety of this biographical data, as narrated by Severian, reads thusly: "I learned (or rather, I thought I did) that his father had been a craftsman; that he had been raised by both parents in what he called the usual way, though it is, in fact, rather rare; and that his home had been a seacoast town in the south, but that when he had last visited it he had found it so much changed that he had no desire to remain." (*Claw*, 87–88) First time through I thought Wolfe was trying to cast Jonas in Christic terms; the son of a carpenter father raised in New Sun's version of Capernaum, who rides not into, but out of Nessus, slouched on a donkey/merychip. A false Son of Man, that is. This all changed obviously with the tinker/gypsy angle. Now I believe the person who provided Jonas's organic parts was sired by a tinker metalworker/smith, spent his youth traveling about with his parents' caravan, and called home the seaside town Jonas mentions, where perhaps the caravan wintered, or where other tinker clans congregated annually, like France's Saintes-Maries-de-la-Mer. The part about his home being so changed he never visits it sounds right out of Thomas Wolfe, but is probably an excuse invented by Jonas to explain his wanderlust to Severian. I also believe that Wolfe's parenthetical qualification—the "or rather, I thought I did"—is a hint that much about Jonas's story is not as it seems—i.e., that it's really the history of his human donor, not Jonas's per se.

CHAPTER 14
BLACK HOLES AND GREEN MEN

1. Cyriaca's tale about the Library of the Citadel, in part, reprises this.

2. Ditto for everyone in league with Abaia, Erebus and the other Megatherians—from Baldanders to the undines to the Vodalarii and the Ascians. "As it was then," explains Vodalus, "so shall it be again. Men of Urth, sailing between the stars, leaping from galaxy to galaxy, the masters of the daughters of the sun." He fails to mention, of course, the carnage and chaos that's also likely to accompany the venture.

3. The green light might also be a luminous mask worn by an exultant. (Cf. "The greenish light grew stronger, and while I watched, still more than half paralyzed with pain and wracked by as much fear as I can recall ever having experienced, it gathered itself into a monstrous face that glazed at me with saucer eyes, then quickly faded to mere dark.")

4. Exploring the dirt maze, Severian finds a ladder and ascends to where there are literally photons at the end of the tunnel. "The square of daylight at the top was at once blinding and delightful" Once free, however, Severian discovers "The great, silent trees stood closer here, and the light that appeared so brilliant to me was the filtered green shade of their leaves," (*Sword*, 167) But could this earlier brilliance—now seen as muted by contrast with the dark—somehow have been engineered by the green man? It is late in the day at high altitude, after all, where sunlight is almost certainly thin and rachitic—hence difficult to believe it's as fulsome as Severian first describes.

CHAPTER 15
SEVENTEEN

1. Notice how in part the *Genesis* quote is echoed by Maxellindis' uncle, the boat captain. Though he does not know it, the night before, he has heard undines and possibly Abaia moving upriver, but in describing the strange activities that have taken place—sort of a Second Coming of the Megatherians—he says, "Sometimes I felt like I wasn't on old Gyoll at all, but on some other river, one that run up into the sky, or under the ground." (*Citadel*, 300)

2. It's possible the zoetic transport ship mentioned in *Urth*, being the future equivalent of Noah's ark, plays to the flood myth, but I feel it's more likely that

the ship will be used to transport live animals to the mountainous Cursed Town—or possibly later to the Whorl.

CHAPTER 16
ABDIESUS

1. See Note 1, PRISONERS.

2. Severian is recuperating in a tent after being rescued by Appian aboard his mammoth[3] and says, in response to a question from the Autarch, "I shook my head and laid it on the pillow again. The softness smelled faintly of musk." (*Citadel*, 191)

3. The elephant scene is straight out of Robert Graves' *Claudius* books. "What fearful destruction you would cause if one day you were to mount on a elephant and take the field in person," Graves has Claudius writing to Herod at one point. Then later to the same: "I shall probably take your kind advice about Britain, my dear Brigand, and if I do invade that unfortunate isle I shall certainly ride on the back of an elephant." Wolfe also imports the bibliophilic Sulpicius—one of Claudius's tutors—and makes him an Autarch, and may have found inspiration for his notion that Camoena is the bride of monkey-like Inire in the following description of the original Cumaean: "I came into the inner cavern, groping painfully on all-fours up the stairs, and saw the Sibyl, more like an ape than a woman, sitting on a chair in a cage that hung from the ceiling…"

4. Severian believes Abdiesus is contemplating his own death—hence the long wait before he's noticed.

5. I've never been able to figure out who this other armiger is; therefore, what his name might be remains a persistent mystery.

6. See *Prisoners* for the possible identity of this woman.

7. Cyriaca is also a cryptonym of fiacre (while Racho is a subcryptonym, requiring two additional letters).

8. Signifying Abdiesus's union with enemies of the state is the cryptonym Abaia.

CHAPTER 17
SEVERA

1. When I asked Wolfe about his tendency to create lost fictional sisters, he responded: "It's having been an only child, with no relatives within five hundred miles. My family consisted of my father, my mother, our dog, and me. No one else." (Personal correspondence, 9/27/2000.)

2. I use the word *quasi-* here without reservation, because this is how Wolfe, in the on-line interview conducted by *People* magazine, responded to the question, "Is Merryn, the witch at the end of *Claw*, Severian's sister?" Wolfe: "I've never been sure...I think that that very well may be the case, but I've never settled that in my own mind. Very likely she is." Wolfe's claim that he's never "settled" the identity of Severa seems very slippery to me and is typical of the author's deviousness.

3. On the other hand I do believe she's the prostitute Thais. (See *Thais*.)

4. Here is the exact quote, again from the *People* on-line interview.

Question: "Are any characters from *New Sun* going to appear in the *Short Sun*?"

Gene Wolfe: "Yes, some will. The two that I'm fairly confident of are Severian and Merryn. Beyond that I'd better not say—I'm still writing these books, and I'm not sure what I'm going to do at times."

Unfortunately, I have seen frequent misattributions of the above claiming that Wolfe said either "Severa" or "Severian's sister" would appear, whereas the word he actually uses is "Merryn." The difference, I warrant, is significant.

5. In Greek Mythology, Myrine was an Amazon queen and means "sea goddess"—another link to Father Inire, since the Palaemon of myth is a fellow marine god. *Oread* may also be a clue to Merryn's alien nature.

6. Sf writer/poet Tom Disch's best guess. Disch, we're told, jokingly liked the notion of Morwenna being Severian's mother, "because [Morwenna's name] sort of rhymed with Ouen's."

7. "The whip mark Dorcas had carried from the Piteous Gate burned on her cheek like a brand." (*Claw*, 198) Severian, in turn, will also acquire a cheek scar when Agia slaps him with the lucivee. "She slapped me with an open hand—there was a pull at my cheek, tearing pain, then the rush of blood." (*Citadel*, 213) Severian links Morwenna and Dorcas yet again in another passage: "Just as Morwenna, whom I had executed at Saltus, must have poisoned her husband

and her child because she recalled a time in which she was free and, perhaps, virginal, so Dorcas had left me because I had not existed in that time before her doom fell upon her." (*Citadel*, 20)

8. My friend Roy Lackey, who helped copy-edit this book in its early stages, believes it was Hethor who introduced the poison to the roses, hoping to kill Severian—and he's probably right. Eusebia, we should note here—or rather the Roman empress named after her—also died of poison, attempting to enhance her fertility, which perhaps supports the notion that Stachys, Morwenna's husband, abandoned Eusebia because she could bear him no children.

9. Marc Arimani of the Urth on-line list was the first to advance Pia's candidacy as Severa.

10. This has not always been so, however. As we learn in *Urth*, the "coast is quake prone, as the old records indicate clearly enough, but there hasn't been one since the river changed its course." (259) This may help to explain Palaemon's earlier confusion about where Thrax is—located up, not down, the Gyoll—especially if he's been timeflitting about in either his ship or mirrors.

11. Appian as whoremaster and the House Azure owe much to Robert Grave's *Claudius* books, wherein Claudius is the doorkeeper of a brothel established by his nephew Caligula and all the prostitutes are the wives of senators and patricians.

12. Compare the following two descriptions, the first of Barbea, the second of Severian (who's comparing his face to the dead man buried in his mausoleum—actually himself):

> "Her face was oval and perfect, with limpid eyes, a small, straight nose, and a tiny mouth painted to appear smaller still." (*Shadow*, 89)

> "My straight nose, deep-set eyes, and sunken cheeks were much like his, and I longed to know if he too had dark hair." (*Shadow*, 22)

13. Another pertinent quote about the witches' sexual license may apply: "The screams we heard through the ports of our dormitory came not from some underground examination room like our own, but from the highest levels; and we knew that it was the witches themselves who screamed thus and not their clients, for in the sense we used that word, they had none." Note the use of *clients* here as a possible synonym for 'johns' or 'customers.' Appian also later calls the visitors to his brothel "clients."

14. Adolescent girls maturing faster than adolescent boys, Severa may have left the Witches' Keep as much as two or three years earlier—plenty of time to have entered a downward career spiral and wound up in the world's oldest profession.

15. After Barbea fails to win Severian over, she returns in disguise as the "Chatelaine Gracia." At least that's how I'm choosing to interpret the following passage:

> Though this girl seemed quite different, there was much about her that reminded me of the 'Chatelaine Barbea' who had come before her. Her hair was as white as the flakes that floated past the windows, making her youthful face seem younger still, and her dark complexion darker. She had (or seemed to have) larger breasts and more generous hips. Yet I felt it was almost possible that it was the same woman after all, that she had changed clothing, changed wigs, dusked her face with cosmetics in the few seconds between the other's exit and her entrance. (*Shadow*, 89–90)

Saint Gracia may also fit the profile in that she, like Saint Catherine, was beheaded.

16. Hildegrin at one point addresses Dorcas as "goldy-hair," and later, after she cleanses the mud of the Lake of Endless Sleep from her, Severian remarks, "Freed of filth, her hair was pure gold." (*Shadow*, 228)

17. Azure is the official designation for blue in heraldry. Hence the appropriateness of *House Azure* for a brothel that features the clones of bluebloods.

18. Severian references the voluminous snow of that night twice more in the course of the narrative, each time using it as background to detail his initial encounter with Appian. (Such repetition of details in Wolfe's work is usually important.)

> I felt his hands, small, soft and moist, beneath my arms. Perhaps it was their touch that told me who he was: the androgyne I had met in the snow-covered House Azure. (*Citadel*, 186)

> "I would be more impressed, if I did not recall you so vividly from our meeting in the House Azure." (That porch, covered with snow, heaped with snow that deadened our footsteps, stood in the silken pavilion like a specter. (*Citadel*, 192)

19. While most of the talk about khaibits seems restricted to female exultants, Simulatio ("copy, imitation") of "The Map" may be a male khaibit.

20. I see nothing lurid nor sinister in this, just a doting father who misses his own daughters, Famulimus and Merryn. In other words, he's not the malign incarnation of Lewis Carroll.

21. If only half-heartedly, Gregory Feeley at least nominates Jolenta as a potential candidate for Severa in his "The Evidence of Things Not Seen" (NYRSF #31, March 1991): "So who is Severian's sister?…The woman who becomes Jolenta prompts some suspicion, if only because we never learn the name she bore before her unnatural transformation, but nothing more can be adduced.

22. "During the Medieval Ages and Renaissance, red-haired persons were often suspected of being witches" (*The Encyclopedia of Witches and Witchcraft*); "At times in England, France, Germany, Spain, and America, red hair has been unpopular and distrusted. At the height of Europe's witch hunts, in the 16th and 17th centuries, many women suffered the shame and pain of being stripped, shaved, and 'pricked' by a witch-hunter, endured torture, and were put to death, simply because they were redheads" (*Hair: Sex Society Symbolism*); "During the years 1483–1784, women with red hair were suspected of witchcraft and endured torture and death through being burned at the stake or drowned. Women who were accused of witchcraft were searched for 'Witch marks'; basically any abnormality including moles, freckles, warts, and most especially obvious differences such as an extra finger, crossed eyes or red hair" (*The Art of Being a Redhead*).

23. Agia's hair is described as chestnut; i.e., red-brown, the redness in her case signifying her association with the academy of magicians Severian encounters in the mountain jungle.

24. I categorically believe that everyone who is lame or limps in *New Sun* is related to Severian. This includes Agia, Jolenta, the old castellan at the Citadel, and yes, Triskele. (See Note 1.)

25. E.g., Severian calls Robert and Marie brother and sister, whereas Marie calls Robert her husband. Also, the dotard Severian persistently identifies as Casdoe's father is almost certainly the father of her husband Becan. (See *Fechin*.)

26. Given the Marilyn Monroe paradigm, it's tempting to see Jolenta's death as suicide. However, Severian knows more than a little of first-aid and surgical redress (recall his operating on Triskele), so it's unlikely he'd mistake a small knife wound for the puncture of a bat bite. On top of which, the wrist wound links her back to both *Saint* Jolenta and the other Son, while the bat itself is traditionally associated with witches—Wolfe neatly tying the two semi-conflicting images together.

CHAPTER 18
THAIS

1. Odilo *père* narrates the short story of the Urth cycle, "The Cat," wherein we learn the old Autarch's name is Appian (a detail never mentioned in the original Book, though it is derivable).

2. Odilo, of course, does not realize that the Hipparch Severian of the Black Tartantines on his raft is the very Severian he's relating the anecdote about.

3. Wolfe provides further ironical resonance here when he has Odilo exclaim to Thais, "But you obviously know nothing of artifice, nor of intrigues carried out daily—and nightly!—among the myriad hallways of our House Absolute." (*Urth*, 314)

4. Actually Marcellina. See *Prisoners*.

5. "Thea," we should note, does not accompany her fellow prostitutes Gracia and Thecla in the sleigh.

6. Besides, that is, his own incorporation into the new pantheon as Oannes, as well as the subsuming of Odilo and Pega likewise.

7. Notice how the diabolically clever Wolfe will have Severian note, "Someone spoke to her, calling her 'my dearest sister,'" and the potential misinterpretations this is likely to generate.

CHAPTER 19
THECLA

1. And which device of the torturers' impels Thecla to commit suicide rather than undergo a second session within it? Why, *the revolutionary*, of course—a very nice bit of irony by Wolfe.

2. I include among these Thecla's violet eyes, as well as her "icy, cold hands," which Severian mentions several times.

3. Further examples include the Domnicellae of the Pelerines—an ancient *sis*terhood of priestesses—who's called Mother; "brother" Severian, spiritual twin and awakener of the mandragora; and various life forms the Hierodules have based their monstrous masks upon ("All are your brothers, though you may recoil"). Also please note that while Wolfe probably intends for us to believe these titles are primarily figurative or symbolic, this does not mean there may not be elements of biological kinship between or among the cited examples.

4. Throughout both the original quartet and its sequel, the old Autarch remains nameless, Wolfe no doubt wanting us to figure it out for ourselves—as he does most of the nameless characters in New Sun—and it is possible to deduce if you know the twin meanings of *apis* and have access to a comprehensive listing of saints. Still, GW must have felt these clues weren't quite enough—hence Appian's eventual name-drop in "The Cat."

5. Odilo has served as Appian's steward for fifteen years, but during his third year Sancha—who has been absent from court with Appian's approval for fifty years—returns. 50 + [15-3] = 62. And yet notice Appian's reaction when "Paeon" tells him that Severian is about to succeed him: "I did not think it would be quite so soon."

6. If there's evidence dating Appian's trip to Yesod, I cannot find it, but it does seem possible to link it to his engagement in criminal activities (since his pandering is related to his mutilation), which begins around the time of Severian's birth. This also allows him plenty of time to sire Thecla, who's somewhat older than Severian.

7. Whereas a daughter born to a khaibit would probably inherit nothing.

8. Thea's face is often described as heart-shaped, so perhaps we're meant to see this woman as the mother of both Thecla and Thea.

9. One other possibility exists. If Thecla's mother is applying her makeup in front of a panel of mirrors, she might appear to be multiplied threefold, especially if Thecla is a mere toddler and unable to distinguish reflection from reality.

10. This indeed may help to explain why Merryn addresses Thecla as "sister" in Severian's fever dream. Merryn—as the biological daughter of Inire and Camoena—and she may have spent time together in Famulorum, Appian's home town. (Merryn, in fact, may be the "Josepha" Thecla mentions three times.)

11. The brown eye is somewhat problematical here since we know Appian has blue eyes (an allele of which may have contributed to Thecla's violet). So perhaps Severian's fever-driven hallucinations have spliced the minotaur bull of Appian with the bovine eye of a real bull—perhaps the one he encountered in the pampas.

12. It's difficult to decide what Appian means here by "influence in the north." He may be referring to the exultant clan that has holdings on Lake Diurturna. Or he may be referring to Thrax, which appears to be the second-largest city in the Commonwealth.

13. Here's the full account as described by Thecla:

> I walked down a corridor whose walls were lined with sad masks of silver and entered one of the abandoned rooms, high-ceilinged and musty with ancient

hangings. The courier I was to meet had not yet come. Because I knew the dusty divans would spoil my gown, I took a chair, a spindly thing of gilt and ivory. The tapestry spilled from the wall behind me; I recalled looking up and seeing Destiny crowned in chains and Discontent with her staff and glass, all worked in colored wool, descending upon me. (*Citadel*, 204)

14. Appian, after all, has learned that Severian will succeed him way back in *Shadow*, when Severian first visits the House Azure.

15. One of the conventions of science fiction is that the future has many branches, and there may be as many potential futures as there are branches. Inire's future—in actuality our past—may be similarly brachiated; hence any number of things could yet happen, including Thecla's non-suicide or, say, Severian's drowning (which does appear to have happened in at least one alternate version of the past).

16. Severian may need to acquire the Claw of the Conciliator, for example, or meet Famulimus, Barbatus and Ossipago.

17. Twice she's referred to as Josepha, one as Josephina. Possibly the former is a diminutive of the latter; equally possible either Wolfe or the book's copyeditors confused one for the other.

18. Unless the female exultants are held as hostages from menarche to menopause and never allowed to resume anything like a normal life.

19. Nicarete and Thecla each confer their names to an insect genus (beetles and butterflies respectively), but this connection seems tenuous.

20. The relationship between armiger and exultant classes is never fully discussed by Wolfe. Presumably, the latter evolved or is still evolving from the former—whence Jonas's comment about how the exultants are "the newest [families] of all" and how "in ancient times there was nothing like them." By tinkering with their own bodies—khaibits provide sera to amplify height and Thecla has had her eyes widened by minute applications of a poison (probably belladonna)—the exultants have further distanced themselves from their roots. Perhaps, however, it's only just a matter of having the financial wherewithal to perform these adjustments that distinguishes the two classes.

21. This adds additional resonance to the Lomer-Nicarete relationship. Lomer has been incarcerated because of a peccadillo he allegedly committed with the much younger Sancha. Sancha, however, may well be Thecla's grandmother and therefore Nicarete's mother. Nicarete thus seems to have pair-bonded with the man imprisoned for molesting her mother. There may be additional threads of

connection between Thea ("divine") and Sancha ("holy") as well as Nicarete (Niki ["victory"] + Areti ["virtue"]) and "Rose the Graced"—aka Sancha.

22. Thecla's perfume smells of burning roses, and when Sancha dies, children quote the famous epigram about Rosamond Clifford, murdered mistress of Henry II. ("Here Rose the Graced, not Rose the Chaste, reposes./The scent that rises is no scent of roses.") Meanwhile, roses bloom annually in both the Atrium of Time and on the Catherine Wheel. It's also probably no coincidence that Gene Wolfe's wife is named Rosemary.

CHAPTER 20
SWIMMING WITH UNDINES

1. As Severian tells Dr. Talos when the latter comes to visit him in the Citadel: "…It is good to see you again, even if you come as the emissary of your master." Talos, looking blank for a moment: "Oh, Baldanders, you mean. No, he has dismissed me, I'm afraid. After the fight. After he dived into the lake." Severian: "You believed he survived, then?" Talos: "Oh, I'm quite sure he survived. You didn't know him as I knew him, Severian. Breathing water would be nothing to him. Nothing!" (*Citadel*, 291–292)

CHAPTER 21
WITCHES, SACRED AND PROFANE

1. To reprise, if perhaps confusedly so, these events: at the behest of Hildegrin the Badger, the Cumaean and Merryn conjure up a living Stone Town, which is reigned over by Apu-Punchau, an earlier iteration of Severian. Hildegrin, it seems, seeks knowledge, explaining, "There was somebody who used to live in this here place we're sittin' on that knew things that could make a difference." But when he attempts to seize Apu-Punchau, the timeline fractures. Severian, while remaining yet himself, also becomes Apu-Punchau—hence sees *two* Hildegrins, one from his own perspective, the other from Apu-Punchau's. Severian—as Apu-Punchau—subsequently attempts to free himself from Hildegrin #1, while ur-Severian attempts to aid Hildegrin #2, who appears to be wrestling with somebody invisible—Apu-Punchau. But when the two Hildegrins approach each other too closely, they wind up obliterating one another, and the timeline rean-

neals itself. *Note*: I've chosen to use upper case when discussing Stone Town (as opposed to the Book's use of stone town with a definite article.)

2. The first best clue comes from *Shadow*, 167: "[The Domnicellae] wore a hood and a narrow cape that trailed long tassels."

3. Not only do the Pelerines take a vow of chastity, they believe the sacred Claw purifies lust. Or so we're told by Agia, who deems order members "professional virgins."

4. This may be an attempt by Wolfe to show that the Pelerines draw their power from the same source as Severian, whose gifts of healing and resurrection at times seem derived from either a geophysical or interstellar dynamo.

5. Cyriaca, who was a Pelerine postulant, tells us more about this gift. "I have the face for a Pelerine," she tells Severian, "though I don't have their eyes. Actually, I never had the eyes, though I used to think I'd get them when I took my vows, or afterward. Our director of postulants had that look. She could sit sewing, and to look at her eyes you would believe they were seeing to the ends of Urth where the perischii live, staring right through the old, torn skirt and the walls of the tent, staring through everything." (*Sword*, 46) The Cumaean may be practicing something similar when young Severian visits the witches' tower and sees her "staring through a glass tabletop at what appeared to be an artificial landscape inhabited by hairless, crippled animals." The "hairless, crippled animals," I maintain, are Famulimus, Barbatus and Ossipago aboard their berth on Tzadkiel's ship. And if not a crystal ball-type analogue or palantir, the "tabletop" may be some sort of monitor device.

6. There may be a subtextual link here with other witches. In Gordon Bottomley's play "King Lear's Wife," two witches, one old and one new, are summoned to prepare the body of deceased Queen Hygd for burial, and it's clear this is part of their regular duties. (The Pelerine parallel is intimated in Mannea's letter of safe conduct, when, attempting to thwart any would-be questioner of Severian's mission, she writes, "As you honor the memory we guard, and you yourselves may in time wish for succor and if need be an honorable internment, we beg you not to hinder this Severian as he prosecutes the business we have entrusted to him.") The same play features characters named Merryn and Wynoc, the latter of whom's called an "old leech" and whose earlier advice—"The Queen should have young women about her bed,/Fresh cool-breathed women to lie down at her side/And plenish her with vigour; for sick or wasted women/Can draw a virtue from such abounding presence"—echoes that of the old leech in Vodalus' encampment. It's equally possible, however, Wolfe

has never read Bottomley and that each simply drew from the same reservoir of Celtic folklore.

7. Alternately, the torturers themselves are skilled in leechcraft, being perfectly capable of self-treatment. Witness young Severian's performance when he doctors mutilated Triskele, displaying not only a wide knowledge of anatomy, but also surgical and suturing skills. Given such training, when we're later told that Severian has reformed (as opposed to abolished) the guild, it seems well within the realm of possibility that he's altered the order's charter to encompass the training of physicians and administering to the sick. The irony of this, of course, is that eventually the Matachin Tower itself could become known as the Tower of Healing. *Historical tangent:* Archagathus, held to be the first Greek physician to practice in Rome, was nicknamed *carnifex*—'butcher, torturer.' (Doubtless, this did not win him many patients.)

8. "I don't really know a great deal about them," Agia first tells Severian, "but we have some of their habits in the shop, and I asked my brother about them once, and after that paid attention to whatever I heard. It's a popular costume for masques—all that red." (*Shadow*, 170–171). This last bit of information, besides prefiguring Severian's encounter with Cyriaca, may also allude to Poe's "The Masque of the Red Death," wherein a figure much identified with Severian—i.e., cloaked Death—appears among costumed and masked revelers. Wolfe, of course, attended an elementary school named after Edgar Allan Poe.

9. At least who hail from the Witches' Keep. Morwenna and the woman known as Mother Pyrexia may be backwater witches, but with no access to the Hierodules' technomagic.

10. Further evidence can be adduced cryptonymically, given that three of the Pelerines' top leadership positions—Conexa Epicharis, the Domnicellae, and Mannea, Head of Postulants—either yield Camoena/Inire, or are backwards derivable therefrom. (See *Appendix* for details.)

CHAPTER 22
WHITE WOLVES

1. This is directly contradicted by Severian in last few pages of *Urth* when he mentions remembering "my flight from the white wolves in the Secret House, and a thousand similar terrors." (*Urth*, 364) The contradiction, however, may be resolved in several ways: (1) the memory belongs to either Thecla or any of the previous Autarchs sharing Severian's brain, both/all of whom are drawing upon

times when white wolves have been more common; or (2) the wolves have been reintroduced by the Hierodules after Severian has written the *Book of the New Sun*, but has yet to depart for Yesod (there being a need to restart the Autarchal method of succession should Severian fail in his mission).

2. This sounds like a dangerous activity. Then again, look what happens every year during the Feast of San Fermin in Pamplona, Spain.

3. Jorge Luis Borges also covers "The Crocotta and the Leucrocotta" in his *Book of Imaginary Beings* and this is perhaps where Wolfe originally encountered them. (Baldanders can be found here as well, along with Talos, undines, the Salamander, and the amphisbaena.)

3. Mistranslations, of course, are part and parcel of all such work. E.g., *lukos*—wolf—has often been mistranslated as *leukos*—light. While a more pertinent example has Severian pondering over the constellation called The Eight, which curiously has only three stars. The constellation he's talking about is our *Octans*, meaning octant—an eighth of a circle—which is triangular-shaped. Hence someone in the future, in compiling his or her atlas of the sky, has mistranslated Octans as The Eight.

4. Alzabo derives from "al-dhi'b," the archaic Arabic word for wolf or jackal.

5. Agricola here is actually commenting on a passage found in *The Twelve Keys*, a famous alchemical work written by Basil Valentine, a Benedictine Monk of the 15th century.

APPENDIX
FIRST RULE OF NAMES

1. I believe, in fact, that Typhon is a Neighbor, which is why he returns as Pas to the Blue-Green system of *Short Sun*. (He's the Neighbor Windcloud, by golly.)

2. I was initially intrigued by the idea that Thea and half-sister Thecla might be alien and found some interesting congruencies (both are tall as Hierodules, Thecla's father has a hedge maze, which would make him the Daedalean Inire, and Thecla and Palaemon each confer names to butterflies), but could never make the theory work in the end. It now lays abandoned and waiting for some other stalwart to perform the Procrustean millwork on it.

APPENDIX B
THE SECOND RULE OF NAMES

1. This, at least, is how Buck Mulligan describes it in James Joyce's *Ulysses*.

2. As I child I was delighted to learn how Count Alucard of *Son of Dracula* confabulated his *nom de schlock*. Subsequently, I tried to apply the technique to everything I read—mostly comic books—and immediately sourced the parent name of Superman's Kal-el. I date my love for cryptonyms from these early days; and though I did not know it then, it is possible I already had some presentiment of my future.

APPENDIX

THE FIRST RULE OF NAMES

By and large Wolfe uses the following scheme throughout the five Sun books, although, as we shall see, in almost every case there are exceptions.

The names of saints are conferred to the human population of the Commonwealth. Aliens, however, attempting to pass as humans may have names based on saintly exemplars (e.g., Palaemon, Merryn).

Names drawn from various mythologies are conferred to *non*-humans. Primarily, these involve aliens, but a notable exception is Dr. Talos. Typhon is seen by some as ancestrally human, but I believe he's pure alien.[1] At least two aliens have names derived from Latin verbs: Inire (to begin, to enter); Venant (to hunt).

Names that have both saintly and mythic exemplars are conferred to characters I maintain are aliens attempting to pass as human. Palaemon and Paeon are the obvious examples here, while Idas comes close. Odd exception: Thea.[2]

Androids in both the *New* and *Long Sun* series are named after metals or minerals. E.g., Sidero, Hierro, Zelezo (all mean *iron*), Hammerstone, Molybdenum, Marble, *et al.* Notice how Ossipago ("bone-grower") does not fit this pattern.

Names that don't quite fit any profile include Baldanders (imported from *Der Abenteuerliche Simplicissimus Teutsch* by Johann Hans Jakob Cristoffel von Grimmelshausen), Loyal to the Group of Seventeen (who being an Ascian may not have a proper name), and Robert, Marie, and Kim Lee Soong (all three hailing from the Age of Myth; i.e., our time).

THE SECOND RULE OF NAMES
(with commentary by Rik Stroeb)

Perhaps my greatest fear in compiling the following list and commentary is that many people will either seek to dismiss it as being equivalent to the search for Baconian acrostics in the works of William Shakespeare or call to mind Stephen Daedalus' strange theory about *Hamlet*: "He proves by algebra that Hamlet's grandson is Shakespeare's grandfather and that he himself is the ghost of his own father."[1] Nevertheless, as I've attempted to prove throughout much of this book, I believe that Gene Wolfe, far from assigning names randomly from a compendium of saints, has used a certain stratagem in naming and matching many of the characters in his masterwork, and that once you realize and accept this stratagem you can employ it to determine many of the hidden, secret, or thematic relationships between various sets of characters—indeed, once the key became apparent, it allowed me to reaffirm a number of previous conjectures, as well as to seek out hidden relationships I'd never suspected before. So let me restate Wolfe's second naming convention one final time: given any two names in *The Book of the New Sun* and its sequel, if the second name can be derived entirely from the letters of the first name, or with the addition of a single letter, there exists a relationship of some kind—often, but not always, opaque to the reader and typically uncommented upon by the books' characters. Such cryptonymic relationships may be biological, figurative, political, indicative of identicality, or other. And while previous practitioners of similar techniques[2] have mainly confined themselves to true or near anagrams (one thinks of James Branch Caball and the various Kinbotian shades of Vivian Darkbloom), perhaps the most likely writer Wolfe may have adapted the technique from, although he does it far less frequently, is J. R. R.Tolkein, with his Sméagol/Gollum and Sauron/Saruman exemplars.

This is not to say, however, that the stratagem (at least as I employ it) is foolproof: with as many names as there are in the five books (by my count close to 300), perhaps it's inevitable that there should be a certain pseudo-incestuousness in a roster of this magnitude. Thus there may be a number of false positives in the list below and a number I thought were patently false—indeed, dozens—I simply dropped altogether. (Perhaps this is a mistake since the industrious reader may be able to perceive relationships where I couldn't; if you're of a mind I invite you to try.) Coincidences too may occur; but I think the vast majority of paired relationships are valid and worthy of further investigation.

Also to the point, I think the frequency of the Inire-Cumaean clusters support many of my central claims about *New Sun*'s subtext. As we shall see, the minions, agents, confederates, and proxies of Father Inire are everywhere, either spying on Severian or attempting to safeguard him from harm or making sure that certain pathways remain open, always with the endgame of ensuring that the New Sun will be kindled, Urth will be reborn, and that the new people of Ushas may go on to become the potential forebears of the Hierogrammates of Yesod.

Parent/Cryptonym	*Relationship*

* = Names not found in *New Sun*.

1. Severian/Severa	Brother/Sister
2. Agilus/Agia	Brother/Sister
3. Thecla/Thea (+c)	Half-Sisters
4. Famulimus/famula	Sisters

Commentary   The famula is this case is Merryn; both are daughters of Inire and the Cumaean.

| 5. Severian/Agia   (+g) | Cousins |

Commentary   Severian, Agia, and Agilus are the grandchildren of Dorcas and Caron.

| 6. Dorcas/Casdoe   (+e) | Identical (figurative) |

Commentary   Dorcas is the grandmother of Severian and Severa; Casdoe is the mother of a Severian and Severa tandem. Dorcas is married to an unnamed old man, while Becan's father is similarly old and unnamed (notice how Caron/Becan fall just shy of being cryptonyms as I've limited them; hence are subcryptonyms).

| 7. Catherine/Herais   (+s) | Severian's Mother/Grand-mother |

Commentary   Catherine is the mother of Big Severian, Herais the grandmother of Little Severian.

| 8. Herais/"Thea"/Thais   (+t) | Sisters (figurative) |

Commentary   Casdoe at one point rather oddly asks Severian if he knows her mother Herais (he's just come from Thrax, where she resides). Her linkage with the cryptonyms "Thea" and Thais suggests she may be a hetaera (with the latter word itself suggesting Herais); i.e., a prostitute—and again we see further parallels between the two families (Severa, I maintain, has been prostituting herself.)

| 9. Cadroe/Casdoe   (+s) | Identical (figurative) |

Commentary   Possibly a member of a parallel family (the Inires playing with multiple timelines in their epic quest), but this one sinister since it's associated with the Seventeen Stones (Baldanders/Cadroe being another close-but-not-quite-cryptonym-pair)

| 10. Morwenna/Merryn   (+y) | Sisters (figurative) |

Commentary   Both may be witches—sisters of the weird. See *Severa*.

11. Piaton/Pia   Brother/Sister(figurative)

Commentary Both are prisoner slaves; Severian himself notes their sibling-like nature.

12. Pelagia/Pega   Mistress/Handmaiden

13. Typhon/Piaton   (+a; $i = y$)   Brothers (teratoid)

Commentary Brothers by artifice only—Typhon having grafted his head to Piaton's body.

14. Eusignius/Eigil   (+l)   Brothers (figurative)

15. Drotte/Eata   (+a)   Brothers (figurative)

Commentary 14,15 Eusignius, Eigil, Drotte, and Eata are all members of the Torturers' Guild.

16. Laetus/Eata   Brothers (figurative)

Commentary Both are shipmates.

17. Maxellindis/Eata   (+t)   Girlfriend/Boyfriend

18. Syntyche/Eata   (+a)   Girlfriend/Boyfriend

19. Emilian/Miles   (+s)   Brothers (figurative)

20. Melito/Miles   (+s)   Brothers (figurative)

Commentary 19, 20 Emilian, Miles and Melito are all members of the same "band of brothers." I.e., they're soldiers in the Commonwealth military.

21. Mineas/Miles   (+l)   Brothers (figurative)

Commentary Severian believes both Mineas and Miles have been returned to life via the agency of the Claw.

22. Baldanders/Abban   Brothers (figurative)

Commentary Both are extremely huge (figurative being literal here)

23. Valeria/Daria   (+d)   Sisters (figurative)

Commentary A likely false positive on first observation, but then Severian himself notes the resemblance—Wolfe perhaps covertly calling attention to his naming stratagem.

24. Zambdas/Zama   Brothers (figurative)

Commentary Both are water brothers—Zama a sailor, Zambdas a fisherman. Perhaps the latter will also drown as Zama has.

25. Mafalda/Zama   (+z)   Mother/Son (figurative)

26. Lazarus*/Zama   (+m)   Brothers (figurative)

Commentary Both are raised from the dead—one by the original Son, one by the New Sun.

27. Roche/Racho   (+a)   Brothers (figurative)

Commentary Both are brothers in lust, patronizing prostitutes.

28. Kimleesoong/Lomer   (+r)   Brothers (figurative)

Commentary Both are antechamber prisoners—Kimleesoong among the first generation, Lomer the last.

29. peryton/pteriope   (+i)   Brothers (winged)

30. Secunda*/Ouen   (+n)   Sister/Brother

31. Secunda*/Cas   Daughter/Mother

Commentary 30, 31 Secunda is the hypothetical second child of Dorcas and Caron. She is almost certainly the woman who nails children to furniture imprisoned in the Matachin Tower.

32. Caesidius/Secunda*   (+n)   Severian's Relatives

33. Caesidius/Cas   Severian's Grandparents

Commentary Cas is Severian's paternal grandmother, Caesidius his maternal grandfather.

34. Gene Wolfe/Owen   Severian's Fathers

Commentary Gene Wolfe is the literary father of Severian—Ouen (synonymous with Owen) is Severian's father in the book. The name Eugene also derives from Owen.

35. Palaemon/Ouen   (+u)   Severian's Fathers

Commentary Ouen is Severian's absentee biological father; Palaemon his step-surrogate.

36. Paeon/Appian   (+i)   Father/Son

Commentary This relationship parallels that of Palaemon and Severian.

37. Fechin/Inire   (+r)   Son/Father

Commentary This relationship parallels that of Palaemon and Severian.

38. Palaemon/Mamas   (+s)   Father/Son

Commentary A perversion of Relationship 36—this Palaemon being the "knowledgeable, evil" leech in the jungle (the original Palaemon) and his catamite charge Mamas.

39. Severian/Inire	Father/Son
40. Catherine/Inire	Severian's Parents

Commentary Catherine is literally Severian's mother, Inire/Palaemon his figurative father.

41. Katharine/Inire	Patron Saint/Patron
42. Catherine/Thea; Thecla (+c)	Severian's Primal Loves
43. Valeria/Severa (+s)	Grandmother/Granddaughter

Commentary Also sisters-in-law because of the temporal anomaly involved.

44. Baldanders/Idas (+i)	Father/Daughter
45. Pelagia/Agia	Daughter/Mother
46. Nicarete/Thea (+h)	Mother/Daughter
47. Nicarete/Appian (+p)	Consort/Autarch

Commentary 46, 47 Nicarete and Appian are quite possibly the parents of Thecla. See *Thecla*.

48. "Rose the Chaste"/Thea; Thecla (+c)	Grandmother/Granddaughters

Commentary Thecla's Grandmother has been called both "Rose the Chaste" and "Rose the Graced" after she dies; she is almost certainly the Sancha of "The Cat" and Lomer's teenage seductress. See *Thecla*.

49. Cyriaca/Cyby (+b)	Niece/Uncle
50. Jolenta/Jonas (+s)	Siblings (figurative)
51. Jolenta/Talos (+s)	Siblings (figurative)

Commentary 50, 51 Jolenta, Jonas, and Talos have all been surgically or artificially enhanced/create

52. Dorcas/Caron* (+n)	Wife/Husband
53. Meschiane/Meschia	Wife/Husband
54. Prefect Prisca/Inire (+n)	Wife/Husband
55. Camoena/Cumaean (+u)	Identical
56. Myrine*/Merryn	Identical

Commentary Myrine may be Merryn's mythic (as opposed to saintly) cognomen. See *Severa*.

57. Josephina/Inire	(+r)	Daughter/Father
58. Josephina/Thais	(+t)	Identical
59. Josephina/Jonas		Mirror Travelers
60. Thais/"Thea"	(+e)	Identical

Commentary 57–60 Josephina (aka Josepha) is one of the more mysterious names in the Book. Cryptonymic evidence suggests she may be another (along with Thais) avatar of Merryn. Thais is also the khaibit "Thea" Severian meets at both the House Azure and Hypogeum Apotropaic; they are reunited at the end of *Urth*. See *Thais*.

61. Palaemon/Paeon		Identical

Commentary Note also the serendipitous presence of *ape* and *pa* in both names—*papa ape* being Father Inire.

62. Burgundofara/Gunnie	(+ie)	Identical
63. Peryton/Purn	(+u)	Identical

Commentary I believe that the peryton Severian sees in the mountains is the shapechanged Hethor—Purn in a later incarnation now Urth-bound. See *Hethor*.

64. Tzadkiel/Zak		Identical
65. Domnicellae/Domnina		Identical
66. Catherine/"Carina"		Identical

Commentary The woman named Carina in "Eschatology and Genesis" and whose real life equivalent Severian sees when he returns to Urth from Yesod is his mother being ushered to safety (almost certainly the clutches of the Pelerines).

67. "Katharine"/Catherine		Identical

Commentary Catherine, mother of Severian, plays Katharine, the Torturer's patron saint in their annual guildsday celebration.

68. "Meschiane"/Camoena	(+o)	Identical

Commentary As Carina is to Catherine, Meschiane is to Camoena—a thespian other. Furthermore, Camoena and Inire are the couple dropped off by the cacogens at the end of *Urth*—symbolically Meschiane and Meschia.

69. "Rose the Chaste"/Sancha	(+n)	Identical
70. Hierodule/Inire	(+n)	Identical

71. Seekers of Truth and Penitence/Torturers		Identical
72. Journeying Monials of the (+p) Conciliator/Pelerines		Identical
73. "Meschiane"/Inire (+r)		Wife/Husband

Commentary Meschiane—the typological equivalent of Camoena in "Eschatology and Genesis"—is married to the real life equivalent of Meschia, Father Inire.

74. Earth/Urth (+u)		Identical
75. Buenos Aires/Nessus		Identical

Commentary A nifty inversion here, the "good air" of Buenos Aires becoming the poisoned waters of Nessus.

76. Neil Armstrong/Nilammon		Identical
77. United States of America/Ascia		Identical
78. John Fitzgerald Kennedy/Navigator (+v)		Identical
79. Ascian/St. Ann (+t; Ann = Anne)		Colonist/Home
80. Arioch/Abaia (+b)		Enemies of the New Sun
81. Blaithmaic/Abaia		Author/Subject

Commentary Blaithmaic has written *The Lives of the Seventeen Megatherians*, a book about Abaia and his league of monsters.

82. Baldanders/Erebus (+u)		Enemies of the New Sun
83. Baldanders/Abaia (+i)		Enemies of the New Sun
84. Abaia/Agia (+g)		Enemies of the New Sun
85. Sabas/Abaia (+i)		Enemies of the New Sun

Commentary Sabas of the Parted Meadow shows up at the Sanguinary Field—perhaps to counterbalance Laurentia of the House of the Harp (who's aligned cryptonymically to the Inires).

86. Diurturna/Juturna (+j)		Confluence

Commentary Baldander's Castle is on Lake Diurturna; he and the undine Juturna (who is perhaps the mother of Idas) may have rendezvoused here.

87. Abdiesus/Abaia		Enemies of the New Sun
88. Abdiesus/Erebus (+r)		Enemies of the New Sun

89. fiacre/Cyriaca   (+y)   Racho Connection

Commentary 87–89 For further explanation of the Abdiesus-Racho-Cyriaca connection, see *Abdiesus*.

90. Abundantius/Abaia   Enemies of the New Sun

91. Abundantius/Agia   (+g)   Enemies of the New Sun

Commentary Both also appear to be members of the same cult of adepts. See *Agia and Agilus*.

92. Vodalus/Talos   (+t)   Enemies of the New Sun

93. Pinian/Abaia   (+b)

94. Baiulo/Abaia

Commentary 93, 94 Zama—who has sailed with Pinian—drowns near Baiulo (both Abaian cryptonyms), but is reanimated by Ceryx (Inire)—perhaps a symbolic attempt at trumpery similar to the Moses and Court Magicians contests.

95. Abaddon/Abaia   (+i)   Confluence

Commentary Links enemies of the New Sun with the abyss of Hell.

96. Pelerines/Inire   Religious Order/Founder

97. Matachin Tower/Inire   Confluence

98. Matachin Tower/Camoena   Confluence

99. Botanic Gardens/Inire   Confluence

100. Botanic Gardens/Camoena   (+m)   Confluence

101. Hypogeum Apotropaic/Inire   (+n)   Confluence

102. H. Apotropaic/Camoena   (+n)   Confluence

Commentary 97–101 The Matachin Tower, Botanic Gardens and Hypogeum Apotropaic represent the three primary operation bases in the Inires' quest to secure the New Sun.

103. Camoena/Mannea   Pelerine Hierarchs

104. Conexa Epicharis/Camoena   (+m)   Pelerine Hierarchs

105. Conexa Epicharis/Inire   Pelerine Hierarchs

106. Domnicellae/Camoena   Pelerine Hierarchs

107. Domnicellae/Inire   (+r)   Pelerine Hierarchs

108. Einhildis/Inire   (+r)   Pelerines

Commentary 103–108 Here the Hierodules' connection to the Pelerines all but shouts to us. See *Witches*.

109. Decuman/Cumaean   Witch/Sorcerer

Commentary Both die attempting to subdue Severian.

110. Mother Pyrexia/Inire   (+n)   Witch/Magus

111. Rudesind/Inire   Allies of the New Sun

Commentary At the end of *Citadel* Rudesind himself reveals he had been working for Father Inire all along.

112. Hildegrin/Inire   Allies of the New Sun

Commentary Hildegrin may be operating in his own best interests as an equal-opportunity shovel, but I find it likelier he is working (given his inside knowledge about the Inires and Severian) as a mole, spying on Vodalus and reporting to the Hierodules.

113. Laurentia/Inire   Allies of the New Sun

Commentary Full name—Laurentia of the House of the Harp—may contextualize the "heavenly" aspect of the Inires. See *85*.

114. Marcellina/Gracia   (+g)   House Azure Prostitutes

115. Marcellina/Barbea   (+b)   House Azure Prostitutes

116. Marcellina/Inire   Allies of the New Sun

Commentary 114–116 See *Prisoners* for a full explanation of who Marcellina is.

117. Yrierix/Inire   (+n)   Sages

118. Yrierix/Ceryx   (+c)

Commentary 117, 118 Perhaps another link or subtextual bridge between Inire and Ceryx.

119. Werenfrid/Inire   Allies of the New Sun

Commentary Werenfrid is an earlier member of the Torturer's Guild, possibly even Inire-in-disguise—which means he could also be the other guildmember who's dispatched to an outlaying town. (The second is the original Palaemon.)

120. Serenus/Inire   (+i)

Commentary Perhaps an attempt by Wolfe to link Jupiter (Serenus) with Jovinian—the true provider of the sword being Palaemon/Inire.

121. Gunnie/Inire   (+r)   Allies of the New Sun

122. Burgundofara/Agia   (+i)   Traitors of the New Sun

Commentary Gunnie immediately bonds with Severian aboard Tzadkiel's ship, perhaps at the behest of Ossipago. Later, as Burgundofara, she betrays him to Typhon's soldiers at Saltus—again, perhaps a necessity, since Severian's capture will aid and abet his growing stature as the Conciliator.

123. Sidero/Hierro   (+h)   Android Shipmates

124. Sidero/Inire   (+n)   Allies of the New Sun

Commentary Sidero is the first person we hear speak to Severian aboard Tzadkiel's ship and it seems likely that he has been assigned by Ossipago to watch over him.

125. Hierro/Inire   (+n)   Allies of the New Sun

Commentary Perhaps another android tasked with safeguarding Severian.

126. Nicarete/Inire   Allies of the New Sun

Commentary Nicarete may be a confidant of Father Inire's, perhaps being placed in the House Absolute's antechamber to watch for (and later protect) Severian when he arrives.

127. Eusignius/Inire   (+r)   Allies of the New Sun

Commentary Another possible spy of Inire's—one closer to Severian's age—in the Torturer's Guild.

128. Maxentius/Inire   (+r)   Allies of the New Sun

129. Maxentius/Cumaean   (+c)   Allies of the New Sun

Commentary Would there be a Severian of the Torturers' Guild if no Saint Katharine existed—and thus no mother Catherine to portray her? So somehow the Inires must have engineered Katharine's eventual demise. (Maxentius in this sense would be an unwilling ally.)

130. Famulorum/Famulimus/famula   Confluence

Commentary Given its cryptonyms Famulorum may well be another, more rural, node of the Inire's Briahtic operation.

131. Ossipago/Os   Confluence

Commentary Ceryx (Ossipago) is encountered and dies in Os. See *Masks of the Father.*

132. Marie/Inire (+n)   Missionaries

Commentary   Robert and Marie clearly represent Inire and Camoena; but when Marie suggests they abandon their missionary work and take a plane home (i.e., return by Tzadkiel's ship to Yesod), Robert chastises her. Isangoma (another aspect of Inire, being Zulu for "sorcerer") then provides further gloss on their mission, reading a passage from the Bible about how Moses has not been allowed to enter the Promised Land—just as the Inires will never see Ushas. Historically, Robert and Marie are probably the Scottish Christian missionaries Robert and Marie Moffat; Robert was trained to be a gardener and both went to Africa to proselytize.

133. Bregwyn/Inire (+i)   Allies of the New Sun

134. Herena/Inire (+i)   Allies of the New Sun

135. Tanco/Canog (+g)   Allies of the New Sun

136. Kyrin/Inire (+e)   Allies of the New Sun

Commentary 133–136   Bregwyn, Herena, Tanco, Canog and Kyrin are all early converts to the Conciliator movement.

137. Maxellendis/Inire (+r)   Allies of the New Sun

138. Grimkeld/Inire (+n)   Allies of the New Sun

139. Hadelin/Inire (+r)   Allies of the New Sun

Commentary   Maxellindis, Grimkeld, and Hadelin are all shipmates of Severian at one time, perhaps no more than synergistic/synchronistic elements in the Inires' scheme, but vital nonetheless. If Hadelin has control over the temporal co-ordinates of his landing site, he may have been ordered by Inire to strand Severian one thousand years in the past so he can become the Conciliator.

140. Maxellindis/Hadelin (+h)   Niece/Uncle

Commentary   Maxellindis' uncle is never named (usually meaning we need to uncover it ourselves), but could it be Hadelin? When last seen Captain Hadelin has gone off to Liti with Burgundofara one thousand years earlier; but just as Severian believes the middle-aged Gunnie will become restless and reboard Tzadkiel's ship, perhaps Hadelin does too, only this time when he puts ashore, he does so in Severian's time. Here he again captains a boat until he dies taverning in—where else?—Liti.

141. Hierogrammate/Apheta (+p)   Identical

142. Hierogrammate/Inire (+n)   Parent/Child

143. Apheta/"*Papa Ape*"   Mother/Child

Commentary   The "Papa Ape" cryptonym supports my notion that Apheta is the mother (by Severian) of Father Inire.

144. Apeiron/Inire

145. Apeiron/Paeon

146 Apeiron/Papa Ape

Commentary 144–146 While pertaining to a procreative aspect of the Increate (at least as used by Severian), Apeiron not only unifies cryptonymically Inire and Paeon with "Papa Ape," but also means "unbound" in Greek—a very descriptive definition of Father Inire's ability to parse time in both directions.

147. Ctesiphon's Cross/Typhon   (+y)

148. Ctesiphon's Cross/Piaton   (+a)

Commentary 147, 148 Procrustean guesswork here: the Parthian city of Ctesiphon was conquered by Roman emperor Septimius Severus—perhaps symbolizing or adumbrating Severian's eventual triumph over Typhon. (The cross aspect does seem to allude to Severian's Christic nature.)

149. Last House/Ash   Residence/Resident

150. Ushas/Ash   Opposites

Commentary Ushas represents the future timeline if the Hierogrammates win. Ash represents the timeline if Abaia, Erebus, and the other Megatherians win.

151. Meschia/Ash   Opposites

Commentary Meschia is deemed "the first man" in Dr. Talos's play *Eschatology and Genesis*. Ash is the last man in the timeline where the Megatherians win (but conversely "the first man" in Norse mythology.)

152. Meschiane/Carina   (+r)

153. Meschiane/Jahi   (+j)

154. Kyneburga/Lybe   (+l)   Maids

Commentary 152–154 All five women are characters in Dr. Talos's play *Eschatology and Genesis*.

155. Kyneburga/Hunna   (+h)   Maids

Commentary Hunna is the finally-disclosed name of Thecla's maid (who's tortured *sans nom* in *Shadow*). Kyneburga is Carina's maid in *Eschatology and Genesis*.

156. The Claw/Thecla   Confluence

Commentary Both abide within Severian, and just as Thecla has come to Severian via the blood-borne route of ingestion, Severian's blood will impregnate the thorn that becomes the Conciliator's relic.

SELECTED BIBLIOGRAPHY

Andre-Driussi, Michael. *Lexicon Urthus*. San Francisco: Sirius Fiction, 1994.

Attwater, Donald. *The Avenel Dictionary of Saints*. New York: Avenel Books, 1981.

Biedermann, Hans. *Dictionary of Symbolism*. New York: Facts On File, 1992.

Borges, Jorge Luis. *Imaginary Beings*. New York: E. P. Dutton & Co. 1969.

Borski, Robert. "Queen of Shadows: Unveiling Aubrey Veil in Gene Wolfe's *Fifth Head of Cerberus*," *New York Review of Science Fiction*, 168 (2002), 16–18.

———. "Wolves in the Fold: Lupine Shadows in the Works of Gene Wolfe," *New York Review of Science Fiction*, 155 (2001), 14–15.

Bottomley, Gordon. *King Lear's Wife*. Boston: Small, Maynard & Company, unknown.

Carroll, Lewis. *Through the Looking-Glass*. London: The Folio Society, 1962.

Clute, John. w/Peter Nichols. *The Encyclopedia of Science Fiction*. New York: St. Martins, 1993.

Clute, John. *Strokes*. Seattle: Serconia Press, 1988.

Cooper, Wendy. *Hair: Sex Society Symbolism*. New York: Stein and Day, 1970.

Delaney, John J. *Dictionary of Saints*. Garden City, N.Y., 1980.

Feeley, Gregory. "The Evidence of Things Not Shown." *New York Review of Science Fiction* 31 (1991) 1, 8–10; 32 (1991) 12–16.

Frazier, Robert. "The Legerdemain of the Wolfe." *Thrust* 19 (Winter/Spring 1983) 5–9.

Graves, Robert. *Claudius the God.* USA: Penguin, 1956.

———. *I, Claudius.* New York, Vintage, 1961.

———. *Greek Myths (Volumes I & II).* Baltimore, MD: Penguin, 1957

Guiley, Rosemary Ellen. *The Encyclopedia of Witches and Witchcraft.* New York: Facts On File, 1999.

Lockwood, John; Smith, William. *Chambers Murray Latin-English Dictionary.* Edinburgh: Chambers, 1933.

Nigg, Joseph. The Book of Fabulous Beasts. New York: Oxford University Press, 1999

Wolfe, Gene. *Caldé of the Long Sun.* New York: Tor, 1994.

———. *Castleview.* New York: Tor, 1990.

———. *Claw of the Conciliator.* New York: Timescape, 1981.

———. *Citadel of the Autarch.* New York: Timescape, 1982.

———. *Endangered Species.* New York: Tor, 1989.

———. *Lake of the Long Sun.* New York: Tor, 1994.

———. *Return to the Whorl.* New York: Tor, 2001.

———. *Shadow of the Torturer.* New York: Simon & Schuster, 1980.

———. *Sword of the Lictor.* New York: Timescape, 1981.

———. *Urth of the New Sun.* New York: Tor, 1987.

0-595-31729-4